DO BOMB DOGS DREAM OF CHASING BUTTERFLIES?

KREGG JORGENSON

outskirts press

Outskirts Press, Inc.
http://www.outskirtspress.com

ISBN: 978-1-4327-6424-1

Original cover art by artist extraordinaire Glen Carey
glencareyartistforhire@gmail.com

Outskirts Press and the "OP" logo are trademarks belonging to Outskirts Press, Inc.

PRINTED IN THE UNITED STATES OF AMERICA

This book is dedicated to my former CBP K-9 Instructors/Trainers; Senior Instructor/Course Developer Scott Zeitner, and the late Sergeant Major J.P. Henderson, USMC. Both true and dedicated professionals. Semper Fido! And to all working K-9 teams, past and present, for their service.

"I've seen a look in dogs' eyes,
a quickly vanishing look of amazed contempt,
and I am convinced that basically dogs think humans are nuts."

-John Steinbeck

CHAPTER

I

Alas! Methinks, perhaps, Shakespeare was vexed.
The dogs of war aren't always let slip or unleashed when someone cries, '*Havoc!*' No, the truth of the matter, at least with working military bomb dog teams serving in combat today, is that K-9 handlers keep their dogs on leash as they both cautiously move towards the mayhem and misery, together.

It's what we do, and given the dangerous and deadly nature of the work involved, and considering that a pressure plate or command detonated IED can turn our kibble to bits in a micro-moment, and at times, have, the '*Sweet swan of Avon*' might've appreciated that it actually is much ado about something.

Max is my U.S. Army K-9 team partner, and when we were temporarily loaned out to work with a Company of Marines on a road clearing operation in Helmand Province in southern Afghanistan during the actual '*dog days of summer*', it only seemed appropriate since the Marines referred to themselves as, '*Devil Dogs.*'

Batoor, the Afghan military interpreter, who accompanied us on the six-day mission in early August, thought that this was hilarious because from all of the enemy chatter that he was picking up on the radio, the Taliban were calling us all *Spi zoe*, which is the Pashto word for, *sonsofbitches*.

"Is funny, yes?" he said, chuckling and enjoying the doggy irony, "But good dogs are ever watchful and loyal, so we are all in good company, too, I think. *Shohna ba shohna.*"

Shohna ba shohna was the Afghan National Security Forces phrase meaning shoulder-to-shoulder, together.

Actually, there was no thinking about it. We were in good company, shoulder-to-shoulder, so the Marines nodded, or said as much. Well, not me, I'm a dog. From me a tail wag is as good as a nod, and a sloppy tongue hanging out the side of my mouth passes for a grin in canine life.

Over the course of the mission with the *Devil Dogs* and with the two of us working our K-9 team magic under the bright Afghan sun, we'd found five of the Taliban's pressure-plate Improvised Explosive Devices, including a particularly nasty fifty-six pound fuel bomb a few kilometers down the road from the sun baked, dust-blown village of Haji Tourjahn.

With the U.S. pressuring Pakistan to restrict shipments of ammonium nitrate fertilizer to Afghanistan that the Taliban use as their primary ingredient for the IEDs, the insurgents turned to importing potassium chlorate for their much nastier, but slightly more cost effective explosives.

The plastic, tub-size, crockpot mix of the white crystal powder, kerosene, and a pinch or two of spite, added an improved fiery element and hellish pain to their concealed bombs and gave them a bigger bang for their '*fuck you!*' buck.

The downside for the Taliban, of course, is that potassium chlorate is a key ingredient in the production of your everyday household matches. Given that electricity is a scarce commodity throughout the countryside, and since kerosene oil lamps and candles are the mainstay for generating the much-needed light at night for the Taliban to cook their food, find their way to the outdoor toilet to do their business, or hey, even plan their attacks, you'd think they would hold matches in a higher regard. Could be, too, that they don't particularly want us here, and maybe hoping we'll see the light, and get the message, one IED at a time.

While the fuel bomb might not have blown the jar heads' up-armored Humvee sky high, it certainly would've incinerated all of those inside of it, including the loyal Afghan interpreter who was riding in the lead military vehicle at the time, so he knew he was in very good company.

"Was good *Spi zoe* mission," Batoor said with a grin, on the way back to Camp Leatherneck.

Max nodded and said it was.

A few kilometers shy of the camp, and just outside yet another small, weather worn village, the convoy slowed to a stop to let an old, stoop-shouldered goat herder bring his semi-manageable flock across the road. The old man was herding the goats back to the village with a walking stick, and like all goat herders with goats that had the dispositions of cats, the *herding* took a little doing. So, we waited.

Glancing out the half-opened window of the Humvee as we were stopped, I smiled to myself when I spied a lone Tulip that comfortably buttressed up against a several good-sized boulders off to the side of the road. The Tulip, that had proudly pushed its way up through the seemingly barren soil, and somehow, in spite of the harsh surroundings and the war, had blossomed, brilliantly.

The bright scarlet, bell-shaped flower was highlighted with a golden fringe that dropped down to a thin, but sturdy, dark green stem to a draping splay of three to four, broad, lime green leaves at its base. The lone flower gave an elegant and serene beauty to the parched and desolate backdrop.

Afghanistan doesn't have a national flower, but if it did, then the Tulip that originated in neighboring Persia, and was celebrated throughout the world, would be one of the country's top contenders.

The lone tulip offered a wondrous display of natural artistry, that, for the moment, gave a sense of tranquility and much needed hope to this end of the world. That is, until one of the goat herder's wandering goats, spotted the proud flower, scampered over, and began making quick work over his serendipitous little salad bar.

"NO! NO! NO!" I growled, climbing up the half-opened window and working myself up to fighting frenzy trying to scare off the soulless little vegan from the vile act. Stuck inside the Humvee with my snout barely out of the partially opened window, there was little I could do but show my anger and contempt by rabid snarling and barking. I knew it, the chuckling passengers in the Humvee knew it, and the once startled goat who had temporarily moved away from the half-eaten flower, was about to realize it, too.

"Easy Thor. Easy," said Max, pulling me from the window and trying to calm me down as the gloating goat went back over to the flower and began chowing down on the rest of the Tulip.

"SONOFABITCH!" I growled.

Yeah, yeah, I know, I know. Technically, that's me, but how do you swear at a goat and insult its lineage enough to get his attention when its crime is feta accompli?

Bull nosing my way under Max's arm I was back up on the window, barking my displeasure at the goat only to have Max drag me back down a second time, this time yanking hard on my collar and reprimanding me.

"I said, EASY!"

The goat had worked its way down the stem, pulling, tugging, and finally latching onto the buried bulb, until there was nothing left of the once majestic flower but several thin strands of dirt covered, stringy roots that were hanging out the side of its mouth as it chewed.

Soon the roots, too, were gone and the goat was smugly running his tongue over his lips and teeth staring at me until the old goat herder walked over and swatted the errant animal with his walking stick to get the gluttonous goat back to the flock. When I began working up a muffled growl at the goat herder who let this tragedy happen, the old Afghan shot me a hard glare over his shoulder.

"Your dog doesn't like goats," laughed a Marine Gunny in the front seat of the military vehicle.

"Or goat herders!" added another Jarhead manning the gun turret above us who, too, was watching on.

Naw, it wasn't about goats, let alone goat herders. It was about the desecration of the only one true thing of natural beauty I'd seen on this mission or in this country in days and perhaps, months! And since I couldn't stop the goat from this profane violation- this outrageous, unholy and vile sin, then at least I was hoping to scare the goat enough to shit out one simple seed.

The convoy started rolling again and, hot and dusty as it was, Batoor and the Marines were in a good mood, again. It was the end of the mission and everyone, and everything, was still intact. It wasn't a win-win, but it wasn't a lose-lose, either.

It was a welcome military homeostasis of sorts; a momentary warm and fuzzy euphoric feeling of internal balance all the while knowing that, externally, everything else could go to shit in an instant.

But Batoor was right. For the now, it was a good *Spi zoe* mission, so much so, that upon our return, the Marines held a small ceremony for us and made Max and me both honorary *Devil Dogs*.

"For Army pukes," said the Company Commander, calling us out in formation and presenting us with a certificate of appreciation, emblazoned with United States Marine Corps gold and red Globe and Anchor, "you and your Malligator did an outstanding job for us and we'll let your command know that it is much appreciated. You're welcome to serve with us any time. Ooo-rah, *Devil Dogs*, and Semper fucking Fido!"

The rest of the Marines in the company formation soon joined in with a raucous and rousing chant of, "*DEV-IL DOGS! DEV-IL DOGS! DEV-IL DOGS!*" and a few Team America's, "*Fuck Yeahs!*"

After the presentation and short celebration, we said our goodbyes to the Marines and made our way over the flight line to catch a helicopter ride back to our Military Working Canine Detachment area at Camp Phoenix, just outside of Kabul.

A Marine Gunny saw us off with a few liter bottles of water and a box of MREs, and we left with the satisfaction of knowing that we had frustrated the Taliban on this latest time out in the sandbox.

The fact of the matter is, as a bomb dog team, we're not just good at tracking down deadly IEDs before they're tripped or triggered we're very good at it.

Fucking A!

Fucking B, however, is that very good doesn't necessarily mean, great.

We've both been wounded in action, previously, in two separate IED triggered detonations. Each time we *ate the blasts*, that's what it's called when you can't make it out of the blast zones and you're caught up in the explosions and somehow managed to survive, we'd been told that we'd been, *lucky*.

That, and the word, *fortunate*, were something we heard, time and again, in both instances from a number of the medics, nurses, and doctors in the various stages of our treatment and recovery. We were '*lucky*' or '*fortunate*' that we'd only come away with mild concussions, some constant ringing in our ears, and several minor cuts and flesh wounds from the blistering bits of splintered shrapnel that had torn, ripped, or burned into us in the blasts. Eating a blast doesn't make for a Happy Meal.

Oh, and on a small, but perhaps timely and appropriate historical note at this time, it was Sir Henry Shrapnel, the British Inspector of Artillery, who in 1804, invented the artillery round that was filled with scraps of metal and sent red hot splintered fragments across a wider, and more destructive area when it exploded. To me, the IEDs are merely the latest evolutions to Sir Henry's design with the same overall desired effect. A shame his name wasn't Sir Henry Chew-toy.

Although we hadn't been caught up in ground zero of the epicenter of the explosions that might've vaporized us, or sent jigsaw pieces of us flying, we'd still been caught within the continuously troubling blast radius zone. Even at something of a distance and somewhat spared a nastier fate, we were still slammed with the deafening, tornado-like force and a wall of heat and overpressure from the blast. It brought Hell in an instant and sent us wind milling and tumbling through the air like Pit Bull tossed Beanie Babies. With it, too, came the blistering splintered shrapnel that tried its best to turn us into reluctant dartboards well before we'd finished tumbling from the blast.

However, in each instance, Max's individual body armor and rucksack, and my modified canine vest that had been fitted with ballistic plates, took the brunt of what had hit us. Body armor and Kevlar helmets, though, are like umbrellas in a downpour; they stop a lot of what is raining down on you, but they can't stop it all. Rain may soak you, but shrapnel will do the same with your own blood.

The assorted nasty scrapes, bumps, and discolored bruises were all bag and baggage that went along with the other damage, but it didn't seem to worry the medical staff as much as it did us. The raw scrapes would scab over and the dark purple, almost black bumps and bruises, that would eventually fade to scarlet and piss yellow were all too commonplace in a war zone. They generally only garnered shrugs or *muy macho* 'suck it up, Rambo' looks or comments, if you whined too much. After all, they had more serious wounds and injuries to contend with and treat.

Even so, each time we'd been patched up in the Emergency Room after getting caught up in the blasts, the Doctors didn't release us right away. Although the force of the shock wave from the explosions had knocked us on our butts, rang our proverbial bells, but hadn't caused too much in the way of outward physical body damage, the doctors monitored us for twenty-four hours afterwards to watch for other troubling signs.

They wanted to be sure that we hadn't experienced something more serious and damaging, internally. The monitoring was part of their learned protocol. The longer these wars went on, the better the doctors, nurses, and medics became at dealing with the myriad of battlefield injuries and horrors that came their way; injuries and horrors that prior to this latest war, weren't previously covered in their medical textbooks. Knowledge, though, always comes at a price, and the learning process in this profession would extract its partial or full payment in haunting, painful ways.

The medical teams soon learned that the kinds of injuries or wounds soldiers can suffer in an explosion depended upon the size of the charge in the IED, and how close the victims were to the epicenter of the blast zone when it detonated.

The initial lesson learned was that hurt radiates out. Those of us who had been caught up in an IED detonation well understood that the closer you are to the epicenter of an explosion, the more bad things can happen to you.

Get caught in the immediate ring of the kill zone and you're dead in a brutal and ugly way. A few more steps outside of the kill zone, but still within the troubling blast zone, if you survive, then your degree of pain will be dictated by distance.

From a better distance, when you hear the blast, your initial survival instincts are to duck, cover, and worry about the shrapnel that can come at you like flying meat cleavers, only there's more than just the hot, splintered fragments of metal that can kill you well before they strike.

If you're within the deadly and dangerous radius of an explosion, chances are you may not even hear it as the first thing to reach you will be the 1,000-degree-plus searing heat that pushes ahead of the noise; the searing heat that can scorch your mouth, esophagus, and lungs, so that even if you somehow survive being blinded and having your lips, ears, eyesight and nose burned away, each breath you'll draw in the dark afterwards will feel like broken glass in your throat and chest.

Then too, there's the overpressure that goes with it; the screaming Banshee of the blast that, even if it doesn't leave you with any or all of the ugly, outward injuries, it can also leave you with something just as horrific internally, like a TBI; a Traumatic Brain Injury.

After an explosion you might look physically okay and uninjured with a TBI because the frightening few outward symptoms of the slowly growing damage are all too easy to overlook with a cursory physical assessment. Other than what initially appears to be mild shock and momentary confusion, there might not be any noticeable outward damage. At a quick once over, and other than ringing ears and being covered in dust and debris, you might look to be relatively normal and okay.

But it's what is initially missed that'll kill you, like the burst blood vessels in your eyes, and the disorientation that soon follows. What goes unseen with a TBI are the small, micro tears in your brain that lowly bleed and cause it to swell until your life lights short circuit and go out.

Forever.

That's why, after we ate the blasts, they monitored us and kept watch for the little signs to make sure that we hadn't suffered TBIs. Our massive, skull-pounding, screaming pain behind the eyes when we moved our heads headaches, instead, were deemed to be just 'mild' concussions.

It could've been worse. Miserably so, and we know it. During our multiple deployments we'd lost good friends to TBIs and IED blasts; dogs and handlers killed, maimed, or horribly disfigured doing the work we do as K-9 detection teams; the work that, by the way, never seems to end over here. We have seen better days.

Talk to me when I'm lying on the ground after I've eaten a blast; dazed, bleeding, and streaked and covered in choking dust, blood, and spitting phlegm, and I might remind you that it's no way to treat 'Man's Best Friend.' That is, if I was human and actually able to speak. But me saying, 'Seriously, what the fuck?' still comes out: Woof?

So, eh…

Woof?

CHAPTER

2

My name is Thor and I'm a six-year-old, lean, but not quite mean, mocha colored Belgian Malinois. I am Man's best friend and a slobbering sweetheart, when you get to know me. Next to fine Belgian chocolate, I can be a woman's BFF, too. I have a leash, so yo! Call me. Let's hook up.

I like long walks on the beach, I'm a good listener, and I like to cuddle. I'll make my heaven in a lady's lap, so, ladies, feel free to think of me as a seventy-four pound lap dog, or something that will gladly keep your feet warm on a cold night. I don't have a cell phone, but if you want me, just whistle.

My official U.S. Army Military Police title is: Military Working Dog, TEDD, T-Thor, tattoo number, T-210. The TEDD stands for Tactical Explosives Detection Dog. And if a bomb dog has ever alerted to an IED that you weren't previously aware of, and that you were about to have a close encounter of the '*you fucking got to be kidding me*' kind, then think of the TEDD as advocating to *Thank Every Damn Dog*.

Yeah well, that's my Tedd Talk and, oh, I don't know, an idea that I think is worth spreading, too. Pass it along.

Max usually calls me, T-*Dogg, Buddy,* or *Buddy Boy*, while more than a few others call me, *Malligator* or *Land shark*, because we Belgian Malinois have a reputation and skill set for chasing down, locking on, and flying tackling bad guys.

As a breed we're agile, fierce, and we just don't take a bite out of crime, we chomp down on it like its feeding time at a Louisiana Gator farm and they're serving some tasty Cajun chicken.

A Military Working Dog's real talent, at least in the war zone, besides guarding key checkpoints in bases or camps or patrolling, is sniffing out IEDs before they detonate. Our personal record is twenty-seven and two, and while on the surface the 'twenty-seven' number is impressive, it's the second number that, at times, keeps us awake at night or becomes the stuff of nightmares when we do finally nod off.

The first time Max and me *ate a blast* was on our very first deployment in another warzone. That was in Iraq back in 2003. Our primary assignment then was working the five to seven mile stretch of highway from the Baghdad International Airport to the front gate of the heavily fortified, ten-kilometer squared, safe site of the International Green Zone in the center of the city. Nicknamed *Route Irish* by our people, the main highway to and from the airport had proved to be a dangerous and deadly run.

For ten months straight we accompanied Humvee and truck convoys back and forth along *Route Irish,* as they brought in new arrivals, equipment, supplies, and a string of VIP visitors to the Green Zone.

Irish is where we earned our proverbial stripes by finding the IEDs planted by some of Saddam's more dedicated and determined holdouts, or their Al Qaeda cousins.

The majority of the IEDs we'd found were your standard basement-made variety pipe bombs or modified pressure cookers with pressure plate triggers, hastily placed, and, at times, not very well hidden. A few others, though, were the more professional individual or intricately linked-together mortar or artillery shells or anti-tank mines, reworked, and reconfigured to detonate by cell phone or a tripped electrical switch.

With each new passing week in the fight, the bad guys were learning how to up their game against us, which meant we had to adapt and up ours to meet the challenge.

As a bomb dog team we'd not only been trained to sniff out IEDs, we were also taught to look for signs of freshly churned dirt and disturbed ground, strategically placed, but casual looking piles of garbage, hastily parked or abandoned vehicles, people in chunky or heavy clothing wandering towards us, or anything else potentially troubling that was conveniently near or next to the section of roadway or overpass we'd be passing. There was a method to the madness, and madness to the method.

The lessons paid off, but there was more schooling to come.

By mid-March, with less than two months left to go on our deployment, we were on our third run of the day, escorting some newly arrived media types and several high ranking NCOs and junior officers to the Green Zone, when the Military Police vehicle leading the convoy stopped well ahead of a small, but suspicious pile of garbage.

The trash pile, that hadn't been there on the previous run, was a little too close to where the convoy would pass. Hackles up suspicious? Oh fuck yeah, and something that needed to be checked out before the convoy moved on.

Since we didn't have any EOD people, those 'Hurt Locker' bomb disposal type expert teams tasked with defusing the explosive devices or safely detonating them in place with us this time out, and since we couldn't remain stopped, or even left lingering on the highway without being subject to sniper fire or mortar attack, Max and me were called up to investigate the suspicious trash pile.

Signs on the convoy vehicles that were printed in several languages warned civilian traffic to keep well back of the convoy, while shouted warnings from our soldiers with weapons raised reminded the locals of the restriction.

It wasn't about military road rage. The restriction was to hinder the occasional Kamikaze-like suicide bombers in cars and trucks, as well as any drive-by bangers from attacking us while we were moving or were momentarily stopped in place.

"It's show time, buddy," Max said, adjusting his Oakley wraparound sunglasses and my doggles. Both the sunglasses and doggles we wore were to cut the glare from the harsh sunlight as well as to protect our eyes from blowing sand and debris, not to mention, that they made us both look pretty freaking cool.

Max hooked me up to the fifteen-foot long lead, patted my vest at the back of our Humvee to pump me up. "You want to find it? Yoooou want to find it? Come on, buddy. Come on, T-Dog, let's find it!"

The hunt was on and we moved in our well-practiced unison, taking it slowly and methodically as we went. The long lead gave me room to maneuver with Max always close by. Five yards ahead of the trash pile, I caught a whiff of explosives in the immediate area. It was a bright, clear day, the temperature was in the mid forties and climbing, and there was a slight breeze.

It was the slight breeze that gave the IED away. My nose shot up to the sky when I caught the scent cone, and like a boxer in the ring doing with a head bobs and weaves, I began to track the odor back to its source.

In the open like this, the odor would rise and swirl with the air current. It soon had me working the scent cone in a round about manner while slowly narrowing it back down to the roadway, which, of course, led me closer to the trash pile. Surprise, surprise.

"What'cha got, buddy? What'cha got, T-Dogg?" Max said, as we inched towards the piled garbage and I suddenly stopped and sat like I'd been taught to do.

Next came my signature swivel head alert of staring at the hidden and trash covered IED, back up at Max, and then back to the trash pile. I'd done my part, now he needed to do his.

"Yes! Good boy!" he said praising me and giving me a couple of quick rubs on my belly and ears for the effort.

"YES!" he said again, praising me as he pulled me away from the trash pile. "Good dog!"

Max yelled back to the Convoy Commander that we had an alert and to notify the Green Zone to get someone out here to deal with it. But the slight pause and hesitation from the Convoy Commander brought on some mild annoyance from Max. Apparently, the Convoy Commander, a Staff Sergeant, didn't think we were close enough to the trash pile to actually sniff out an IED. What came next was reluctance.

"You sure?" yelled the NCO, only to have Max frown back at him and stand his ground.

"That's affirmative," he said, confidently and maybe a little annoyed. "Call the Green Zone and get us some EOD people out here. It's an IED. It's there."

It was there. I smelled it. At best, humans have five million olfactory sensory cells while dogs like me have two to three hundred million or more, depending upon the size of our snouts.

That's right, size matters, and with our muzzles stretching into our olfactory cortex we can pick up on odors and identify scents that you humans can't even begin to fathom. The nose knows.

The rest is up to the handler to recognize the interest we show and the alert we provide. It's all about the training, or the lack of it. And maybe more importantly, it's about trusting the dog, which wasn't always the case. The Pentagon spent millions trying to come up with new gadgets to detect IEDs only to discover that we dogs provide the best results.

Even from the distance, I could smell the Staff Sergeant's wavering uncertainty that smelled very much like his newly issued uniform he received when he arrived in-country three weeks earlier. He was still new. He hadn't learned to trust us, yet. He wasn't alone.

"The VIP Sergeant Major we picked up at the airport doesn't like the idea of waiting on this highway out in the open. He's thinking we should drive around it," the Convoy Commander yelled to Max. "You copy, Dog boy?"

"Yeah, I copy," Max said, eyeing the thin shoulder of the road the convoy would most likely take. "But I don't give a rat's ass about what he thinks unless he's a bomb dog handler, and I guarantee he wouldn't like it any better if, his vehicle gets blown to shit by the IED that's hidden in the trash pile or any secondary device that may be waiting, if we try to drive around it. Call for EOD. I'm sure it's a spider. It'll need to be blown in place," said Max, back over his shoulder as he rubbed my ears and patted my vest again. A 'spider' was our slang for a hidden explosives device.

"Good boy!" he said to me, because, well, I was.

"We got an Ali Baba on a cell phone!" yelled one of the MPs on the convoy's security team. The soldier was down behind the gun sites of the M240b swivel mounted machinegun in the turret of the lead vehicle scanning the immediate area.

The Military Policeman was focused in on a much too calm-looking Lookie-Loo, who was peering out of a second story window of an adjacent building, a building that was conveniently clear of the blast zone. The MP brought the machinegun up on the Iraqi who appeared to have a cell phone in his hands. An *Ali Baba* was the GI slang for a local bad guy.

"Shit!" swore Max, turning me back towards the convoy as he saw the Ali Baba glaring at us before he disappeared from the window opening.

Someone in our convoy was yelling at us.

"RUN!" he yelled, and we took off on, an aptly named, dead run, and were quickly trying to put more distance between us, and the trash pile. We had gone maybe twenty to thirty yards when the Iraqi pressed the send button on his cell phone that triggered the explosion.

In an instant, the blast wave bowled us over and sent us sprawling, well before we heard the thundering boom. A hive of angry, stinging wasps in the shape and swarm of splintered shrapnel and loose rocks, quickly followed. Behind us a cloud of black, acrid smoke flecked with dirt, dust, and debris rose in a thermal column in the sky from the center of the blast.

Through the buzzing and wah-wahhing in my ears I could make out small arms fire, but none of it seemed to be aimed at us. Max and me were both down and struggling to breathe as our world was spinning like a bad carnival ride. The small arms fire was over in a few minutes and was immediately replaced with yelling. Yelling was a staple of combat. Swearing too, for that matter.

"CEASE FIRE! CEASE FIRE! Goddamn it, I said, cease fire!" yelled the Convoy Commander while the cry was echoed up and down the length of the convoy.

"Watch the buildings!" he yelled. "WATCH THE BUILDINGS!"

"FUCK!" yelled Max, flat on his back and staring up at the roiling, dust-filled sky through what was left of his twisted and broken sunglasses.

Slowly rolling over, he tossed aside the twisted and broken sunglasses, as he pushed himself up to his hands and knees, and rested there for a moment trying to clear his head and desperately trying not to vomit. His lungs were burning and his vision was blurred. When he finally regained some better focus and coughed up some dust from his lungs and blew out what was clogged in his nose, he found me seven feet or so away lying on my side.

"Oh, Jesus...no!" he said, crawling towards me as best he could.

My doggles were all cracked and hanging all doggywampus and askew, I was covered in dirt and debris, and I was bleeding from a small tear in my right hip. Our dinged and dented individual body armor, our IBAs with their much-appreciated ballistic plates, took the worst of the flying shrapnel. Covered in a layer of fine dust we looked like the ghosts we almost had become.

"Hey buddy, you okay?"

I was on my side and thinking that if every dog has its day, then this one wasn't mine. As Max sat and pulled me into his lap, he glanced back at the small crater in the road behind us.

It was a pressure cooker IED that had left the three-foot wide hole and sent us sprawling. Had it been a larger or more sophisticated IED, then the crater would've been deeper and neither one of us would've been alive to feel this miserable.

The MP, who had taken out the Ali Baba bomber seconds after he detonated the IED, was still down behind the sites of the machinegun, scanning the immediate area searching for other targets. He had fired several hundred rounds, in short four to six round bursts, and even so, the barrel of the machinegun glowed a dull and fading orange.

"You're okay, Thor," Max said, assuring me that perhaps I was. He had upped the volume since his hearing and mine was still a little muffled. As he ran a hand over my fur, he came away with a few bloodstained fingers. "I got you, buddy."

I had my head cushioned in the crook of his elbow and let it rest there for a bit. *Okay* wasn't the human word I had in mind. Blood was slowly oozing out of the wound. Retrieving a gauze bandage from the

First Aid kit he carried in his right front pocket, he scraped away a patch of dust and placed the bandage over the bleeding hole. He gently applied pressure trying to stem the slow, but steady flow of blood. For the moment, the combined steady pressure and the gauze bandage was doing the job.

"I got you, buddy," he said again, running his free hand over my ears. "I got you."

Max had a few bleeding rips and tears himself, but the bulk of his attention and focus was on me. That's my partner, that's my boy.

Seeing us stuck out in the open a medic came racing up with several other soldiers to help get us behind cover. They shouldered us back behind an up-armored Humvee where the medic began conducting a better evaluation of our injuries and treating our visible wounds.

"You're banged up a bit, but you're going to be okay," he said, applying gauze bandages and tape to a small wound on his right tri-cep and a gouge to his right, front thigh. As he spoke he was also checking Max's eyes and ears.

After a quick once over, the Medic said, "Dude, you're lucky."

"What?" Max was having trouble hearing the medic. A slow trickle of blood was falling down his left ear and he was cleaning out debris from his other ear.

"I said, you're lucky!"

"In a shit lottery, maybe."

"It's all pay to play once you've enlisted," nodded the medic. "How's your focus?"

"My what?"

"Your eyes. How's your focus?" said the medic, upping his volume.

"Better than my hearing, apparently."

"I suspect you blew out an eardrum."

Max gave a slight nod. Anything more would've hurt.

Not quite satisfied with what he found from our wounds, but not screaming for a body bag, either, the medic added, "We'll get you back to the Green Zone, get you to the CASH, and have you checked out to make sure you don't have a TBI."

A CASH was a Combat Support Hospital, the new MASH for this

latest war; a portable surgical hospital that served the military in the field.

Max nodded, even if he could probably only make out every third or fourth word. The explosion had our ears ringing like Quasimodo on crack yanking on the church bell ropes with gusto and maniacal glee. It also left us dazed, off-balance, and stumbling like drunks. We weren't dead, even if it felt like it.

"You're going to be okay," the medic said again, while Max offered a small, resigned smile in return.

'*Okay*' was the operative word here; not good, not wonderful, just okay.

"Hey Doc, can I get a better bandage for Thor?" Max asked the Medic.

"Thor?"

"My dog."

"Your dog?"

"Yeah, he's wounded, too. The bandage I had is too small."

The medic shrugged and nodded. "Sure," he said. "No problem."

The medic dug into his aid bag and pulled out a clean ten-by-ten bandage pad and a paper-covered lump of wrapped gauze. Removing the smaller, blood-soaked bandage that Max had hastily applied earlier, he began treating the wound.

"Your German Shepherd just saved a few lives," said the medic, wrapping and tying a knot over the clean bandage.

Max didn't take offense at the '*German Shepherd*' insult, and neither did I. For the moment, we were above the noise.

"Let's get you out of here. There could be a secondary device," the medic said once we were stabilized and then helped us back to the safety of the vehicles where we were loaded us into the medic's Humvee for transport.

Secondary explosive devices were sneaky ways to double up on ambush pain. By planting a second remotely controlled IED and waiting for others to run up to help rescue the wounded and recover the dead, after the first IED went off, the Ali Babas would then trigger the second blast, and take out more of we hated Infidels.

Fortunately, there was no secondary device and the convoy rolled on unmolested. At the hospital back at the Green Zone, we were X-rayed before the Emergency Room team cleaned out our wounds and removed what shrapnel splinters they could locate and get to. Well, at least the ones they could get to without complications.

After the easy pieces of jagged metal had been pulled or cut out, and the wounds stitched, an attending Radiologist and another Army Doctor went over the X-rays together.

"Some small pieces here and here that shouldn't be an issue," said the Radiologist, a tall, prematurely balding man in his mid-thirties.

"Mmm," agreed the second Doctor, a short, dark haired Asian woman with Harry Potter-like glasses. The nametag on her uniform read: CHAN.

"Shrapnel just missed the femoral artery here," said the Radiologist. "He was lucky."

"His dog, too, according to his Vet."

"We good?"

"Mmm."

Max was seated on an examination table looking very much like he'd gone the distance with a much better MMA fighter in an octagon of hurt and grime. I was at his feet and the dog in his fight. Clean bandages and tape covered seeping wounds and we had been given working medication for the accompanying pain.

We were deadbeat tired, we smelled like bad Tuna, and were covered in a sad film of dirt, sweat, and semi-dry blood from the blast.

Back to us Doctor Chan said, "No bad news, well, not real bad news, anyway, Sergeant. We removed the large pieces of shrapnel. However, you both have some smaller fragments in you that will stay put for the time being. Also, you have a mild concussion and suffered some hearing loss."

She paused and Max replied with a small shrug and smile.

"We'll need to send you for an Audiology consult to confirm it, but that'll come later. The good news is that the shrapnel remaining in you shouldn't cause any real problems and, barring any serious infection, your wounds should heal. All in all, it could've been a whole lot worse. You're lucky."

There was the 'lucky' thing again. This time with a nod and another 'Mmm,' this time from the Radiologist.

"Other than maybe setting off a few metal detectors when you go through TSA at the airports, you should be fine," Doctor Chan said with a small grin.

"You won't take them out?"

"No need, actually," she said, dismissing them. "Any surgery would be too invasive and cause more problems than the shrapnel itself. The body will either force the small bits out or encapsulate the fragments, but other than that you're fine. Just keep copies for your records so that when you leave the Army you'll have them, if you ever need to file a claim with the Veterans Administration."

"Ma'am?"

"My father is a Vietnam veteran. The VA lost his records in a fire at the records center in St. Louis back in the 1970s. Proving he got shot took more than the through and through bullet scars on his thighs, so hold onto copies of your medical records is all I'm saying."

"Yes, Ma'am," said Max.

"Oh, and Sergeant…"

"Yes, Ma'am?"

"File a claim," added Dr. Chan, "because, given your MOS and the nature of the work you do, especially with regards to the concussion and hearing loss, and, if you'll excuse the pun, this might come back to bite you."

Max gave them another small smile.

Because our wounds were only considered 'minor' and the concussions' 'mild,' we spent the next week to ten days on light duty. While our wounds healed we exercised within our limits and continued our training. Max cleaned kennels, and ran errands for the Detachment Commander and the First Sergeant while I got in some odor detection work and gradually improved physically.

The Officer-In-Charge of the canine unit in Baghdad at the time lobbied to get us more stand-down time but she was overruled by the higher ups. This, she was told, had to do with the shortage of available bomb dog teams, and the non-serious nature of our wounds.

She didn't necessarily agree, but left with little choice, she carried out her orders. As an Army Military Police Captain, she took her job seriously, professionally. She looked out after her working K-9 teams, as did the First Sergeant, showing that we were more than just grease penciled names on an operational duty roster. However, she did send us back for a follow-up visit to the Doctor for one last evaluation.

At the follow-up visit, the Doctor who had treated us for our wounds said she'd give us an additional week to recuperate, if we wanted it, but Max said it wasn't necessary. We were *good-to-go*, he said, which earned a surprised look from the doctor.

"You sure, Sergeant?"

"Yes, Ma'am. Time to get back to work."

"Sniffing out roadside bombs."

"Yes, Ma'am."

The Doctor stared at Max quietly for a moment, processing her thoughts, and concerns.

"Your call, Sergeant," she said and then looked at me and grinned.

Humans do that to me from time to time. I'm fucking adorable. "How's your dog doing? I understand he took some shrapnel, as well."

"He did, but he's fine. Aren't you, buddy?"

Max was scratching my latte-colored ruff and smoothing down my ears.

"Woof!" I said, because, like I said, I'm a dog, and 'Take the second week, you dumbass' still comes out, Woof, regardless of how many times I bark it. You see the problem with this whole not talking thing? Yeah well, we dogs see it, too. Woof?

Oh, and here's a little tip for you if you ever find yourself in combat when something wicked this way comes, and things go horribly wrong in a hurry; if you don't really give a rat's ass or second thought about medics, nurses, doctors, or Veterinarians before you get wounded, you certainly will afterwards. They work hard. They do good things in always stressful and trying situations, so treat them nice.

Wag your damn tail.

CHAPTER

3

There were a few more close calls during the rest of the deployment, but we left Iraq without any new wounds or serious injuries. Max and me happily returned stateside, this time to Fort Gordon, Georgia, a few miles outside of Augusta and two hours east of Atlanta on I-20 for people who don't want to Google.

In 1735, the British Colony Governor, James Olgethorpe, named the then town, Augusta, to honor the German born, English Princess, Augusta of Saxe-Gotha, who, probably never ate a peach, said, *'Y'all,'* or *'Go Bull Dogs'* to her homies.

Oh, and yes, I know I said, 'Max and me,' again. If it bothers you or say, puts you in a furor, Herr or Frau Goebbels, then, you probably don't really understand the unique bond and special relationship working military dogs share with their handlers. To me, the *me*, is grrr-matically correct, colloquial speech, even if it comes off as a poke in your I.

It's also nostalgic, because it always takes me back to the very first moment we partnered up. We were younger then, damn near puppies, in fact. Max was a brand new, fresh-faced handler and I was an eighteen-month-old just out of canine training. When we were introduced, Max stepped into my cage in the kennel, dropped down on one knee, and held out a hand for me to sniff. As I did, he reached in, started scratching me behind the ears, looked me in the eyes, smiled and said, "Looks like it's you and me, buddy."

It was his smile and the words behind it that sealed the deal. We bonded, and it has been Max and me ever since, year after year, deployment after deployment, and IED blasts and all that went with them.

Like all change of duty stations, Fort Gordon was a temporary assignment and not necessarily a bad one at that. Georgia was experiencing a glorious spring with blossoming sweet Magnolias, blue-violet hanging wisteria, bright red canna Lilies, Daffodils, and butterfly favorite Honeysuckles, all amazingly aromatic and flavored with wafting smoke of mouth-watering grilled chicken, steak, sausages, or ribs from a dozen or more different hickory, mesquite, or charcoal burning grills and smokers on any given weekend.

There were butterflies and lightning bugs to merrily chase and snatch at in the gloaming, too. And on our early evening walks or runs, it made for a nice little bonus activity, as did the satisfaction and contentment that came with running over freshly mown lawns, peeing on interesting smelling trees and brush, and marking the dog territorial fire hydrants.

Max seemed to enjoy it as well, as women here walked their Golden Labs, Retrievers or fru-fru yapping dogs in Yoga pants…eh, the women were in Yoga pants, that is, not the dogs. Other than their collars and leashes, the dogs were *au natural* naked, give or take a King Charles spaniel or two, and maybe the occasional Toy Poodle or Chihuahua wearing, swear to God, ugly doggie sweaters.

Doggie sweaters? Seriously, humans? Doggie sweaters!

On the job we worked patrol and continued our proficiency training, with Max tasked to teach a few new handlers some combat tricks of the trade. It was a relatively easy assignment for us, but the joy of returning home didn't last. Our stateside duty was short-lived.

After only seven months in Georgia we were redeployed back to Iraq. The war was heating up and there was a shortage of bomb sniffing K-9 teams and especially experienced K-9 teams, so Max had volunteered for another go at it.

Al Qaeda, and their locally grown affiliates and friends, had introduced ESPs, the Iranian made 'Explosively Shape Penetrators' explosive devices that were causing considerably more damage than their previously basement-made variety of IEDs, so the bomb dog teams for many of the units they served were much appreciated.

Also, Max had just broken up with *Notice me! Notice Me! Red Lipstick* Michelle, his prissy poodle of a girlfriend from Seattle, which also might've had something to Max's decision to volunteer to return to the warzone.

I'd only met *Notice me! Notice me! Red Lipstick* Michelle once when she flew down to Georgia to spend a weekend with Max for what I sniffed was a troubling trip. After checking her into a Best Western Motel in town he brought her on base to the kennel to meet me.

She looked very hesitant and uncomfortable as she entered the kennel and was much out of place dressed in an expensive white blouse, dark cotton pants, and glossy red high-heels that matched her glossy red lipstick and glossy red manicured nails. She scrunched her nose over the smell of the kennel and didn't look all too happy to be there.

"Hey sweetie, this is Thor!" he said as he brought me out of my cage only to have her reel back in disgust as I bounced towards her.

"Oh God, no! These pants are Armani," she said, holding out open palms to stop me from jumping up or even moving closer. Not that she had anything to worry about as Max had me on leash and in control.

"Ew... dog hair!" she cried as she started wiping away the dog hair that wasn't there.

She didn't put out her hand to let me sniff it, nor did she pet me, or seem all that interested in wanting to pet me. Try as I could I really couldn't get a good whiff of her beyond a fog of perfume and the thick layer of foundation makeup, carefully applied blush, bronzer, Luminizer, lash mascara, eye shadow, lip liner, gloss, filler putty, spackle, chipped paint fixer, and airbrushed dent repair she had on that was a walking billboard to the high-end cosmetic counter she worked at the one of the high-end chain stores in the mall.

I couldn't tell you for certain what lay beneath the surface, either. She could have been pretty, plain, butt ugly, or even say, Jimmy Hoffa in some weird government witness protection program disguise. When she made no mention of organizing a union to Max, I realized Jimmy was still encased in concrete in some football stadium End Zone and that *Notice me! Notice me! Red Lipstick* Michelle was just a much-pampered pooch.

"Come on," pleaded Max, playfully. "He won't bite!"

"No," she said, backing away, and when Max started to walk me towards her again, she backed away even further.

"I *said* NO!" she said, angrily and shooed me away. She wasn't having it, any of it.

Max got the message and so did I.

"Maybe later, buddy," he said, putting me back in my cage. Max was more than a little disappointed while she didn't seem to notice, or perhaps, care.

"I'm hungry," she said, changing the subject. Her tone was lilting, but somehow managed to remain whiny. "All they had on the plane was those small bags of peanuts and pretzels. Can we get something to eat?"

"Sure. Where do you want to go?" Max said, locking my cage and hanging up my leash. "What would you like to eat?"

"It doesn't matter."

"There's a great little Barbeque place just off base…"

Notice me! Notice me! Red Lipstick Michelle scrunched her face threatening to dangerously crack the makeup fault line and shift her tectonic plates. "Ew, no," she said. "No Barbeque."

"Chinese food?"

"Nooooo," she said, drawing out her reply as she shook her head. "No MSGs."

"Italian?"

"Uh-uh."

They were still working their way through a list of eateries as they left the kennel with Max offering additional suggestions and her making more faces and declining each in turn.

Other than really seeming to care about something she said really didn't matter when it came to eating, it was obvious she didn't like dogs, too, which told me something more about her. That she was there that weekend to break up with Max told me the rest, and maybe all I really needed to know about her or wanted to know.

Besides the breakup sex, I sniffed that stateside duty, hadn't provided Max with enough of an adrenaline rush as he had in Iraq, so, once again, it was back to combat. It was once more into the breach.

CHAPTER

4

This new deployment, we were told, would be for six months, unless Max decided to extend the tour of duty, which of course, he did for an additional one hundred and eighty days, five months into the deployment. That was too much math for my simple canine brain, and all I knew was that we weren't going home anytime soon.

On this second extension, of this second deployment, we were stationed two hundred and fifty miles north of Baghdad to the city of Mosul. There, the bulk of our missions were spent with the famed 101st Screaming Eagles Airborne Division, working with the paratroopers in and around the disputed 'liberated' city.

We would learn much about Mosul, its people and its history, and how it would all come to blend and work its way into our own lives and histories with this latest deployment. Mosul would no longer be a distant thing or name on a map to Max and me, anymore. It would take on new and personal meaning, just as it had to the soldiers who fought there.

Prior to the war, before the fighting, the population of Mosul had hovered somewhere around two and a half million, with the bulk of its inhabitants occupying the better west bank of the famed Tigris River. It was a prosperous and important city where deluxe Mercedes, Porches, and even the occasional Lamborghini could be seen cruising the grand boulevards and streets dotted with outdoor cafes and trendy shops.

Just upstream from the city stood the massive hydroelectric

dam- the Saddam Dam- that was the fourth largest in the Middle East. Constructed in the mid-1980s, it was a showcase dam for Saddam's regime that generated the bulk of the country's electrical power and much needed irrigation to the region and country.

Once upon a time, and even hours before the 'shock and awe' bombing campaign that kicked off the war, Mosul had been one of Iraq's and Saddam Hussein's most prosperous and notable cities. It had a well-respected University, a top-notched Medical College, and was the financial site of the large and imposing Central Bank of Iraq.

The beautifully marble covered, forty-meter tall, beige-colored National Bank once held the bulk of the nation's wealth, and only a small fraction of Saddam Hussein's own personal fortune, along with the monies and valuables of what belonged to his supporters.

Rumor and even some intelligence sources, had it that Saddam had also squirreled away hundreds of millions in banks around the world through a dozen or more alleged Iraqi ex-pat proxies. His 'just in case' money.

Lest the proxies forget whose money it actually was, Saddam would send out a few enforcers from the *Jihaz-al Mukhabarat al-Amma*, his Secret Police from time to time, to pay visits to remind those that the funds deposited in their own names, actually, weren't theirs to spend. They might enjoy allowances but they would never enjoy the fortunes the bank balances represented.

The Secret Police visitors occasionally paid unannounced social calls to a few of the wayward proxies whose financial indiscretions came to light. During the home visits, Saddam's henchmen might clip off one of the thumbs of their wives or favorite children with pruning shears so that the responsible husband might better understand the error of his fiduciary ways.

Still, it was the Central Bank of Iraq where Saddam could keep a better eye on the nation's real wealth and the millions more it held. The bank's large and impressive state-of-the-art vault was lined with walls of safety deposit boxes. The boxes were reportedly filled with the ruling elite's gold bullion, silver ingots, diamonds, gems, fine jewelry, rare art, and other valuables that Saddam, one day, might take an interest in, say, if one of his wealthy supporters fell out of favor, and, say, accidentally shot himself in the back of his head, twice, while cleaning a pistol he never owned.

It was said that the Central Bank's vault floor held several rows of shrink-wrapped pallets, piled three-feet-high and deep with more than a billion dollars in stacks of Dinars, Euros, Swiss Francs, Rubles, and U.S. one hundred dollar bills.

There the money and wealth remained until the day before U.S. troops entered Baghdad. That was when Saddam had his son, Qusay, and a team of his henchmen, make a little withdrawal from the bank, for what they claimed was 'necessary security money.'

"Hi, my dad's Saddam, and I know that I don't really have an account here with you, but these are my guys and these are our big ass guns pointed at your faces, so I'd like to make a little withdrawal from everybody's accounts, please."

"Eh…how much would you like to withdraw, oh, benevolent Dictator's psychotic, bank robbing son?"

"Psychotic son? No, no, no. I am Qusay. You must have me confused with my big brother, Uday. I am the good son. Same father, different mother, less of a whack job."

"Ah yes, of course, of course, the good son!"

"Yes, that's me! I will only shoot you in the eye, if you ignore my request. Uday will stick an electric carving knife in it and swirl it around a few times like he is mixing hummus. Should I get him on my cell phone for you to see if he and his carving knife are available?"

"No, no, that will not be necessary. I am glad to be able to assist you today, oh benevolent Dictator's less psychotic son. And how much will you be taking out of your non-existing account?"

"900 million or so will do."

"900 mil…"

"Yes, 900 million. Oh, and do you validate parking?"

Qusay Hussein's haul was considered by many to be the biggest bank heist in modern history and went off without a hitch. Of course, it did. The bank manager might momentarily balk, but no Iraqi in their right mind would ever refuse an order from Saddam or his sons, without serious consequence, especially a bank manager who initially mistook Qusay for his bat shit crazy brother, Uday.

The bank manager complied.

Let me walk this in a few circles before I lay down why Uday and Mosul are linked to this tale of sound and fury.

Uday Hussein, Saddam's oldest son by his first wife, Sajida Taifah, was the scheduled heir apparent to the proverbial throne. He was an untouchable and as such, he reveled in mind numbing privilege and excesses. He was also someone who was prone to sporadic violent outbursts and acts. It was said that throughout the 1980s and 90s, he made vicious assault, kidnapping, rape, torture, and murder, all seemingly part of his weekly routine and sick agenda.

Rumor had it that he had killed his first man at age 16, and that by his thirties, the heir apparent, had upped the number considerably. Because of his explosive anger that quickly turned into out of control rage, he was well feared, not just by those who opposed him, but by those within Saddam's elite circle of trusted friends and advisors, who were forced to deal with him and his antics as well.

And, although, they might never openly acknowledge it, or even in private, whisper it, the dislike and distrust of the volatile son was there. It ran deep, with good reason, especially after a drunken Uday killed one of his father's friends during a state dinner party to honor the wife of the President of Egypt.

Uday, though, didn't just kill the man. He gutted him with an electric carving knife.

An outraged Saddam had his son arrested, tossed into prison, and had even ordered his execution. Uday remained in jail for three months before the death sentence was lifted, as many suspected it would be, and he was, instead, banished to Switzerland.

In Geneva, he was told he would serve as an Assistant to the Iraqi Ambassador, while in reality, Uday continued serving himself. He partied too much, got belligerent when he did, and carried on with his mad dog antics, which was why his stay in Switzerland was short lived and the Swiss Government booted him out of the country on his Babylonian butt.

With his tail tucked between his legs, he returned home, somewhat cowed. Back in Iraq, and to keep him out of getting into more trouble, and perhaps, away from his inner circle and electric carving knives, a frustrated Saddam put his first-born successor in charge of the Iraqi Olympic Committee and the nation's Football Association.

Uday, of course, was given a free hand in running the organizations, and soon brought his own unique coaching style to the job. He even implemented a new and unique way of motivating Iraq's top athletes to bring glory and acclaim to his father's regime.

Win an event or match and a happy Uday personally received, hugged, and lavishly praised and celebrated you. You were his new, and momentary, best friend. Ah, but lose an event or match, and you were dragged down to the basement of the Sports Training Center to be sexually humiliated, beaten, and even tortured, if, say, Uday felt that you hadn't given it your all and done your best.

By not winning or even medaling, Uday reasoned that the athlete had not just disrespected Iraq, but had disrespected him, personally. Male or female, it didn't matter. As an equal opportunity sadist, he gave the athletes the individual beatings and humiliation he thought they deserved.

Some track team members said that the shot fired from the starting pistol at the beginning of a race was a reminder of what might happen if they didn't win or place in the track and field events.

There was whispered talk, too, of a boxer who had lost an important regional championship bout and had been brought back to the Sports Center's basement for a motivational adjustment. A team of Uday's 'motivators' bound and tied the boxer to a chair, and then took turns punching and kicking him until he was little more than a bloodied, semi-conscious lump. Not wanting to be left out in the act, Saddam's semi- pride and joy then took a cattle prod to the helpless victim.

Other national athletes would later claim to have been stripped and beaten with hoses and canes before being dragged naked across rough concrete floors and tortured in what were reported as 'shameful and unspeakable ways' by Uday or his motivational team. An unfortunate few of the athletes who hadn't demonstrated enough remorse in their performances were simply 'disappeared.' There were rumors that those who were 'disappeared' had been fed into man size wood chippers and shredders. True or not, the threats were there and the rumors grew.

By the close of 1996, Uday Hussein was so hated and despised that several Iraqis tried to assassinate him in the up-scale Mansour district of Baghdad. It happened during one of his weekly outings cruising in his Porsche convertible searching for desirable young women to kidnap and rape. While the assassination attempt failed the would-be assassins, however, did manage to cock-block his lechery by shooting him seventeen times.

The well-coordinated attack with several shooters had taken a less than a minute to carry out, and left little to no time for Uday's bodyguards, who were following at a prescribed few cars behind, to catch up and confront the attackers. A running gun battle ensued but several of the attackers had managed to get away.

The attack was partially Uday's fault, since he was on one of his usual predatory outings and had his bodyguards hang back while he slowly drove the streets and sniffed around. By the time the bodyguards reached the badly wounded Uday in his shot up Porsche, Uday was a bloody mess.

The attack left him partially paralyzed with a bullet lodged in his spine. The bullet that couldn't be removed, had also left him with a permanent limp or possibly two, as it was generally believed that a few of the bullets had hit him in the groin and neutered him on the spot.

The hushed talk spread, with many quietly relishing, and enjoying the irony that Uday's deranged dogma had finally got hit head-on by his own oncoming Karma. Well, everyone, but a few of his bodyguards who Saddam had 'disappeared.'

As a result, Uday, the once heir apparent lost the title to his younger brother, Qusay, who Saddam officially announced would now succeed him as Top Dog. However, both brothers would lose out to the 101st Airborne in Mosul in July of 2003, when a tip from another angry Iraqi, had the paratroopers surround a villa in the city where the two brothers and others were allegedly holed up and hiding.

The 101st soldiers and a group of Ninja Special Operators, along with some air support from an Army Kiowa attack helicopter and an Air Force A-10 Warthog ground attack jet, took out the snarling pack in a roaring gun battle.

Humans like to call someone as perverted as Uday, a *'twisted, sick puppy.'* But here's the thing; no dog I know, or dog I have ever known, young or old, not even the most wild eyed and foaming at the mouth, Old Yeller rabies wannabe, would ever make torture a sport, which is something else we don't understand about humans.

WTF- woof?

That Uday was finally put down in Mosul may only have been a small footnote in the overall history of the city since world-renown scholars and archeologists knew that Mosul held more remarkable historical significance and worth than a dictator's son.

In terms of its cultural value, it was a city rich in antiquity. Mosul laid claim to the ruins of one history's prominent sites; the ancient and Biblical Assyrian capital of Nineveh, whose large and impressive ruins rested on Mosul's less populated eastern bank.

For several thousand years, Nineveh had been conquered and re-conquered by anyone who had a bone to pick with the Assyrians. As a result of its many invasions, the population of Nineveh, and what eventually became Mosul, became an ethnic mix of tribal Arabs, Kurds, Assyrians, Iraqi Turkmen, Yazidis, Armenians, and Shabaki people.

There may have been others, but it was hard to tell the ethnic or cultural differences between them since the sneers we received patrolling the city all looked the same.

With over six miles of massive mud brick and stone walls, and winged bull men carved into the massive Mashqi gate, the *Gate of God,* that guarded the city, Nineveh's ancient remnants whispered of its important Biblical past and grandeur. In the Bible, it could be found in the Old Testament Book of Isaiah, Chapter 36, along with the lost glories of its once mighty ruler, King Sennacherib.

"Verily, I say unto Hezekiah in J-town, 'King S is the schizzel, yo...'

The archeological site held the grave of the Prophet Jonah, as well, and had once served as a major religious site for Ishtar, the Babylonian goddess of fertility and sex, all of which became the topic of one loud conversation in the vehicle we were riding in on a resupply run to the Dam.

This we heard on an up-armored Humvee troop carrier conversation on a memorable ride with the Combat Engineers working at the hydroelectric dam. We shared the troop carrier with five 101st soldiers, who were part of the number that were riding shotun on the convoy.

The convoy was delivering a few tons of cement and three truckloads of rebar that the American and Iraqi engineers needed to re-grout and support the existing structure that was slowly chipping and wearing away.

One of the paratroopers sitting behind us was saying that the ancient ruins of Nineveh held Jonah's tomb and that the ruins, that were thousands of years old, were still revealing more of its past glories with each new excavation and unique find.

"Old swords and shit. Some gold artifacts, too. Well, at least before the war," said the soldier with an afterthought. "I don't think too many archeologists are doing much digging now."

"Seriously? Jonah's Tomb?" said the PFC driving the vehicle. "Like, Jonah from the Bible?"

"Yep, the very same."

The Humvee's driver, a newly arrived Private, was impressed.

"So is there, like, you know, a tomb for, like, the whale?"

"The whale?" said a somewhat bewildered Platoon Sergeant seated next to the PFC in the front passenger's seat while chuckles were rising from the back of the vehicle.

"Yeah, that swallowed Jonah."

"Seriously?"

"Yeah-huh, because, you know, like Jonah's grave and all," said the PFC driver, nodding like a Kindergartener hoping to get a gold star on his progress chart from his teacher for not eating a crayon.

"You understand we're in the middle of a fucking desert, Private?" the Platoon Sergeant said.

"Could be, like, a miracle...you know, or something," replied the PFC.

"A miracle might be that you actually passed the written test to get into the Army," replied the Platoon Sergeant. "Maintain a safe operating distance from the vehicle in front of us and, like, I dunno, shut your blow hole."

Ishtar, and the whole Easter thing soon carried the rest of the drive. A Specialist-4, named Sanchez, who was standing in the turret and manning the fifty caliber machinegun, was saying that Ishtar was where we get the whole Easter thing with rabbits and eggs, while another soldier in the back with us, disagreed.

"No, it's from the Germanic pagan goddess, Ostara, who was the goddess of dawn who had a rabbit as a lover," argued the paratrooper seated behind us.

This was too much for the Platoon Sergeant.

"Ishtar was also a shitty movie! Now shut the fuck up, Rick Steves, and keep your eyes on the alleys and rooftops!"

It was quiet for another block or so until the young driver spoke up again.

"Who's Rick Steves?'

"The god of roads less traveled, but with more reliable maps than we're issued," replied the Platoon Sergeant.

"But this is, like, one of the main roads, right, Sarge?"

The Platoon Sergeant sighed, rubbing his eyes. It was going to be a long ride to the Dam.

It was also a necessary ride.

The American and Iraqi engineers needed the cement and rebar rods we were delivering to keep the Dam from breeching. It was a Herculean task, but this wasn't Greece and there were no ancient gods working on the project. If the Dam collapsed it would cause catastrophic flooding. The inland tidal wave would inundate a third of the country down river and kill an estimated one million people. It would be a flood of Biblical proportions, and interestingly enough, probably on the same flood plain that gave rise to the story of Noah. The cement and rebar would be a godsend in the form of a 101st Screaming Eagle convoy.

Betting money, though, was on one ethnic faction of bad guys angry at another ethnic faction, would give the breaching a push with a shitload of Semtex, which was another reason why Max and me were accompanying the resupply convoy to the Dam.

We were saving lives, either by delivering the much needed patch kit, or by keeping someone else from blowing it up. Either way, it was an important mission, especially for Mosul and the people living further downstream.

First, though, we had to get to the Dam, and in an active war zone, getting from Point A to Point Z, was seldom an easy go. The Platoon Sergeant had a right to be concerned, as did the Convoy Commander up ahead in one of the lead vehicles. Burnt-out cars and abandoned trucks littered the road out of town as we went.

When the convoy came to a tight turn at a roundabout on the edge of the city, an abandoned and suspicious looking old and dented white Honda Civic that was conveniently resting a little too close to the roadside, gave the Convoy Commander, a Mosul streetwise West Point Lieutenant, pause for concern. Several nearby run down and abandoned buildings gave the roundabout a nice spot for an ambush.

"Hold up! HOLD UP!" came the call over the radio from the Lieutenant, who eyed the suspicious vehicle from a tactically safe distance as the vehicles in the convoy behind us jerked to gear-grinding, mechanical stops. Diesel engines knocked as they idled and nervous hands rested on weapons that went from SAFE to FIRE.

The Convoy Commander took in the abandoned looking buildings as he took out a radio frequency jammer to block cell phone calls or hand-held radios used to trigger IEDs. The jammer's range, however, was limited, and the bad guys knew it.

"Looks like we have a *Papa Oscar Sierra* V-bied that could be a problem. Dismount, secure a perimeter, and send up the bomb dog," he called over the radio back to us.

A V-bied was a vehicle borne IED, a car or truck bomb. A '*Papa Oscar Sierra*' was the military phonetic offering for the initials, P.O.S. that was slang for: *piece of shit.*

The convoy was a good hundred meters or so away from the abandoned Honda, well clear of the potential kill zone. The IED might explode and send shrapnel flying, but not enough to cause any real damage to the convoy at this distance. As the Screaming Eagle paratroopers scurried out to cover the surrounding area, Max and me unassed the Humvee we were riding in, and readied to go to work. He'd be working me on a long leash.

"Heads up and swivel! Watch those windows, doorways, and rooftops!" shouted the Platoon Sergeant to the other soldiers, something that Max and me were counting on. I wasn't so much worried about snipers as much as I was about a bad guy with a cell phone or an electric switch that could and would trigger an IED, given the opportunity. A shouted warning from one of the soldiers could very well save our lives.

Max adjusted our IBA's, kit, his new ballistic sunglasses, and my doggles and we moved out at a cautious walk as he glanced at the darkened doorways every so often. Shadowy doorways and windows always presented potential problems. Well before we reached the abandoned car Max held up and took a knee. One of his bootlaces had come undone so I came back to him to wait at his left side.

When you're searching out bombs and booby-traps you don't need to be tripping over your own feet. Max was still down on one knee retying the bootlace and I was sitting next to him when the abandoned *Poppa Sierra Oscar* Honda exploded.

Because the soldiers were carefully watching the surrounding area the bad guy with a cell phone had to keep his head down, which meant he guessed how close Max and me would be to the vehicle as he triggered the device. He couldn't see or know that Max had stopped to tie his boot.

Frustrated or angry that the convoy stopped well short of the car bomb, the Ali Baba decided that if he couldn't take out one of our vehicles, then he'd at least take out the dog team that foiled his IED ambush. We were to be his target of opportunity, his small victory.

Because he had dropped down behind cover, Mister Baba's timing was off. He assumed we had entered the kill zone when he detonated the charge. We hadn't, but his fallback plan had almost worked, regardless.

There was a blinding, bright flash, instantly followed by a massive eruption of heat, debris, and noise that hit us in a man-made tornado. The abandoned *Poppa Oscar Sierra* Honda that was once parked up ahead was no more, only a deep ten-foot wide crater in its wake.

There is no making sense of dumb luck or perceived miracles in combat, of why this or that happened, or didn't happen. If you survived something that you shouldn't have, then you took it as good fortune and counted your blessings, well, if you had the fingers remaining on your bleeding hands.

When the car bomb detonated the massive explosion sent the Honda's hood flying at us up right like a small wall. As it slammed into us, the upright hood proved to be a fortunate and painful blessing. The metal hood that bowled us over, however, acted as a shield and took the brunt of the shrapnel, stones, and debris from the blast.

We were down, dazed, and Quasimodo was back. The invisible bells were, once again, wildly clanging in our ears. Still we were alive.

However, words like *fortunate* or *blessing* aren't necessary the first words that come to mind when you're on your face in the dirt, bleeding, with the wind sucked out of your lungs, and you're struggling to breathe. Not to mention that you're still stuck out in the open in a warzone. Yeah, there's that, too. Other, seemingly more combat appropriate words might immediately come to mind.

"Are...you...fucking...kidding me?" Max said, struggling to roll over and sit up. His sunglasses were broken and hanging from his face that was covered with a layer of fine dust.

When he finally managed to sit up and hold himself steady without falling, he reached up and tossed what was left of the broken and loose hanging pair of sunglasses.

Well, everything except for the splintered pieces of the expensive frame that had speared his right eyebrow and the bridge of his nose. Wincing and gently pulling the thin metal shards of the sunglass frames out of his face, he started wiping away some of the dust and debris that clouded his vision. The dripping blood would have to wait. For now he was trying to find his breath.

Still seated and feeling like a coal miner who'd been caught in a cave in, he began searching for other survivors, in this case, me. I was only a few feet away, where I'd been tossed in the blast, but I was still partially hidden by a blanket of churned-up dust and dirt. The long leash kept us reasonably close together.

As the dust cloud began to dissipate and settle, Max found me on my side and struggling. Crawling over on all fours, he reached out and pulled me into his lap. A razor sharp piece of shrapnel had sliced across his right cheek leaving what he would later call, 'my dueling scar.'

While his Filipina mother would worry that it had scarred her baby's handsome face, his American father, with his deep German roots, would quietly think of it as the mark of a man.

"You good, buddy?" Max said, wiping away a small stream of blood that was dripping from his eyebrow where the broken arm of the sunglasses had impaled him.

"How you doin', boy? You okay?" he said, brushing away dirt from a small wound on my back where shrapnel had sliced away some fur and meat and was badly bleeding. Slapping on a bandage he taped it in place with duct tape before checking me for additional wounds. As he was working on me, he opened and closed his mouth from time to time, shifting his jaw back and forth trying to clear the ringing in his ears, not that it helped all that much. The bells would be ringing for days. I had a few more cuts and bruises, but nothing significant, or at least, nothing that looked significant.

"Good boy," he said, running a hand over my ears and staring me in the eyes. "You're a good boy."

A baby-faced toddler, disguised an as Army Medic, was racing up to treat us, but before he arrived we had already taken our own inventory, all the while gaping at the large car parts that lay around us.

Twisted and sheared pieces of the shattered car, including the engine block and twisted drive shaft, were blown out of the V-bied's epicenter and were embedded like interpretive monuments within spitting distance in the surrounding ground.

The up-right hood from the car that slammed into us had protected us from the larger chunks of car parts that had blown straight at us in the blast. The hood that now lay on its battered side was gouged and pitted from the severed metal in the explosion. However, while the car hood had offered some protection, it didn't offer all.

Although nothing felt broken, there were going to be a number of nasty bruises to go along with yet another concussion and a few new rips and tears in each of us.

The Individual Body Armor- the heavy thirty-two pound IBAs with front and back ballistic insert plates, we wore, once again, helped block whatever got around the door, but it only covered most of the vital organs. We both had metal fragments or splinters that stuck into the body armor like iron porcupine quills.

But the body armor vests didn't cover the pecker or balls, which, oh, I don't know, to some of us in this crazy business, ranks pretty high up there on the *vital* scale. Those, too, were areas we checked and breathed a sigh of relief when we found no damage.

The body armor vests also didn't really protect our faces or necks, paws, hands, arms, legs, thighs, and other exposed swaths of flesh were subject to hits with pieces of flying shrapnel and deadly debris that grazed or tore into them like badly flung darts and forks.

These were always the more vulnerable areas and where we had taken some hits. The hot metal that had cut into us burned as well, but we smiled stupidly at each other, happy to be alive.

"Sergeant! Look at me!" said the puppy-looking medic, now at our sides and quickly checking over our wounds. "Where are you hit?"

"Eyebrow...here. Feels like I sat on a nail gun with my left thigh as well. Big fucking head ache, too," he said. "My dog took some shrapnel in his back. I bandaged it, but would you look at it for me."

"Duct tape?" said the medic, staring at Max's work.

"It stays."

"It does," said the medic, "the bandage has stopped the bleeding. He's going to lose some fur when it comes off."

"But it stopped the bleeding."

"It did," said the medic, "Now let's have a look at your eye."

Blood was still dripping down his face, and the wound left a one-inch tear across the eyebrow, but the sharp shard hadn't damaged his eye, the eye socket, or his skull. Still, it left a nasty looking wound.

The medic wiped away much of the dirt and blood on the brow before slapping on a bandage and then wrapping it with a ring of gauze around Max's head.

"Anything feel out of place or broken? Neck? Back? Legs? Shoulders? Arms?"

"Not me, but I'd like to get my dog X-rayed."

There was ready relief in the young medic's eyes when he knew that our wounds didn't appear to be life threatening.

"You were lucky, Sarge. It looks like it's all small hits."

Cold comfort that. After pulling out small splinters of shrapnel that the body armor didn't cover, he taped on gauze bandages to cover the remaining puncture wounds.

"I'm done here so let's get you back to the vehicles and transport you to the field hospital. They'll check you out and catch anything I missed. Hopefully, it's all in the fat and nothing else."

"Fat?"

"Good! You're paying attention," he said, grinning. "You passed my shock test."

Max gave a painful nod.

"If it makes you feel any better, most of the small pieces of shrapnel deeper in will eventually work their way with time."

"That's been the practice."

The medic stared at him for a moment before he spoke again.

"I take it, then, this ain't your first Purple Heart?"

Max gave a weary smile. "Naw, it's our second, Doc," he said. "We're still carrying some shrapnel from another IED explosion last year in Baghdad."

The puppy, who was a surprisingly good medic, snorted, and shook his head. "Well then, fuck! You two must have magnet asses," he said. "Let's move before anything else comes flying at you and hits me by mistake. You able to move?"

Max said we were. We were still woozy, but that didn't matter.

"Good, then let's get you and your pooch out of here," the medic said helping Max to his feet. "There could be a secondary device."

"Roger that."

"Not to mention that we're easy targets out here in the open like this, even for their worst shooters. No offense, Dude, but I don't want a Purple Heart."

Neither did we, but they were stacking up, regardless.

No one shot at us and nothing blew up as we made our way back to the convoy. Back at the field hospital the medical staff methodically went over our wounds and injuries. We were X-rayed, cleaned up a bit, treated, bandaged with slathering Neosporin, and eventually released. The medic was right about some of the shrapnel working its way out of our bodies.

Every now and then, a small metal fragment would push and work its way out through the muscle and skin. It would appear one day looking like small, ugly and raw blackhead pimple, only the shrapnel didn't just pop or fall out.

The first time one of the shrapnel zits appeared, Max had the medic remove it. After that and realizing it was no big thing, when the next ones began to push through the skin, Max squeezed the metal splinters out between his thumb and index finger or plucked them out with tweezers.

I even knocked one out of my hindquarters with a thumping back leg scratch like I was going after an annoying flea. When it fell out, I sniffed at the bloody metal fragment, grumped at the reminder, and then brushed it aside with my paws.

The deeper penetrating shrapnel, hopefully, would encapsulate and wouldn't move or push into any of the vital organs. If they stayed put, then they wouldn't present that much of a health hazard or danger.

Combined with the other bits of shrapnel we had received during our first deployment, it was likely Max and me would die of rust before we'd ever die of old age, let alone, cancer.

"Hey, are those freckles?"

"Naw, hood ornaments."

CHAPTER

5

We completed our second deployment and the extra four-month extension with no new wounds and with everything relatively intact.

Muzzle and nose in place? Check.

Paws and hands and feet in place? Check.

Eyes, tail, balls? Check, check, check.

Nervous twitches and budding cynicism?

Yep, those were there, too.

The rotation back to the states, back to Fort Gordon, and back to the land of lush, green grass, pee-able bushes and trees, the always aromatic fire hydrants, and trash piles or cars that didn't explode when you passed them on the street, made for a nice homecoming. After the first few weeks, we seldom hesitated or cringed when we passed parked cars or piles of debris, although we often gave them a wide berth.

Dog teams didn't usually return stateside together, but someone, somewhere either thought we both should, or had cut the wrong travel orders. Either way, it worked for us.

Half a year on, though, with the fighting heating up in the two war zones, and because the working military canine teams were stretched thinner that they ever had been, Max volunteered for a third deployment and we were on our way.

This time it was to Afghanistan, a land that some prominent historians referred to as, *'the Graveyard of Empires.'*

'*The Graveyard of Empires.*' Now there's something I imagine a host of visiting armies throughout history must have missed in the fine print of their travel brochures ever since Alexander the Great stepped off of the tour bus, took one look around the Adventure Land theme park, and proclaimed, 'Hey, it's all Greek to me.'

It was the Persians, Greeks, Genghis too, saying 'Yes, we Khan,' the British, and Soviets, that all helped add to the travel brochure copy. Their blood, sweat, and frustrated tears all served as the ink, while ours would only mix and add to the editing until we too, eventually would give up and go home.

Our first and temporary home here in Afghanistan was a Military Police Company in Kabul at Camp Eggers. A few months later, we were relocated to a small kennel detachment at Camp Phoenix, six pot-holed miles outside of the capital.

Our unit, Detachment Sirius, is an interim command serving field operations for combat units in temporary need of K-9 assistance. Like all military units, we go where we're told to go, and do what someone, somewhere higher up in command, thinks is a good idea or working plan at the time.

It's temporary, of course, and all subject to change. In the three months we've been assigned here, and the eight months of its existence, Detachment Sirius is still temporarily operational serving a seemingly non-temporary need. Ours is not to reason why.

At one time, Camp Phoenix had solely been a U.S. military installation, but this Phoenix that had risen from the ashes of an old junkyard, went on to become a halfway decent NATO military base, courtesy of Brown and Root Construction. Some of the old timers, or private military contractors who had been around for a while still called it the '*Scrapyard,*' or '*The Land of Dormant Shrapnel.*'

To us, though, for the deployment, Camp Phoenix is home. And like any new home it would take some getting used to, beginning with the setting and culture. By *setting*, I mean the *other* Afghanistan that is out beyond the camp's high walled perimeter, manned guard posts, high-tech security systems, and wrapped in razor wire.

By *culture*, I mean the locals who live beyond the camp's high walled perimeter, always manned guard posts, high-tech security systems, and razor wire that we'd seldom interact with, except for some locals who work in the camp or from what we see from our patrol vehicles in passing or our run ins with the Taliban. Like Iraq, the missions here are the same, and of course, uniquely different.

It didn't take long for the differences between Iraq and Afghanistan to become apparent. It's more than just the feral edge or feel here or the different odors and smells of the country.

Iraq is a modern country at war; sometimes with us, sometimes with itself, and the various ethnic, tribal, or religious factions that make up its citizenry. Afghanistan, on the other hand, has a more feral, tribal feel with distinctive lines between 'us and them,' whoever the *us* or *them* happened to be.

For the most part, it is a visual and cultural time machine trip to the past; complete with rustic and rugged mud-bricked villages and walled ancient settlements spread out over vast stretches of sun burnt, sepia toned, or pale dust-colored ground, all under an azure sky that has given up on its dreams of reigning over placid times.

It is also a deeply divided country, steeped in traditions once thought passed; a weary nation at odds with itself and seemingly, a calendar. The city of Kabul, with its three million plus inhabitants, is modern enough. However, join a patrol to the countryside, or just beyond the city's limits and you'll come to where modernity ends and the time travel begins.

An hour out of Kabul can quickly take you back centuries and transport you into a seemingly long lost era, or perhaps, one that can shy away from being found or brought to heel.

It's not the land that time forgot, as I've heard some say it is, but more like the land that time just glanced at like a broken watch, said 'Fuck it, ours is the hours of our discontent' and tossed it in a drawer with other things that didn't seem to work, but still one day might hold value. Stay on a dirt road long enough through the deserts and barren mountains and you'll be thrust back through the millennia.

Outside of the larger cities and towns the colors seem to wash out and wilt as the Afghanistan hinterland takes on a tint and tone of a series of vintage photographs. A Pashtun or any of the members of a particular tribal clan in his rural village today would look and probably feel right at home in his Great, Great Grandfather's time, well, minus the cell phones, Kalashnikovs, RPGs, and the many pock-marked bullet holes or holes made to the dwellings from incoming 12.7mm Dushka heavy machinegun fire.

As you drive by on patrol and if you momentarily stop on the road at one of the distant villages, you'll find women and girls clad in bulky blue or dark burkas, or head to foot flowing *chadrei* robes, cooking flat bread in open ovens, hauling water, or involved in any number of other mundane chores before they warily turn away and slip into the shadows.

You might even smile watching laughing children chasing chickens, or each other, or give an appreciative nod to those working in their farmed fields and small orchards. That is, until they see you staring and they'll stop stock still and guardedly stare back, cynical of your intent, as they watch and wait for you, the uninvited visitors, to move on.

Stare at them long enough and they'll squint their dislike or even cold distain through hazel or dark eyes for those of us that represented the latest foreign invader, or perhaps, just the others from the next province or tribe over.

99% of the population is Muslim, but that doesn't necessarily mean they see eye to eye as evident by the animosity the Sunni have towards the Shia, and vice-versa. Still, there's more because besides the Pashtuns, there are the Tajiks, Hazaras, Uzbeks, Aimaks, Turkmen, Balochs, the Pashai, Nuristanis, Ghiljis, Arabs, and a dozen or so others, as well as a smattering of Hindus, Buddhists, and Zoroastrians, who all have their own unique takes on, guess who's coming to dinner, and how they're received.

Distrust here goes back even further to a time when a young Alexander of Macedonia was good, but not yet, Great, and, maybe even earlier, still. The magnitude of misery is on display with ancient to modern ruins as a reminder that something wicked this way comes.

Try to learn something of the various social or ethnic differences and you'll soon understand that old feuds in Afghanistan run long and deep like cracks and splits in emotionally cold glaciers, plotting their time to splinter a fragile stability. It is also a land steeped in revenge and honor.

New feuds form with a sudden outbreak of violence, and the real lesson comes in learning or trying to figure out which side of the old or new feud, you, as the interloper, fall into, and knowing that regardless, whether you're in a deceptively peaceful looking village in a distant province, or even in bustling city like Kabul, you'll only be momentarily tolerated, and always looked upon as a foreign invader.

What lies just beneath the calm and placid looking surface can be a brutally dark and dangerous undercurrent. Afghanistan, after all, is still a war zone with more than a few painful historical reminders dotting its age-old map; reminders that don't even have to reach all that far back to get the point.

In the 19th and 20th centuries it is where clannish Afghans annihilated over 16,000 retreating British and Indian soldiers and their family members that were promised safe passage during their retreat from Kabul in the First Anglo-Afghan War.

It is a land where the rebelling Afghans won the battle of the Maiwand Pass in the Second Anglo-Afghan War that claimed 1,000 more British lives. While the Afghan War lords would lose that war to the British, the victory at Maiwand would go on to boost their national pride over invading armies.

Less than a hundred years later, when the Soviet Army invaded and occupied Afghanistan from 1979 to 1986, the Afghans accounted for 15,000 Soviets killed in action and 30,000 more wounded, in yet, one more seemingly winnable war. After seven years of vicious fighting the Soviets, like the Persians, Greeks, Mongols, and the British before them, withdrew.

Enter the U.S. and the ISAF combined forces a decade later, hopefully with a better exit strategy. The casualty numbers of this latest war are yet to be fully tallied.

On a literary side note, it was the Battle of Maiwand Pass that provided Sir Arthur Conan Doyle with the wound and slight limp he gave to Doctor John Watson, the chronicler and sidekick of the legendary consulting detective, Sherlock Holmes.

It makes one wonder if perhaps Holmes and Watson might've been able to figure out and better explain why Pashtunwali, the code of behavior for Pashtun people in Afghanistan, prescribed hospitality and protection to those who asked for it, including we outsiders, and was rigorously adhered to, while with other tribes, say, in the next province over, an interloper might be greeted with unleashed hostility and say, a knife through the eye.

Policies, laws, actions and behavior often were dictated by National and Sharia Law, and supplemented by what came from a council of elders and leaders in a Jirga in a particular village, while slights and injuries to pride and honor set other acts in motion.

The war only brought about new sinister doings, so perhaps it wasn't a mystery at all. Maybe we didn't need the famed detectives to tell us that the Afghans just wanted us gone, so they could go back to fighting each other.

Drive by a back-country village while you're out on patrol and stop, and happy children will rush out to greet you with smiles, clamoring for treats that soldiers sometimes carry and give to the kids as gestures of goodwill. Elders, too, might even invite you in for tea and conversation.

Pull up to the next village over and you might be greeted by a nine-year-old boy strapped with a suicide vest running towards your lead vehicle, or directly at you and your buddies, courtesy of an Elder who had helped the kid into the vest.

It's not business, it's just personal.

Unless we're specifically requested by name, Max and me seldom work Kabul. The majority of our missions take place out into the hinterland, working with various combat teams and units in critical need of our services. Despite the many differences between Iraq and Afghanistan, the one constant and common denominator are the IEDs.

Odds are that Max and me will be wounded again one of these days doing what we do, but we hold tight to our daily ritual and mantra which is this: We stare each other in the eyes, nose to snout, and he says, 'Not today, buddy. Not today.'

That's it. Nothing big or fancy. Just 'not today.'

It's a simple ritual and mantra, and a good one to have because we don't play the odds. Instead we pay close attention to detail; like the odor of hidden explosives riding on air currents and scent cones, looking for telltale sign of foot prints and disturbed ground leading to or away from piles of garbage or freshly churned earth next to the roadways.

We scan the surroundings searching for something out of the ordinary, carefully keeping an eye out for civilians and yahoos standing off in a safe distance holding cell phones, and eyeballing us with the kind of vitriol, bitter invective, and unbridled animosity usually reserved for rival football team fans or divorce courts.

Attention to detail: that's what saves lives, not quick, cluster fuck searches or any foolish notion that our numbers are up rather than what's really in play. *Wise and slow. They stumble that run fast.* Good advice on lessons learned.

Early on, sniffing out training aids or IEDs was always fun, a game. And I thought of it as a game, too, until we got caught up in the second IED explosion in Iraq. I don't know why, but I didn't associate the first explosion with finding the buried device. No initial stranger danger, just finding the thing- the IED- that emitted the odor, and getting a 'GOOD DOG,' atta boy praise from Max for doing it.

I was a good dog, a highly trained one at that. So I wrote the first blast off as a one-off fluke, something bad that had happened that had nothing to do with playing our game. However, by the second blast there was no more mistaking the relationship between the two. The game, at least in the field, became deadly serious afterwards; a game we now played with considerably more caution and care.

Our two previous deployments had provided us with a working amount of valuable experience, with knowing what to do, as well as, the just as critical, knowing what *not* to do as we worked. Nothing brings that lesson home more than eating two blasts.

The IEDs were a sign of the Taliban's dominance in the once

thought safe roads or well travelled tracks. As a sign of my own dominance, and maybe a very personal and angry personal response to the Taliban who were trying to kill us, I'd taken to peeing on the IEDs we'd uncovered to mark my territory from the bastards who had planted the devices. Yeah well, I may be a working military dog, but I'm still a dog, and this country has a serious lack of fire hydrants.

I've been taught to sit and drop down when I sniff out weapons or explosives. I've also been trained to knock you on your ass with flying jaw-clenching tackle, given the command.

It's all fun and games until it isn't, and until your whole world, or at least the small part of it that's everything you know at the moment, literally goes up in smoke.

That being said, getting caught up in two triggered explosions just makes pissing a little easier. In fact, it's a whiz!

CHAPTER

6

After the Devil Dog mission, and after a few days of stand down, our Detachment Commander, Lieutenant Kelly had another mission for us.

"Ah, there you are, Sergeant!" the West Point graduate said, limping into the kennel and finding Max running a wire brush down my back coat, grooming out some dust and loose dog hair. Every time Max hit just the right spot, my right back leg happily began twitching and kicking air. What? You don't have a spot on your back near your shoulder blades, that when scratched, is damn near orgasmic? Don't judge.

"Got a mission request for you and Thor, by name," said Kelly.

"By name, L-T?"

"Your fame precedes you. You two up for the task?"

"Yes, sir. When and where?"

"You'll be flying out to Bagram Air Field and working with the First CAV in Parwan Province."

"The CAV doesn't have their own dogs?"

"Apparently, not an available one this time out. It's short notice, I know, but I need you packed and ready to go in forty-five minutes. Drop what you're doing, and pack what you'll need for a three to four day patrol, including travel time. Hooah?"

"Hooah."

Max put the brush aside and reached for my Canine vest, brushing off some dust and dog hair I shed in the process.

"And oh, that reminds me," Kelly added with an afterthought, "First Sergeant Hallatt has a new ballistic vest for your Malligator. That one is looking a little raggedy."

Max shook his head, waving off the gift. "Thanks L-T, but we're good to go. Thor likes his old vest."

"You sure?"

"Roger that, Sir. The vest fits him comfortably and lets folks know he has been around the block, a time or two. It has some good Ju-Ju. Saved him from a few nasty shrapnel fragments."

"Superstitious, are you?"

"Not me. It's Thor. He doesn't like black cats, either."

"Yeah well, I imagine he doesn't like any cats."

Max shrugged and chuckled. "Or baths, for that matter."

I shuddered at the mention of the B-word. I looked and smelled just fine, thank you. No need to bring soap into the conversation.

Two years out of West Point, Kelly was the Detachment's Alpha male. He was short, sturdy, smart, and dogged in his leadership. He was our competent Top Dog.

"So, the First Cavalry Division, huh?" Max said and the Lieutenant nodded. Kelly, though, winced as he shifted his weight and reached down to rub the back of his left calf muscle.

"One of their Recon Scout units from their Brigade Combat Team. Black Stetson Cavalry cowboy hats and all."

"Does that mean we'll be riding in Scout track vehicles this time out?"

Kelly shook his head. "Negative," he said. "I'm told you'll be flying by helicopter into the mountains to a staging area, and then humping the rest of the way in to the objective."

A Chinook was a CH-47 large, twin-engine, tandem rotor, heavy-lifting helicopter that served as the workhorse for the military. This improved variation of the ones that served during the Vietnam War could easily hold a thirty-man platoon of fully equipped soldiers, along with its pilots and crew.

The downside is that the big birds tended to lumber along and made for easy anti-aircraft missile targets, let alone well-aimed RPGs.

The upside is that Chinooks were a lot more spacious and comfortable than Apache helicopters.

"They say what the mission is?"

"Something they're calling, *Operation Avon*. That's all I have, but I'm sure the CAV folks will fill you in on the rest during the mission briefing once you get to Bagram. However, *my* mission objective for you and your Malligator is to not to get blown up again because that would leave me with a shitload of paperwork to do, and I hate paperwork. It's annoying."

"*Shitload* an official military designation, is it, Lieutenant?"

"No, but it should be."

"We'll...then in that case, we'll try not to get blown up, again, if only to save you from all of that troubling paperwork, sir."

"Spoken like a good underling," he said. "Did I mention the bothersome little paper cuts that go along with it?"

"No, sir. You didn't."

"Yeah well, they're painful at times as well."

Kelly was wincing again as he gently patted the calf muscle one more time.

"Menstrual cramp, L-T?"

Kelly's attention turned from his leg back to us. He smiled. "Ah, enlisted humor," he said, sarcastically. "Very clever, Sergeant."

"If only to help to lighten the burden you carry, your worship."

"I wish it would lighten this nasty bug bite," he said, pulling up his pant leg and craning his head and neck to check on what was bothering him, and revealing an angry looking, pus-filled pocket on the center of his calf muscle. A ring of festering flesh surrounding the inflamed bite was a mass of red and piss yellow.

"What the fuck, sir!' Max said, reeling in disgust. "You seriously need to get that checked out."

Max pulled me away from the Lieutenant's calf, only not before I got close enough to catch a whiff of the infected bite and cringed. It wasn't good. One in our pack was injured. I looked on with genuine concern, first to Max and then to Lieutenant Kelly.

"I will, but after I get you and your Malligator on the helicopter to Bagram," Kelly said, lowering the pant leg and straightening his uniform. "You two stay safe. No super hero shit on this mission, you hear me?"

"Roger that, L-T."

"If your Spidey senses start tingling, you step back and let the EOD people do their thing."

Max hooahed and said he would.

"Get your gear, and whatever else you think you'll need for a week in your Go-Bag, just in case. Once you have it, load it up in the back of the Humvee," he said, pointing to one of two of the detachment's vehicles parked next to the Orderly Room. "Your First Aid kit for you and your dog good to go?"

"Hooah," Max said. "And I've added a few new things to go with it, sir."

"New things? Like what?"

"Duct tape and a roll of sandwich wrap that I cut in half."

"The Duct Tape, sure, by why the sandwich wrap?"

"It works well holding bandages in place to seal up wounds, L-T. Slap on a pad of gauze and then quickly wrap it around an arm or leg a few times, or whatever, and it keeps the wound clean."

"Where'd you hear that?"

"A Ranger Medic told me about it. Said it has proven useful on some serious wounds with his people in a few firefights. Figured it couldn't hurt to toss them in our First Aid kit. They don't take up much space or weigh all that much, either."

Lieutenant Kelly thought about it for a moment and nodded approvingly.

"Well, I guess until Tupperware starts making containers big enough to handle you two, I suppose it couldn't hurt to have them in your kit. By the way, did I mention that you and your dog smell like week-old meatloaf?"

"Explains your Tupperware reference, sir."

"All part of being a wise, and yet, sensitive, leader. Seriously though, you and Thor take it easy out there. Hooah?"

"Hooah."

Max saluted Kelly and the Lieutenant returned it, before painfully limping from the kennel back to his office.

Hooah, by the way, is the Army's all-defining response for things like; 'Do you understand me? Get the job done,' 'Go kick ass,' or any of the other one-sided questions or comments that don't require anything more than a positive response.

Hooah!

Say it a few times. '*Hoo*'… okay, now add in a ballsy '*ah.*'

Put it together…Hooah!

There you go.

Max had even taught me to say it, too. After a month or so of working on it I could knock out a convincing 'Rhurr-rah,' which is close enough to earn a doggie treat and a vigorous '*good boy*' pat from him.

He's proud of that trick and shows it off to the soldiers and Marines who seem to enjoy it too, as they chuckle, laugh, and shoot a video of it on their cell phones that occasionally shows up on social media. Me? I'm proud I can lick my balls, which, by the way, is a trick I taught myself.

'Rhurr-rah!'

When Lieutenant Kelly dropped us off at the flight line he handed Max two small, oval shaped embroidered patches that he pulled from one of his BDU pockets.

"Here you go!"

"What are they?"

"Pocket patches. The First Sergeant and I had them made to add some pride to who we are and what we do."

"Headquarters authorized them, Lieutenant?"

"Officially, they're unofficial, which means we'll all wear them until someone reigning above us says we can't. Hooah?"

"Hooah."

The small Velcro-like patches were military green and black thread that showed the larger Sirius star in the Canis Major constellation pattern and carried the words; DOG STAR across its face.

"Pretty cool, huh?"

"Hooah!" said Max, and slapped one on my vest and then on his own since we were, and are, Dog Stars. "Oh, I almost forgot. I put you in for an Army Commendation medal."

"For what, sir?"

"Well, according to one Marine Captain you saved some jarhead lives."

"Thor did. I was just lucky to be attached to the other end of the leash when he found them in time."

"Which is why I also ordered a box of yummy doggie treats for him."

"I'd be happy with a maple bar, sir."

Lieutenant Kelly smiled and shook his head. "Naw, no maple bars for you, Sergeant, as both myself and the Army has rightly determined that pastry would not look good on your dress uniform, which is why you're getting the medal.

"Also, I need to sit you down and give you your re-enlistment talk when you get back. It's possible, though, that there might be a maple bar or two involved with the sales pitch. First Sergeant Hallatt said he'd even make his Keurig coffee maker available. For some reason he seems to think you're worth keeping around in his army."

"The Green Mountain, rich Columbian Roast?"

"No, no. The much lesser, watered down, gas station/mini-mart, too long on the burner blends. You are, after all, a lowly enlisted man."

"Ah, what was I thinking?"

"We try to save the good coffee for officers and senior NCOs."

"Goes without saying."

"Or should, of course."

"Of course, sir. I seem to have forgotten my place."

"Which is why we're here to help and remind you of your place, and your betters."

"That would hurt, Lieutenant if I wasn't a K-9 handler, and didn't know that we have no betters."

"Too true, and all joking aside, the Marine Company Commander was adamant about putting you in for the medal. I agreed, so it was submitted and approved. You earned it. We'll hold a Detachment awards ceremony on your return. That being said, you two stay safe out there. You hear me?"

Kelly's demeanor and tone turned serious, the banter gone.

Max's response was a chin-up nod and another Hooah.

"K-9 leads the way!" the Lieutenant said before driving off.

"Roger that, sir."

Max liked Kelly. The West Point graduate was a good leader, a good Commanding Officer, and someone who actually looked out for his people and the dogs. The same could be said of the First Sergeant. They were not only professionals, but they actually gave a shit about us, and that mattered, too.

Max also liked being a K-9 handler, although maybe not so much here in this latest war zone. Still, he felt he had purpose, was doing something noble, and that he was making a difference by saving lives. However, the Bronze Stars for combat heroism from the previous deployments, the two, costly Purple Hearts, and one too many close calls had scraped off some of the job's luster. While he'd enjoy the coffee and maple bars that would accompany the reenlistment talk with Lieutenant Kelly, Max wasn't going to reenlist.

He had other plans in mind, and partially in place.

Before we were deployed to Afghanistan, he had taken a twenty-one day leave and flew back home to Seattle. The visit was, ostensibly, to see his family friends again, although he'd also timed it to take the written test, the PAT, and the actual physical for the Fire Department.

The PAT was the Department's Physical Ability Test that had strength and endurance tests and everything the Department thought were crucial and necessary to do the physically demanding job.

The timed stair climb, hose carry and run, ladder climb, and other fitness events that had run him ragged, had earned him some approving nods and impressive finish times.

Max had been worried about the hearing portion of the physical exam, but had managed to pass with a borderline score. He thought he'd done well on the written test, too, but the test results weren't posted before he had to leave on our new deployment.

We were a month into the latest tour of duty before he had learned how he had done. When he opened the e-mail informing him that he had placed within the top ten, and that upon his return he'd need to go before an oral board, he was immediately pleased, happy beyond all get out, and then suddenly worried and sad, as he was left wrestling with a troubling dilemma.

Leaving the Army meant leaving me, and that was something he told me he wasn't ready to do, yet. Cupping my face into his hands, he smiled sadly, and said, "I love you, you frigging little fleabag, so what am I going to do if I pass the oral board and they offer me a job? Huh? What am I going to do?"

I didn't have the answer for that. The fact of the matter is, as a Working Military Dog, I am Government Property, and as such, I wasn't his pet or anyone else's. I was property.

Never mind, that he has been the only dog handler and partner I've ever worked with, shared a cot with him on missions or slept at his side in the field, and bled alongside in the field, the Army owned me.

If, and, when an opening at the Fire Department came up, then Max would have to make some serious decisions about his future and mine. But that would come later.

For now, though, there was just the war where the word, 'Safe,' was only something the manufacturer etched into the selector switches of soldier's rifles, and where any sense of a normal civilian life was as remote as the possibility of the Taliban no longer using IEDs.

There was the world as it is and the world as we'd like it to be, and the many difficult lessons in between that taught us all the difference.

CHAPTER

7

We were met at Bagram Air Field by the Scout Company's First Sergeant, who after introducing himself, escorted us over to a series of large, tent style Quonset huts just off of the air field's flight line. The two orderly rows of sand-colored Quonset huts, and a small parade ground nearby, served as the Company's temporary holding area.

"You two are in here," said the Scout First Sergeant walking us into one of the huts closest to the Operation's Center. The combat patches on his BDUs showed a 75th Infantry Ranger scroll, a Combat Infantryman's cloth badge, and a Paratrooper's embroidered winged parachute patch with star showing that he had made a combat jump. His name patch said his name was TODD. If he had a first name, he didn't offer it.

"Make yourselves at home," he said, pointing to an empty folding cot just inside the doorway. "You'll be sharing this with a few of my Platoon Sergeants. They're conducting a gear inspection and getting their people ready for the mission. They should be filtering back in a little later."

"Hooah."

"I told them to expect you."

The First Sergeant then said he was heading back to the Ops Center, and would have someone bring us over some MREs and several liters of bottled water for both Max and me.

"I'll get you signed into the chow hall and have someone show you where it is," he said. "We'll need you back here for a briefing at 1800 hours. Hooah?"

"Hooah," replied Max, setting his rucksack down on the cot.

"Word is, you and your pooch are some Top Dogs," said First Sergeant Todd, stopping in the doorway of the Quonset hut.

"He's got a good nose."

The First Sergeant nodded, but it was a half nod, a 'we'll see' nod. "My EOD people can handle any IED we encounter, but it's finding the damn things that's the problem. We ran into one last month on a village sweep just north of here."

Max listened and waited. He knew the Scout First Sergeant wasn't done.

"The Haji's packed a soccer ball with fifteen-pounds of explosives with bolts and scrap metal. They set the ball next to the doorway of the third house we were searching. My people didn't think much of it because there was a ratty pair of kid's tennis shoes next to it. They missed the electrical trigger wire."

"Easy to overlook."

"Killed two of my people. Wounded three more."

"If it's there, he'll find it."

The Scout First Sergeant looked to me, again, and then back to Max. He didn't say anything more. Instead, he just gave the second half of his first non-committal nod as he turned and headed back to his temporary Orderly Room.

We made ourselves comfortable or as comfortable as we could in the sparse hut that could've easily doubled as homeless shelter. There were a handful of empty cots, an old, and battered looking folding table, and a number of folding chairs arranged in a half-circle around the table.

A handful of rucksacks were leaning up against the back wall, ready to go. An open case of water in liter plastic bottles was next to the last rucksack in line, but other than that the hut was empty and looking very much abandoned.

I sat beside the cot as Max dug through his rucksack, pulling out my collapsible water dish, his woobie, a study guide for his on-line course on Shakespeare, and, more importantly, several MRE rations.

We skipped the chow hall and made the best of a Cheese and Vegetable Omelet MRE that Max decided would serve as our dinner. I was finishing chowing down my half of the Omelet and the hash brown that went with it when the four Platoon Sergeants, who owned the rucksacks, eventually found their way back to the hut.

As they came through the doorway they greeted us with chin up nods and 'Hey, how you doin?' comments. Max nodded or said, 'Fine,' as they went about settling in before the 1800 mission briefing.

The briefing took place in an open area, four huts down, where we found a ginger-haired Captain and First Sergeant addressing a small audience of junior officer Platoon Leaders and a dozen or so junior and senior NCOs.

The Platoon Sergeants joined their platoons while Max and me stood off to the side, away from the others, the known unknown watching on. We were visitors. Also, some people didn't like dogs or were intimidated by us, so Max, like most handlers, found that keeping a little distance from the GIs or civilians was an easier way to deal with any potential problem. However, the awkward little problems didn't end there.

There were always one or two dog lovers who, when they saw me, ambled over, and immediately tried to pet me or play roughhouse. Both were something Max, and other handlers, frowned upon, and had to remind the dog lovers that it wasn't allowed or okay to do without at least asking permission.

This usually happened with the Labs and Retrievers, but not so much with we saw-toothed Malligators. Max's warning earned a few quick apologies and one or two scowls. It was understandable. Dogs reminded soldiers of home, and Afghanistan, at times, seemed like a million miles from their own zip codes.

During the mission briefing we were told that *Operation Avon* would be a village sweep of a suspected Taliban waypoint just on the edge of the Province that bordered the remote Panjshir Province. We would board the helicopters and depart shortly after sunrise.

With the briefing over and the Platoon Leaders and Sergeants off to brief their people, Max and me returned to the Quonset hut, after a short walk, and three or four back leg lifting marking stops.

One by one the Platoon Sergeants began filtering back to the hut and readying for some shuteye. After the NCOs checked over their rucksacks and weapons and hitting the shower room and latrine, the overhead lights were turned out and the long night began.

Given the new setting, the odd new noises of Bagram familiar to the airfield, and the round-the-clock helicopter and other aircraft noise from the flight line, finding sleep would take a little doing. But sleeping anywhere at night on a mission always took a little doing with unfamiliar sounds and settings. Once again, it would be an uneasy sleep, even here in Bagram on a base that was as well guarded and protected as a strong box.

Outside, the night was clear and cold. Inside, an annoying blower pushed heat through the hut on and over an even colder slab cement floor. As I crawled up and onto the foot of Max's cot and after walking in a few awkward circles, he shifted his feet and legs to give me some room. It would be a one-dog night because one is the loneliest number.

After we'd both did a little jockeying for space, Max settled in beneath his *woobie* blanket, and then gave me his usual three 'all was fine' pats on my back. Soon Max was out and snoring. All might be fine, but I kept watch anyway. The flight line noises didn't seem to bother him.

There was a slight whistling sound coming out of Max's nostrils as he slept, but that wasn't what had me lying awake in the dark, watching and listening for a good while afterwards. I didn't sleep well on these missions. I never had, and this night was no different.

When I did close my eyes and lower my head to sleep it wasn't for long. Every so often I came up on alert when someone passed by the door outside crunching boots on the crushed rock walkway and when one of the Platoon Sergeant's in the hut got up to take a piss. The unfamiliar settings and noises always made the nights pass slowly. Tonight would be no different.

Somewhere near dawn I was up and so were my hackles. I was

working up a slow and growing growl, ready to spring at the shadow in the dark, only to have Max's hand rub my head to calm me down.

"Easy boy," he said just before the lights in the Quonset hut were turned on by one of the Platoon Sergeants, who had heard the growl and was now nervously smiling at me.

"First Call," said the Platoon Sergeant a little uneasily.

It was 0430. We had thirty-minutes to get up and ready. After a quick trip to the latrine for Max, we greeted the predawn morning with our daily mantra ritual, another one of the boxes of MREs, and a short walk outside so I could do my business. This would also give Max time to take part in his weird little fetish of standing by and watching as I do my business.

Seriously! I just don't get it. It's embarrassing and quite frankly, a little on the pervy side. Worse still, when I'm done, he even has his own plastic bags he uses to scoop up and save my poop like its found treasure or something! I'm not kidding! He scoops it up, ties the bag in a knot, and then finds a nearby bin to store it, where, apparently, others with similar bizarre festishes, collect it.

Early on when he were first partnered up, I thought Max was a strange, strange man, until I noticed that the other handlers were doing it as well, even the women handlers. Then, it hit me that they were all strange people, which I figured was maybe part of the criteria for being a dog handler.

After awhile, though, and figuring who was I to judge, I decided to save Max some of the trouble and help him with his twisted hobby. Only, when I started pooping at his feet in the ranks, or at the end of his bunk in the morning, that didn't earn me the least bit of gratitude or thanks.

With one too many loud *"NO's!"* and *"BAD DOG!"* rebukes, I went back to waiting until he had his plastic bags ready.

Humans, go figure?

Even now, here at Bagram, I did my best to retain some sense of dignity and not look at him as he scooped up my leavings with a small plastic bag, and then deposited the bag in a nearby bin. With dignity restored we returned to the Quonset hut.

There, donning our combat kits, we followed several of the NCOs out to the flight line where they began forming up their Platoons in company formation.

The pre-dawn sky was star-filled and the color of amethyst that was slowly giving way to the thread of a pale, creamsicle glow rising from the east. The day was breaking, but we were still in at thin veil of shadows.

Standing off to the side of the formation, Max and me received some curious looks and sleepy-eyed stares, but not as many as the young female soldier from the CST- the Cultural Support Team, who'd accompany us on the mission. She was a dark haired, brown-eyed young woman who stood all of five-feet-five in her boots, but stood taller with the way she carried herself with pride and confidence.

The nametag on her BDU uniform read, VALENCIA. Her shouldered M-16 rifle, holstered Beretta pistol, body armor, battle gear, and warfighter stance and attitude said that this wasn't her first rodeo, and that she was ready for whatever came her way when the Cultural Liaison aspect failed, and any immediate return fire was needed.

Out on the flight line helicopter pilots and crews were making their way over to their parked aircraft with the kind of comfortable gait and swagger that seemed unique to those who rode mechanical mounts through the skies and air currents.

On the parade ground the four platoons of soldiers were soon joined by a handful of Company Officers and the unit's First Sergeant who took up their customary positions. The Company was called to attention, reports were given by each of the Platoon Sergeants in succession, and once done, the First Sergeant turned and waited until the ginger Captain strode out and took his position in front of his First Sergeant.

The First Sergeant saluted the Company Commander and gave his report and the ginger Captain gave the order for men to stand at ease. There, we all waited. Judging from the way several of their heads swiveled from time to time towards the flight line road and how they frequently checked their watches, they appeared to be waiting on someone with more rank and authority. Waiting was a mainstay of military life. You hurried to wait and then hurried again.

The 'someone,' we were waiting for in this case, was two 'someones,' who rolled up a few minutes later in a Battalion Headquarters Command Humvee. A middle-aged Lieutenant Colonel and a tall, sturdy, and older looking Sergeant Major climbed out of the military vehicle, straightened their uniforms, adjusted their Black Stetson Cavalry hats, and made their way over to the CAV Scout Company Commander and the rest of us.

The black Stetson Cavalry hats were a tradition with U.S. Army Cavalry units as were the earned spurs they were presented with in ceremonies, each hard earned and in place, and all adding to the CAV's pride and *esprit de corps*, which was on full display by the Battalion Commander and his Command Sergeant Major.

"FIRST SERGEANT!" called the ginger Commander.

The Senior NCO turned and called the Scout Company to attention as the Battalion Commander walked out to meet the young Company Commander. The two saluted, and the Captain gave his report.

While this was happening the Command Sergeant Major walked over to where Max and me were standing, and nodded his approval.

"That's still a damn fine looking Malinois you have there, Sergeant Ritchie," the Sergeant Major said, smiling. Max gave him a Hooah in return as he tried to figure out where he had seen the Senior NCO before and came up short. To his knowledge, he had never seen the Command Sergeant Major before.

The Command Sergeant Major saw his obvious confusion and smiled.

"The last time I saw the two of you was shortly after we left the Baghdad airport and were heading down *Route Irish* towards the Green zone."

"Route Irish?" Max said, nodding but still not recalling the meet.

"You and your dog here alerted to an I.E.D. that was hidden in a trash pile that some dim-witted convoy commander didn't think was actually there."

"He was new in country, Sergeant Major."

"And so was I, and, as I recall, I was somewhat annoyed that you had us all stopped out on that open road and forced us to wait for an EOD team, for even what I thought looked to be nothing serious."

Max remembered the incident but pretended he hadn't since he also remembered swearing at him at the time.

"I think I even bitched about it to the Convoy Commander to try to get us moving again while you, though, didn't budge. Good thing, too, because the fact is, you saved the lives of a few soldiers that day, myself included. Look after my Scouts the same way, Sergeant Ritchie."

"Will do, Sergeant Major."

"Hooah!"

"Hooah," replied Max.

The Command Sergeant Major nodded.

To our front the helicopters that were parked on the flight line mechanically began to whine to life as their pilots and crew started running their pre-flight checks. This coincided with the Command Sergeant Major walking out to the Battalion Commander, who, after the saluting ritual, turned the pre-game pep talk over to his to finest soldier he had personally known.

"COMPANY!" bellowed the Senior Non-Commissioned Officer only to have the Platoon Leaders in turn echoed the command.

"PLATOON!"

"STAND AT..."

"STAND AT..."

"HEEASE!"

"HEEASE."

The soldiers went from the rigid position of ATTENTION to the Army's AT EASE version of a quite literal, more relaxed, and casual standing stance. Army humans, too, have their own big dog posturing poses.

Looking over the company formation, the Command Sergeant Major gave a satisfied smile. His face was as lined and time-weathered as Methuselah's showing a facial roadmap of his long career. When he spoke he came across with a mix of George Forman doing his impression of a black John Wayne in the movie, *The Green Berets*. His voice was tempered from several decades of smoking unfiltered cigarettes, and possibly a little, or maybe, more than a little Jack Daniels.

You could toss in several decades of grumbling and shaking his head over enough, 'Seriously? What-the-Fuck Second Lieutenants,' and perhaps, one too many Forrest Gump-like GIs, who didn't have the excuse of diminished IQs, let alone the Ping-Pong playing skills, or any other noticeable talents, and were dumbasses anyway- all of which had helped to form his learned, early morning soliloquy.

The Sergeant Major and veteran soldier, was very clear about what the Army, especially the First Cavalry Division, meant to him. His words and delivery made for an interesting send-off.

He began by saying that he had served with the First Cavalry Division with the 1st of the 9th Cav in Vietnam and Cambodia in 1970. To the majority of us, 1970 was what, way back in the Stone Age, when the bulk of us who hadn't been born yet, assumed that Rock n' Roll might've had something to do with rolling rocks. As he spoke I kept wondering if he actually knew Fred and Wilma, and their purple pet, Dino.

What? You don't think dogs watch cartoons? We do and we smile to ourselves every time you laugh when Scooby-Doo says, 'Ruh-oh!'

We watch a lot of things, we listen to your books on tape, and quietly take it all in, like what was playing out now.

The Sergeant Major, center stage, continued his recital. "I was eighteen-years-old when I began my military career," he said, "and not much older than most of you troopers are now. The Ninth and Tenth Cavalry were the original Buffalo Soldiers, and as a black man, I was proud to be a part of the historical link and significance it carried."

He was now preaching his sermon with a tent revival fundamentalist's gusto and enthusiasm, telling us that since Vietnam and the incursion into Cambodia, he had taken part in other wars, conflicts, and minor dust-ups around the world in the years and decades that followed.

He'd fought in Grenada, Panama, the first Gulf War in Iraq, the second Gulf War: Part-Two, and was now on his third and final deployment here in Afghanistan.

"I wasn't always in the CAV in some of those fights, but I always carried the CAV with me in here," he said, thumping his chest for emphasis. "It is a proud brotherhood, and I am proud to be back with the First Cavalry Division as I finish up my military career and proud to be back amongst the best soldiers in anyone's army! Hooah!"

"Hooah!" came the loud and collective response.

There was no denying that the Sergeant Major was a proud black man, or that he was a proud and accomplished, professional soldier. His uniform was festooned with a variety of subdued and impressive army school tabs, cloth military parachutist badge, combat patches, and enough stars over his Combat Infantryman's Badge to mesmerize Neil deGrasse Tyson. The stars above the wreath-wrapped musket patch represented a different war.

"Make no mistake about it, we are the CAV, the *real* CAV," he said as his head and gaze started sweeping over the audience like a lawn sprinkler covering the cultivated ground. "We are the Cavalry that chased after Geronimo and other renegade Apaches in the Indian Wars, stormed San Juan Hill and Kettle Hill on foot in the Spanish American War, and chased Poncho Villa's ass back into Mexico. We served honorably and valiantly in World War II in Japan, in Korea, Vietnam, Panama, and Iraq before charging into this latest fight here in the 'Stan. Hooah?"

"HOOAH!" roared the Scouts.

"For any of you ignorant sonsofbitches or wet-nosed Second Lieutenants, honorably and valiantly means with big pecker manly pride and mother fucking resolve. In Vietnam, we pioneered Air Assault, and not the 101st Airborne that some high ranking lame ass, policy making, know nothings somewhere in the puzzle palace that's the Pentagon opted to let run the Army's official helicopter Air Assault Course at Fort Campbell, Kentucky. Graduates from their two-week course earn their Air Assault badges and only pretend they're actual CAV. Can I get a Hooah?"

"HOOAH!" yelled the soldiers around us. Max, too, got caught up in the fervor and Hooahed along with them. Some young soldiers, who had their cell phones out and were videoing the speech, were told to put them away. Some did, others were more discreet and kept recording. After all, this was good theater.

Meanwhile, the Battalion Commander, who was standing off to one side, could be seen wincing at the politically incorrect places in the speech, but also could be found chuckling at times as well.

The Sergeant Major was old school Army. He said he was finishing up his career, and later, we would learn that this was his last tour of duty. He would be retiring in less than sixty days, and would send the soldiers under his command off to combat with the same fervor and passion he carried as a lifelong warrior.

Whether his pep talk was YouTubed or not, this was his last hurrah and wartime Hooahing. The Sergeant Major was making the most of it. There was nothing so fervently dogmatic or entertaining as a true believing Command Sergeant Major firing up his death-dealing flock in combat.

"While the 101st may have the official school and award the official badge it was the CAV in the Nam that showed the world how to chopper in on the skids of Hueys in combat assaults in hot Landing Zones under enemy fire like those landing craft on D-Day beaches…Hooah?"

"HOOAH!"

"And when there weren't landing zones, we in the 1st of the 9th, rappelled into the jungle to rescue downed air crews, carried the wounded to open spaces in the jungle that served as our make-shift Landing Zones, and then guided in the Dust-Off Medevac helicopters to get them back to safety. We hooked-up the downed aircraft beneath Chinook helicopters and continued the mission. We called in our Cobra attack helicopters to rain fire and brimstone down upon our enemies from the air and smote the fuck out of them with boots on the ground. Make no mistake about it; boots on the ground is always what wins the fight. Good boots with CAV spurs. Hooah?"

"HOOAH!"

"Oh, and speaking of fights, Hey Marines! We even ended the stranglehold that that little Lollypop guild member, General Giap, and his North Vietnamese Army of midgets had when they surrounded you at Khe Sahn, so you're fucking welcome! That's our lineage, and that's our shared collective pride!

"Today, you young stud warriors are carrying on the proud legacy of the CAV and spanking the Taliban like the sniveling little women-beating bitches they are. We are a hard-charging outfit, even if we no longer ride in on horseback with drawn sabers, and bugles blaring. The CAV is still saving the day, one mission at a time. Hooah?"

"HOOAH!"

With the curtain coming down on the First Act, the Sergeant Major closed with the Rules of Engagement for the mission. He was listing the Do's and Don'ts that earned a half-hearted Hooah from the audience.

Rules of Engagement are the one-sided End User Agreements for the U.S. military now. There're too many to really digest or understand so you mentally scroll down to the I AGREE box, check it, and go game on. Some make more emphasis than others and the Command Sergeant Major outlined those.

"Don't shoot unless you see a weapon and it's pointed at you, and only if you have a clear, imminent threat," he said.

"Do be respectful to the people, their homes, and their religion.

"Don't talk or flirt with any of their women or young girls, as they may someone's wife or wives.

"Don't destroy their crops in their fields and don't call them goat fuckers, even if you catch them naked and applying lipstick and green eye shadow to what they say are only casual acquaintances.

"HOOAH?" said the Sergeant Major, wrapping it up.

"Hooah," came a lackluster response from the Cavalry soldiers who all knew that the Taliban leaders probably weren't putting the same restrictions on their fighters.

"Now go and save the fucking day. Watch over your buddy's six, and know that you're all adding to the CAV's proud legacy."

They Hooahed again.

Of course, they did.

While the CAV's horses and flashing sabers may be gone their black cowboy Stetson hats, spurs, and red and white unit guide-on flags are still around, though, and in the rear areas, especially during awards ceremonies, the CAV's officers and enlisted men wear them with more than a little pride.

However, for this mission the CAV's headgear is Kevlar helmets, and all of the latest instruments of what they call 'battle rattle' and when they 'saddle up' they'll mount the large, cumbersome looking Chinook helicopters.

As the Company Commander shouted out the order that his junior officers and NCOs repeated in turn, each of the four platoons hurriedly made their way up the back loading ramps of the big helicopters.

The harmonized mechanical whines grew in intensity. The Chinook we were in shook, rattled, and lifted off. Soon, we were whop-whopping our way towards the designated landing zone deep in the Hindu Kush in the morning light.

We had joined the Company Commander, his First Sergeant, and the First Platoon in the lead helicopter. Specialist Valencia, the female soldier from the Cultural Support Team, and who, in fact, represented her entire team, travelled with us. Once there were boots on the ground the young Army Captain said he wanted us with him when they began the village search.

Above the noise of the helicopter the Captain said that he, too, was happy to have us along on the mission, primarily because he knows that having a military working canine team along is a lot like having Sherlock Holmes and Doctor Watson on the case trying to stop a few murders before they happen.

"My people are there to cover you while you do your thing," he yelled above the noise, although he was only seated across from us. "We'll have your six, twelve, three and nine."

"Roger that," replied Max, probably thinking what I was thinking; it was nice to have time on our side.

The game is afoot and a paws too, for that matter and it's time for Max and me to solve the IED mysteries in the distant settlements.

I am the hound of the Bastard Villes.

CHAPTER

8

Our target area for *Operation Avon* we were told in the briefing, is the small village of Keley, deep in the Hindu Kush Mountains, in the distant reach of the province, and on an almost forgotten back road to the Salang Pass.

The bucolic village, whose name in Pashto, literally translates in English to 'village,' is little more than an *Old World* way station on an age-old smuggler's route that only became the focus of interest to the ISAF joint Military Intelligence Center in the intensified search for Osama Bin Laden.

There was no hard Intell that he was actually there, or even in the Province, but the Higher-Ups wanted a boots-on-the-ground recon look-see to eliminate it as a possible hide-out, as well as to have a first-hand understanding of who and what was actually there.

Allegedly loyal to the Taliban, there was no mistaking that the village would nonetheless be steadfastly loyal, regardless, to its Pashtun culture and roots, and, of course, loyal cultivators to its overly abundant poppy crop. Afghanistan supplies 90% of the world's opium supply, and, even when there isn't a war on, business is booming, and perhaps, only slightly less noisy.

It's no secret that the Taliban relies on the opium crop to help finance their fight. Some suspected that even a few of the die-hard War Lords were siphoning off more than a little of the money the opium brings in to finance their in compound-like villas in neighboring

Pakistan, expensive vacation condos in Qatar, private Swiss bank accounts, and on lavish shopping sprees to the world's most exclusive malls.

"No! No! I want hand-tooled, fine leather from the *Damn Near Extinct and Rare Endangered Animals Collection* for the seats in the top of the line, tricked-out Land Rover! And can you tell me where can I buy me another gold Rolex watch, only this time with bigger flawless D-grade diamonds and rare rubies on the bezel?"

Holy Wars aren't always about living on a prayer, which is why bribery and corruption seem to go hand-in-hand with politics here, and well, probably everywhere else in the world, too, for that matter. Politicians who bark that they can't be bought seem to have no problem with being leased and leashed.

What a piece of work is man! How noble in reason, how infinite in faculty! In form and moving how express and admirable! In action, how occasionally like a dick.

What can I say? I'm a cynic, especially when, during the briefing, we were reminded once again, about the order not to destroy the poppy crop or raw opium stashes we come across on the mission.

This, too, from the Higher-Higher ups, who catered to the politicians at the State Department, who appeased the Afghan politicians and province chiefs, who placated the War Lords, and well-armed others with vested financial interests and clout in this shaky part of the world.

Opium and hashish production is, and has been, a mainstay for the Afghan economy. Dope is so abundant and rampant here that Loki, one of the longest working military dope sniffing dogs in our detachment no longer goes out on missions in the field. Pete Kannemeyer, his Army Reserve handler, is resigned to the decision.

"Back home a large opium find like the ones we've come across would be big news and cause for celebration," Kannemeyer said, one night over a game of Poker. "But over here it's off limits, even when it's right in front of us. Go figure."

Part of the decision to remove the drug team from the field has to do with the overwhelming number of working poppy fields in the countryside that had Loki alerting to drugs long before the helicopter or vehicle he had been riding in had arrived at the search destination. Also, the previous Army Veterinarian had reported that Loki, perhaps, suffers from 'combat stress.'

The previous Veterinarian, though, was going by Loki's former habit of biting Kannemeyer every time Pete tried to pull him off of an alert. Kannemeyer has seen twenty-one stitches in both of his forearms that the Veterinarian attributed it to 'canine anger issues'. The Vet also noted 'a certain listlessness' in Loki when he isn't working, so he labeled the symptoms as canine PTSD. But here's the thing; it isn't actually canine PTSD.

The fact of the matter is the inadvertent Malligator biting goes hand-in-bleeding- hand with working with us. PTSD may be part of it. However, the fault is not in your scars, but in our selves. We're Malligators. We're not mean. We're just enthusiastic, like sugar high toddlers in a bounce house with sharper teeth.

As for the 'listlessness,' well, actually Loki's just toasted from one too many patrols through the poppy fields and marijuana plots, not to mention his getting into a thin, cloth package of raw opium in one village before Kannemeyer managed to pull him away.

Loki chomped down on the tar-like opium bundles and almost overdosed. Afterwards, he became very spacey. The upside is that the mellow Loki no longer bites Pete or anyone else, for that matter.

His only real job now is occasionally getting called out to run drug checks here at Camp Phoenix or at Camp Eggers. Mostly, he spends his time in the detachment area kennel, laid back, glassy-eyed, and smiling like only a happy, happy dog can do. Also, he is only military working dog I know who wags his tail in time listening to old Grateful Dead or Phish CDs, and whose 'woof' sounds more like, '*Dude!*'

Both Loki and Kannemeyer are scheduled to rotate home in three weeks. A new drug dog team arrived three weeks ago to replace them, and they're working together to integrate the new team into the unit. With the stories Kannemeyer has been telling the new drug dog handler, Specialist Len Connor, the new handler seems happy he and his dog, Lulu, a hubba-hubba looking Golden Lab, won't be going out to the field.

Two new bomb dog teams arrived in country with Connor and Lulu, but they were kept in Kabul. Someone at the NATO ISAF co-alition Headquarters decided they would remain at Camp Eggers to work there for the time being. The plan is to break the two new teams in slowly before they are eventually assigned with the Detachment here at Camp Phoenix. The underlying hope is that they don't break when then get tasked for high-speed missions like ours in the field.

The new teams were assigned to the camp's main gate, working with the U.S. and Afghan Military Police manning the checkpoint. Eight days into the shift work and only twenty-two days since the new teams arrived in Afghanistan, a suicide bomber in a packed suicide vest detonated the device at the main gate.

The suicide bomber, along with a local Afghan policeman, and the working military dog, a sweet little black Lab named Sadie, died in the explosion, while the critically wounded handler, who had lost his left eye and three fingers on his left hand, was medevaced to the U.S. Military Hospital in Landstuhl, Germany.

Any notion of a gradual break-in period came to an abrupt end as the second working K-9 team was immediately put to work at the main gate, where they would remain for the duration of their deployment.

On the job nobody talks about the fissures or hairline cracks.

CHAPTER

9

Two AH-64 Apache Helicopter gunships were doing lazy circles in the indigo sky overhead, covering our insertion into a dry swath of open ground a thousand-meters from the target area.

We took no immediate enemy fire when we landed, but that didn't foreshadow the rest of the morning. Too many visiting armies over the ages knew that Hell is empty and all of the demons are here.

We were in the heart of the rugged Hindu Kush, the legendary mountain range that traverses central Afghanistan to the eastern reaches of northern Pakistan. Everyday life here in the heart is a challenge from the harsh environment, the war and many wars that preceded this latest one, and the dislike and disdain for the outsiders who gave it arrhythmia. Today, its pulse and rising pressure, was subject to another unwanted visit.

When the lead Chinook helicopter touched down carrying the first platoon, the Command Platoon that we were attached to, quickly exited through the back ramp, and raced for protective cover, as was the standard procedure. Find cover and use it.

Once the helicopter had noisily lifted off, it was unnervingly quiet as the CAV Scouts secured the Landing Zone, ready for the fight that didn't follow. Nobody spoke. Like the curtain going up on tragi-comedy play, everyone watched and anxiously waited for the show to begin.

Simultaneously, three identical helicopters were dropping off each of the remaining platoons in different, pre-planned, and strategically placed locations. Each of the four platoons in the company would carry out coordinated tasks on the mission.

With the old village tucked down in a surprisingly fertile bowl-shaped valley, surrounded by bleak, copper-colored mountains, two of the platoons would secure the high ground to the north and south before the Command platoon would enter the village from the east.

The second platoon- the mortar platoon, would set up in an over watch position in the hills to the north with a clear view of the village and the east-west mountain road leading in and out of the village.

The third platoon would take the high ground to the south while the fourth platoon would serve as a blocking force on the road west of the village.

The small village could've easily been mistaken for old ruins from a time when men in armies of shields, swords, and bows first sacked it ages ago. It was the freshly tilled and well-maintained fields and orchards that had said it was still occupied and in use.

The village, more of a poor hamlet really, maybe had two-dozen or so mud-brick, haggard-looking, flat-roofed houses, stretched out over a gradual incline that overlooked the small valley. The small bowl-shaped valley had good sun and water and the crops in the fields had proved productive.

Each dwelling was surrounded with its own ten-foot-high wall. Separate gated entrances led to individual courtyards with outdoor rock ovens close to each house and pit latrines tucked off in discriminate corners.

Narrow and twisted, packed dirt alleys, and shadowy passageways linked the labyrinth-like maze to the houses, animal corrals, and to a larger, common gathering courtyard outside of the village Headman's dwelling.

At one time the village had a twelve-foot-high stone and mud wall securing its perimeter, but as the decades and centuries had passed, the wall had given way to crumbling decay, neglect, and one too many obvious breechings by an invading army of one ilk or another. Truck-size holes and dark, pockmarked battle scars, and ugly man-made blemishes showed the signs of old, and even more recent attacks.

We would need to make a cautious approach.

The Company Commander, the ginger-haired Captain, held us in place until the other platoons were set up and ready. Once that was done he would give us the order to move out. A short time later when the radio calls came in that they were in position and tactical, we moved on the primary objective.

The road into the village, like most of the other roads throughout the remote mountain country, was a long, twisting, pot-holed dirt track that snaked its way through the rugged mountain range. A rusted Russian tank and Armored Personnel Carrier, lost in the 1980s to land mines and frenzied fighting, littered the approach to the village and served as an omen.

In the dry season the road would be parched and dust-blown. In the winter the heavy dust would turn the serpentine track into an undulating river of mud. With frequent rockslides from the surrounding mountains, any going would be painfully slow and drawn out in and out of the mountains.

But we were between the conflicting seasons, not that it mattered much either since we wouldn't be taking the road anyway. The plan was for us to hump to the village through the tilled fields and small orchards that paralleled the west side of the road. It was a slow advance and a strategically cautious one.

The air smelled of wood smoke, flat bread baking in stone stoves, and mixed with the earthy odor of working farm fields. Fifty yards from the village the early warning system went out from some of those tending the cultivated fruit trees, vegetable patches and poppy fields, as we came into view.

The cries echoed into the village and the villagers, as expected, frantically began hiding and stashing away their weapons, their best looking wives and daughters, bundles of raw opium, and any of their other best possessions they thought the latest round of interlopers would take a fancy to and carry off.

As we advanced, the half-dozen or so villagers, that were still in the plotted fields and orchards and knew it might be dangerous to run, were herded together and escorted back to the village by the soldiers in the point squad. Even if they didn't like it, the villagers well understood the ground rules in play. There would be no discussion or arguing. They walked quietly towards their homes under gunpoint.

Just shy of the crumbling perimeter village mud wall we immediately dropped down pumping adrenaline as gunfire erupted from the far end of the village. Staccato bursts of automatic weapons and several explosions echoed through the valley.

"GET DOWN! GET DOWN!" yelled one of the Platoon Sergeants to the group of villagers, who did just that as the soldiers accompanying them motioned them down and kept a watchful eye on the group.

A small fight was on, but well away from us, so everyone around us held their fire. There was more small arms fire, the CAV scouts and the Taliban's, and then, nothing. As quickly as it had begun, the fight was over. Excited radio traffic from the blocking platoon on the west road out of the village confirmed a brief firefight, and that they had five heavily armed Taliban, KIA. An RPG, four AK-47s, ten grenades, two pistols, and one satellite phone had been recovered. The road out of the village was now secured.

With a cautious 'go ahead' hand signal from the ginger-Captain, we were on our feet again and moving on the village. The Command Platoon stopped just inside the perimeter wall that faced the communal courtyard and a large house beyond as the rest of the platoon hurriedly took up covering positions.

An old and beat up Ghaznavi 150cc motorbike with a flat, front tire and a small, dust-laden carpet serving as a seat pad was leaning against a pitted courtyard wall. Sunlight danced on the back of a chrome-plated handle bar mirror. A shout from inside the darkened doorway of the house across the courtyard called out to us. When no one on our side immediately responded, the shouter tried again.

"He say he is the Village Headman," said our Afghan interpreter, translating what was said to the ginger Captain. "He and two Elders are coming out to greet us. He say, please, do not shoot."

We called our interpreter, 'Terp' so as not to give away his actual identity to the Taliban who would brutally murder both he and his family given an opportunity. The helmet he wore, along with dark sunglasses, and a scarf that covered much of his face, offered a certain amount of anonymity. The one-time University Philosophy Major was hoping to stave off a governing system that wouldn't burn books or have his sister whipped or beaten for listening to her favorite George Michael CDs. Here WHAM took on a whole new meaning.

Loyal interpreters were valuable assets for us, which tended to make them and their family members, targets.

"Tell them to show themselves," said the ginger-haired Captain. "Tell them if they have any weapons to put them down, and walk slowly towards us with their hands up. We need to know it isn't a trap."

To his soldiers the ginger-Captain shouted, "Civilians coming out! Don't fire!"

The First Sergeant repeated the command and his voice boomed across the village.

Terp made the translation and the Village Headman and two other geezer Elders slowly emerged from the dwelling, leaned their bolt-action rifles against the front facing wall, and stepped out into the open with gnarled, upraised hands.

The three were dressed in traditional Pashtun shalwar kameez clothing; the white, loose fitting linen trousers, long shirts, and the flat sleeveless coat-like dark vests, with the round and brown woolen Pakol caps atop their heads.

All three wore dark shemagh, wrap around scarves loosely hanging from their heads and necks. One man was in scuffed, brown boots while the other two were in sandals.

They walked towards us until Terp gave them an order to stop a few yards away. They were old men who looked to be in their nineties, but were probably only in their 60s. The lines and creases on their stern faces served as roadmaps to the region and the hard lives they'd lived.

The grim expressions they wore were only partially hidden beneath long and scraggily white or henna-dyed beards. These were the Village big dogs. Their growls or bared teeth dictated life in the communal pack and the consequences for any who challenged them, and, of course, we interlopers.

The ginger-Captain left them standing in the open for a few uneasy moments. Once he and his First Sergeant were satisfied that his Scouts had covered the doorways, windows, roofs, and the thin, winding passageways that could cause a problem, he would greet the Headman and Elders. For the moment the main courtyard and village were quiet, accented only by a swirling dust devil that rose out of the courtyard, danced briefly, and then died.

"*As-salaamu alaykum!*" called out the ginger-Captain in greeting to the Headman as he, his First Sergeant, and Terp walked forward and made the necessary introductions.

"*Wa-Alaikum-Salaam*," came back the cautious response.

"Peace be unto you" takes on a different sound when an armed stranger says it, smiling while those in the small, but heavily armed platoon of soldiers behind him were not.

As part of the small entourage, Max and me took our place a few yards behind the others, which gave us time to look around while they talked. Not surprising, there were no dogs anywhere to be found in the village. This was nothing new. Afghans tend to be skittish towards dogs, and maybe with good reason as I was smiling like an alligator swimming up behind a slow swimmer.

While the formal introductions were taking place, I had my first opportunity to take a sniff around. The breeze that was pushing through the village sent the scent cones swirling. With those air currents, I caught a whiff of gun oil, curry, anger, more curry, and a heavy dose of fear that wafted from the surroundings. The eyes may be windows to the soul, but with dogs, it's our noses that'll tell us what that soul smells like in detail.

Close as we were, it was easy to see that the rifles leaning against the wall of their house were two old, but well-maintained British Enfield and one Russian, bolt-action Mosin-Nagent. Still, there was something more. I could smell it.

"He say they are not Taliban," Terp said, but the Village Headman was fidgeting.

"Taliban flee!" said the Headman, pointing to the far end of the village where the firefight had occurred.

The ginger-Captain's eyes followed the line of sight of the Headman's out-stretched arm and then returned to his sun-lined face. Behind him the two Elders were getting twitchy. It didn't go unnoticed.

"Tell them to keep their hands where we can see them," said the ginger-Captain to Terp, who told the two men to stop moving. The Captain then had him explain to them why we were here and what we intended to do. We would conduct a search of the village for other Taliban fighters who might be hiding, as well as any weapons they might have hidden.

"We need for all of the people in the village to come out from where they're hiding so we can do our search as quickly and efficiently as possible," added the Captain.

Our Interpreter made the translation, and although the village leader didn't appear all that happy with what was proposed, he turned around and gave the loud command, anyway. The Elders behind him echoed the command.

While this was happening, Specialist Valencia, from the Cultural Support Team, replaced her helmet with a hijab headscarf and removed her sunglasses, showing that she was, in fact, a woman. Her M-16, locked, loaded, and ready to rock, showed that she shouldn't be underestimated. The Beretta pistol at her hip only emphasized the point.

Slowly, and with nervous caution, men, women and children, including a few of the Elders' ten and eleven-year-old wives, began to show themselves. They came out in wary clusters like bypassed shelter dogs that had given up hope of ever being rescued.

Soon they began to fill the main courtyard, joining the Headman, Elders, and those from the fields that we brought in with us. Although there were no weapons visible the CAV Scouts remained alert.

Most of the adults and teens assembled in the courtyard wore fearful, frustrated, or angry expressions, with the exception of a number of very small toddlers and young children who hadn't yet learned that they shouldn't smile at these latest invaders. One of the two Elders turned and barked something at several of the women who reined in the toddlers.

When it appeared that everyone was in the courtyard, and the Village Headman said as much, the ginger-Captain and said, "First Sergeant?"

"Sir?"

"Let's get it done."

"Roger that, Captain," said the First Sergeant, who turned and gave Max a nod. "Dog team, you're up."

"Hooah," said Max.

Valencia would deal with the women, girls, and toddlers. The Scouts in the Point Squad would physically search the men and boys, if it came to that. Afghan custom and ISAF policy dictated that the village women would not be spoken to directly by our men, let alone physically touched or searched, which under their religion and culture was *haram* or forbidden. One sure way to make an enemy in any new or strange land was to violate the customs, norms, and mores they held dear. Toss in religion, pride, and honor and it gets even more precarious.

Our policy was that, if, at any time, I alerted to any of the women or children, then Valencia would take over the search from there. She'd discreetly conduct the pat downs. Lest you think her job was easy, keep in mind that the Taliban weren't above wiring up children with suicide vests and triggered explosives and taking out female soldiers.

Before starting towards the first house in line we casually made a pass by the assembled group of women and children. Afterwards, I shook my head to Valencia and she gave me an almost imperceptible nod in return. So far, so good.

The Point squad trailed Max and me, covering us in our search as we moved from the farthest house or structure in the village and worked our way back to the courtyard and main gate.

Besides the mud and stone houses in the individual family compounds behind the walled courtyards, we cleared passageways, common areas, chicken coops, animal pens, and the small corrals that held the villagers' small herds of goats and donkeys.

Every so often Max had me work off-leash so the task took less time than if he had me hooked up for the entire search. No IEDs were found, which made sense since the Villagers didn't have much in the way of advanced warning we were coming.

However, I did sniff out a hidden cache of six RPG rounds, seven AK-47s assault rifles, a Chinese anti-tank mine, a crate of grenades in a hidden beneath a woodpile next to one house, and a stockpile of Soviet small arms ammunition to go along with the assault rifles and pistols beneath a carpet-covered trapdoor in the floor of the Headman's home.

A search of a crumbling and seemingly abandoned outdoor oven by some CAV Scouts turned up a hidden stash of roughly thirty kilos of raw opium. A young Lieutenant with the search team passed along both finds to the ginger-Captain who told him to leave the opium in place. The weapons and ammunition were another matter. The Lieutenant's pointing and whispered conversation gave away the discovery to those who knew, or suspected, what was found.

Even before the CAV Scouts began hauling out the hidden stash of weapons and ammunition, the Village Headman loudly began shouting something to the Interpreter with, of course, all of the accompanying, arm waving gestures and accompanying rancor.

"Whoa! Calm down!" said the ginger-Captain with up raised hands, stepping in to calm the Headman down. "What's he saying?"

"He say the weapons and ammunition you found belong to Taliban. The Taliban hide them and warn them not to tell you," Terp said, passing along what the Headman was yelling about and still yelling to make his point. "The Taliban fighters run when you come."

The Elders were echoing the Headman's words when the ginger-Captain cut them off.

"They tried to attack and kill my people," said the ginger-Captain. "Tell them those who ran didn't get far."

Terp pointed off in the direction of the blocking force where the brief firefight had taken place and explained as much. The Company Commander listened to the interpreter as he translated his words and those of the Headman and Elders.

The officer nodded every now as he studied their faces and, and more importantly, their reactions to the news with more than casual interest. It was like reading the faces of your opponents in Poker, only here the stakes were considerably higher.

As we made our way back to where the ginger-Captain and the villagers were waiting, we passed by the Headman's entourage where I caught a whiff of gunpowder and explosives residue on two of the Elders. I gave my alert and went down on all fours.

Max gave me a concerned look, as did the two Elders. "Good boy!" Max said and then leaned in and whispered something to the First Sergeant.

"Excuse me, Captain," the First Sergeant said interrupting the Company Commander, who was on the listening end of a three-way conversation he was in with the Village Headman and Terp.

The First Sergeant leaned in and whispered what Max had told him, which had him tap Terp on the arm. "Ask them if they're carrying any other weapons on them? And would they mind if we patted them down?"

With enough weapons aimed in on them, they didn't mind, at least not too loudly. One of the Elders nodded while the second man replied with an audible, irritated sniff as the Interpreter began the frisk.

The first pat down produced an old, Soviet Makarov handgun and holster with an extra eight-round magazine. Terp handed the weapon and the extra magazine over to the First Sergeant as he moved on to the next Elder in line. But before he started in on the pat down, the man held his hands up, and told the interpreter that he had something, too.

"To protect from Taliban," he blurted to Terp, who translated it to the ginger-Captain.

"Yeah, I'm sure that must be it," said the ginger-Captain, with more than a touch of skepticism.

When the Elder started to reach for the weapon he had hidden on him, Terp yelled in Pashto for him to stop. No one needed to translate that command. The shout could be well understood in any language and so could the weapons that immediately came up on the Elder.

The Elder quit fumbling with his clothing and stood stump still as the Terp stepped in and did a pretty decent pat down. Bringing out a Soviet grenade, he passed it over to the tight-lipped First Sergeant. Terp completed the rest of the frisk and came away satisfied that there were no more hidden weapons.

"All good," he said, after he had finished.

The Village Headman said something more to the Interpreter who passed along what the old man said to the unit Commander. "He say they keep weapons to protect them from Taliban and bandits."

"What's your take? What do you think?"

Terp considered the question and then gave the ginger-Captain a thoughtful shrug.

"Maybe," he said. "Maybe not."

"And the grenade?" asked the First Sergeant.

"He take from Soviets in the war before this one."

The First Sergeant thought about it and added a shrug of his own. "Could be," he said. "A couple of these guys look old and mean enough to have taken a sword from Conan, the Barbarian."

The ginger-Captain gave the First Sergeant a chin-up nod in agreement. None of the women in the village were crying or weeping for the dead Taliban, which told him that, maybe, they weren't welcome either. The ginger-Captain let out a long, slow breath before he spoke again.

"Tell him we will hold onto these for now, but that we'll give them back before we leave," he said to the interpreter who made the translation, unsure if it would, in fact, happen. The look the Headman gave the Army officer said he didn't believe it, either.

"However, we'll be taking what the Taliban left behind."

That, though, was something the Headman and the Elders did believe.

"And the opium?"

"He say they hide their crop from Taliban and bandits."

In a nearby stall six donkeys and a pile of empty canvas panniers we'd seen spoke to an upcoming trip to sell the bulk of their opium crop. It is, after all, the harvest season.

"They sell the opium in Surobi, Jalalabad maybe," said Terp. "Maybe for food, clothing, and more guns. They are not Taliban, I think."

"But you're not certain?" asked the much too young ginger-Captain, removing his helmet and running a hand over his sweaty, copper-colored hair.

Terp shrugged. "No," he said, honestly.

Wrestling with his next decision as he put his helmet back in place and secured the chinstrap, but remaining true to his word, the ginger-Captain had the First Sergeant return the now unloaded pistol, extra magazine, grenade, and ammunition to the surprised Elders. They could keep their opium, too.

"To protect yourself from the Taliban or bandits just in case they come back to raid your village or try to take what is yours," the Company Commander said to the surprised Village Headman through the interpreter, who was surprised as well.

"*Khoda hafiz*," said the ginger Captain saying farewell to the Headman.

The Headman nodded, said nothing in return, but I could sniff out his displeasure with us behind his benign acceptance. Try as he did to mask it, he was clearly annoyed. We dogs knew human annoyance. We've been familiar with it ever since we decided that there was something to domestication as we crawled up on your most comfortable cave couches, started gnawing on your leftover Mastodon bones before ripping apart your Saber-toothed fur lined throw pillows.

With the village search completed, the weapons and ammunition confiscated, the ginger-Captain gave the order to move out towards the designated pick-up zone. Valencia was replacing the headscarf with her Kevlar helmet and soon her sunglasses were back in place, as was her readied rifle and CAV demeanor. Her Civil Affairs job was done and her war fighter face was on.

As we were reaching the pickup zone the radioman passed along to the ginger-Captain that the in-bound helicopters were fifteen-minutes out, and that they had an 'eye in the sky' above them. The 'eye in the sky' was an armed drone that was on-station, taking real-time pictures, and covering our extraction, and the immediate area surrounding it.

Thousands of miles away the drone pilot and others running the drone's camera had an unobstructed three-hundred-and-sixty-degree view of the pickup zone and was providing us with immediate feedback. All was good.

Once we were on board the helicopters and headed back to Bagram, the drone would go back to working its primary mission of monitoring and hunting along the Salang Pass.

With the pick-up zone secured and a successful mission completed there was little to do but sit and wait for our ride. Leading us over to a truck-size boulder the ginger-Captain told Valencia, the Radioman, and Max and me to make ourselves comfortable, which we did. Meanwhile both the ginger-Captain and the First Sergeant remained standing, surveying the PZ and quietly nodding at how his young Lieutenant and NCOs in the platoon had positioned their people.

Yep, all was good, but neither the Captain or the First Sergeant would be comfortable until everyone in the Company were on the helicopters and we were all safely back at Bagram. Valencia was locked in a conversation with his RTO, his Radioman, while Max leaned up against the boulder and pulled out a dog-eared paperback from his left military cargo pants pocket.

Finding the bent page where he'd left off in the book, Max settled into his reading. I was down on all fours at his feet.

"Shakespeare, huh?" said the Captain, eyeing the book in Max's hands.

"Yes, sir, Selected Works," he said, and then patted the now empty cargo pocket. "I'm taking an on-line course. My dog likes it when I read it out loud, and also, I figure the book is thick enough to stop a piece of shrapnel or two."

"So then what's in the other pocket, Great Western Philosophy?" asked the First Sergeant.

"Sort of," Max replied. "Louis L'Amour's, the Sacketts."

"Which one?"

"*Lonely on the Mountain.*"

The First Sergeant brightened. "Ah, Tell Sackett. Good choice! He's tough enough to stop anything coming at you, that's for sure."

"Good job finding the hidden cache," said the ginger-Captain.

"It's all him," said Max, tilting his head towards me.

"Well then, we'll just let the chain of command know that he did a good job. Thor, right?"

"Yes, sir."

"I'm told you're on your third deployment, so this must seem like no big thing to either one of you. I imagine you guys find small arms caches all the time?"

Max shook his head.

"More IEDs than anything else, sir," he said.

"You find a few?" the First Sergeant asked, taking an interest.

"Twenty-nine and counting. Two that didn't explode."

"Say again?" said the First Sergeant after a slight pause where both he and the ginger-Captain, stood stock still, staring at us wide-eyed and open-mouthed as they did the math.

"We've been caught up in two blasts."

"Two?"

That admission drew Valencia's and the radioman's attention as well. Both were staring at us and waiting for the rest of the story.

"Uh-huh. Had our bells rung and took some shrapnel." Max pointed his arm and leg and my left back leg. "Nothing big so far, knock on wood. Well, I mean I would knock on wood if there were any damn trees around here."

The ginger-Captain chuffed, holding back what he was thinking but not his First Sergeant, who wanted to know more. First Sergeants always wanted to know more and usually did, which was why they were *first*.

"You like your job, do you?" asked the First Sergeant. "Finding IEDs?"

"Well, preferably finding them before they explode, First Sergeant. Sure."

"Kinda dangerous, though, don't'cha think?"

The ginger-Captain looked to the First Sergeant, who was still staring at Max and me like we were nuts. With a wry smile and shrug Max pointed to the cloth Jump Wings with a wreath enveloping a star above the parachute canopy on the patch on the First Sergeant's uniform.

The small black thread embroidered patch indicated that the Senior NCO was parachute qualified and that he had made a parachute jump in combat. Then, there was the combat 75th Ranger scroll attached to his right shoulder.

"You jump out of perfectly good airplanes, First Sergeant. Apparently when people are shooting at you, it seems," he said. "The last Ranger combat jump I read about was, what? Christmas of 1988, when the 75th Rangers jumped from five-hundred feet or less at the Rio Hato Airfield in Panama under heavy enemy machinegun and anti-aircraft fire."

"It was 1989 but yeah, you could say we had a bit of a rough welcome."

"Would you mind if I asked how many parachute jumps do you have, and let me say again, out of perfectly good airplanes?"

"Just that one at Rio Hato."

"One, seriously?"

"Yeah, seriously. The others before or after were all just practice."

Max chuckled and then pointed to the Captain's uniform. "And I do believe that's jump wings and a Ranger tab on your uniform, too, Captain."

The First Sergeant and the ginger-Captain briefly exchanged startled looks, shook their heads, and then laughed. Max had made his point and now the CAV Scout Company Commander wanted to make his.

"You two both have big brass balls, I'll give you that," he said, digging into his cargo pocket and finding what he was looking for. "I'll also give you this."

The officer handed Max a First Cavalry Division Scouts Recon challenge coin. It was the size of a silver dollar with a Division patch-First Team on one side and crossed sabers and Recon Scouts in relief on the reverse.

"If you show it to any CAV Scout when you're in a bar and he doesn't buy you a drink, then just give me the dumb shit's name and I'll slap him up alongside his head," said the First Sergeant.

"Hooah?"

"Hooah," said Max.

CHAPTER

10

Physically and mentally, I'm in the zone. Professionally, I'm a highly trained, combat tested, extremely effective explosives sniffing, Hooah, military working canine.

All-Star status. Three deployments and extended tours, running.

In human years, I'm in my prime, which makes me a little older than damn near most of the GIs I work with over here in this giant sandbox.

And that's another thing, Iraq and Afghanistan are, indeed, two giant sandboxes, and since cats love sandboxes, why aren't those hairball-hacking, don't-really-give-a-fuck, puff-faced feline freeloaders over here looking for nasty things that explode?

They brag about having nine lives, which means they can actually spare a few. So, why aren't they in the fight?

Oh, that's right, they can't do it. They don't have it in them. They never have.

Throughout recorded history dogs have been loved and celebrated, both in fact and fiction for the genuine affinity we enjoy and share with humans. We share a unique and an unparalleled bond with you upright bipeds, complete with natural likings, sympathies, and empathies. You're happy, we're happy. You're sad, we're sad. You have your doubts and we give you paws for concern.

It's all there in fine print and on film; everything from Homer's faithful dog, Argos in *The Odyssey*, to Hachiko, forever waiting in bronze at the Shibuya train station platform in Japan.

They're not alone. There's Laika, the celebrated street dog from the former Soviet Union, who was the first dog to go into space, St. Guinefort, the 13th century French dog that, for awhile, was recognized as a saint, and how about that Wicked Witch barking, Toto, from *The Wizard of Oz?* In addition, there's Tin-Tin's reliable Milou in France, or Buck from Jack London's, *Call of the Wild*, Rin-Tin-Tin, or Bullet from TV westerns, or the multi-dimensional K-9 of *Doctor Who* fame, whose name literally is K-9. Then, of course, there's everyone's all-time favorite, *Lassie.*

You remember *Lassie*, don't you? He's that loving and loyal, lion-maned Collie who's forever saving accident-prone Timmy from, yet, one more crumbling cliff ledge, a train trestle and run-away train, or an abandoned well.

Pet Lassie and ruffle his noble neck, Timmy's Mom, and oh, while you're at it, smack some sense into your dumbass son of yours. The kid has some serious safety issues. Just saying.

By the way, we dogs are noble and one of us even had officially been crowned with nobility. Ever heard of the Dog King of Scandinavia? Nope? Well, legend and a few semi-contradictory historians say that after a Swedish Viking king won a victory over a Norwegian Viking king in the 9th century, the Swedish king put his son on the throne to govern. When the Norwegians rebelled and killed the son, the vengeful Swedish King once again subdued the unruly Norsk neighbors and gave their defeated cousins a choice of picking the king's favored slave over a dog named, *Saur. Saur*, by the way, translates to English as, excrement. Shit. The much-enlightened and apparently contrary Norwegians, with zero fucks given, chose the dog. A wise choice, if you ask me. We're kind, benevolent, and wise. All bow wow down before us or at least scratch our ears.

Seriously though, the wise can sometimes even be scary smart, too.

In a series of well-documented, scientific studies by the University of New South Wales, Australia, in conjunction with Osaka University in Japan in 2001, a four-year-old Australian Border collie named, Snooper, correctly picked out more than 900 different items arranged for the test. The wily black and white Einstein located the items that those conducting the test named.

Let me emphasize that number one more time to let it sink in, 900 items.

In trial after trial, Snooper didn't hesitate when it came to locating an orange ball, a brown brush, or a stuffed white, red, green or blue bunny when he was given the command, which from what I've observed from my time in the military can't necessarily be said of your average new Private or Second Lieutenant.

On the other hand, before you think that Snooper is *all that*, keep in mind that given the option or opportunity, he'd happily rather roll around in the nearest pile of cow shit for hours, so maybe there's a real downside to being a know-it-all.

Snooper isn't a one-off oddity, either. He has since been upstaged by a six-year-old Australian Border collie named, Chaser that correctly identified over 1,000 assorted items earning him the title as, '*The Smartest Dog in the World.*'

Chaser was even featured on ABC News, USATODAY, and 60 Minutes, where he wowed the reporters and helped celebrate the extent of his doggie IQ for the accomplishment. Think about that for a moment. Chaser could accurately identify the 1,000 items, including differentiating between objects and their colors.

What, you say? You heard someone once say that dogs can't see colors? Well both Snooper and Chaser proved them wrong. The fact is, all dogs can recognize colors. We just don't see a need to because, like math, it doesn't really matter to us. You say you have three green doggie treats in one hand and three red doggie treats in the other?

No problem. We'll gladly eat them all and then wonder why you even foolishly bother to count them, let alone why another human would think that artificial food coloring dye would make a red one taste yummier than a white or green treat in the first place. We sniff and taste flavor. We don't sniff and taste color. Our consciousness is elevated beyond that.

What's more, we're loyal, brave, and willing to protect and serve mankind of any size, shape, color, or creed. Womenkind too, for that matter, well, with the exception of those crazy-ass cat ladies, who seem to mistake a dozen purring cats for a meaningful orgasm. And I'm talking women who cackle to themselves and have spiders living in their hair, and who will one day die in their sleep only to be found a week or two later by a social worker with their faces half-eaten, and gnawed on by their famished feline eh, friends.

Cat got your tongue? Well, it's possible. Just saying.

Dogs? We're here for you in a number of good, and sometimes, even in great ways. Just give us a task. We're up for the challenge. Ever heard of a Guard Cat? Nope? Ever wonder why? How about a Sheep Kitty that herds the pre-yarn they seem to love so much? Nope, again. They're not dogs. They don't have it in them to do what we do, which is, to protect and serve.

We guide the blind, protect your homes and property, guard military bases or security sites, and work as service or companion dogs for any health condition or emotional issue you might have. Without being prompted, we've snatched up snakes crawling towards babies, chased away bears, and when we're not teaching humans how to dog paddle, we're rescuing them from downing.

We chase after mechanical rabbits so you can win money at the racetrack, sniff out some cancers, find lost children or loved ones in the woods, and can even locate trapped survivors in the rubble after a tornado or earthquake.

Saint Bernards might even show up to dig you out of an avalanche and then offer you a sip or two from their keg of brandy! We have a calming influence on patients in hospitals, make old people feel better about being warehoused in Old Folks Homes, and- *ahem*- we can even locate things that explode.

No thanks necessary. We're happy to do it. We actually like you.

Cats? Yeah well, you can't teach them squat, but you'll still happily hang up their mouth-vomiting calendars on your kitchen bulletin boards or refrigerators, giggle or smile at on-line videos of cats dressed in pirate costumes, pretending to play piano, or battling yarn. Like what? Yarn is a big problem for you, Fluffy?

Oh, and don't get me started on that Hello Kitty crap, either. You'll slap that damn sticker on any and everything, including the allergy medicine you need because, guess why, you own a fucking cat!

Swollen, itchy eyes? Blame the cat.

Asthma? Blame the cat.

Rash and hives on your face and chest? Blame the cat.

Stinging eyes from foul smelling, dried, cat urine? Yeah well, it's a pisser, but hey, you get the picture.

And, before you argue that cats are smart, too, let me just say, you're right. We dogs know it. They are smart but they're also sneaky.

Don't think for one moment that they're not trying to pull one over on you. Here's why. Cats provide nothing of real or genuine value to humans in return, and yet you bipeds spend ridiculous amounts of your hard-earned money on their Vet bills, carrying cages, cat beds, stinky-ass litter boxes, cat collars with little bells on them, and all those stupid rubber toys that squeak for the entertainment for those sloe-eyed little shits.

Never mind that they scratch up your curtains and favorite chairs, drop dead mice or birds at your door or in your kitchen, unroll your toilet paper in the bathroom, or shred the foliage of your best house plants, you still foolishly believe they might actually like you, let alone, love you.

But here's the thing, when they're sitting and purring in your laps, they're not being lovingly content. What they're really thinking about are better ways to shit in your favorite pair of shoes. Yeah, yeah, but you say you like it when they calmly sit on your lap. Eh, hello? Ever heard of a lap dog? They don't mind if you ladies are in your old sweat pants, ratty tee shirt, and re-watching *Love Actually* for the umpteenth time, they'll happy sit there and watch it with you because they love being with you. It is love, actually. Pass the ice cream.

You say, 'okay, but I don't like dogs that bark.' Fine. Get a Basenji. They don't bark. They yodel! And they'll yodel with love as you rub their bellies.

Cats, on the other hand, don't love humans! They think you're beneath them, so they use you.

However, the real difference, the critical difference between dogs and cats, and I want you to listen carefully to what I'm about to say here, because it all comes down to this; cats aren't loyal. Dogs are.

That's right, we're loyal. Say, for instance, your house catches on fire. If that happens then your ever loyal, ever faithful, and loving dog, will yip, whine, and bark to alert you to the house fire. The dogged and determined hero hound might even try to drag your sorry ass out of the burning inferno to safety, if you're incapable of getting yourself or your loved ones out.

This too, has been documented, time and time again. Its why Law Enforcement, the Military, and civilian organizations have K-9 courage and bravery award ceremonies to honor the deserving canine heroes who go above and beyond the call of duty.

The British even have what's called, The Dickin Medal, a high honor awarded to animals that demonstrate conspicuous gallantry under fire and courage in the face of battle. The Dickin Medal was enacted in 1943 and serves as the animal and bird kingdom's Victoria Cross. One side of the medal reads; *For Gallantry* while the reverse is inscribed: *We Also Serve.*

The prestigious honor has been awarded forty-four times to dogs. Let that resonate for a bit.

Forty-four times for acts of Gallantry.

In 2000, it was awarded posthumously to Sergeant Gander, the mascot for the Royal Rifles of Canada and other Commonwealth Forces during the defense of Hong Kong Island in December 1941.

In bitter fight for the Allied island, the large, black dog defended small groups of wounded Canadians and Brits by charging into a band of attacking Japanese soldiers and halting their attack, not just once, but repeatedly. Then, when a grenade landed near another group of the Allied wounded, this Ram-bow-wow scooped it up in his mouth, and ran it back at the Japanese in a game of fetch they hadn't planned on. Sergeant Gander, of course, was killed in action stopping the attack, but he saved some lives at the cost of his own. He is just one of the forty-four dogs to have well earned the Dickin Medal for extraordinary courage.

Now, guess how many cats have received this highly honored and prestigious award? Go on, guess?

Never mind. I'll save you the time. The answer is: one.

That's right, one. *Uno, ein, un, odin,* or in this case, *yi,* for the number one in Chinese and the number of times the medal was awarded to, and I want to hack up a hairball just saying this, a cat.

The cat, in question, was named Simon. Simon was the ship's cat on the HMS Amethyst, and he was wounded in action when the British ship was shelled by Chinese Army artillery 100 miles up the Yangtze River in 1949.

So what, exactly, did Simple Simon do to earn the award, besides being wounded, you ask?

Well, according to the official citation, he, eh... '*bore his wounds with quiet dignity,*' old boy. That's it, *quiet dignity,* which, if you're not a cat person, is actually blatant, ho-hum fucking indifference.

Now let's go back to the house fire example for a moment. While a faithful dog will certainly alert you to a house fire, a cat, on the other hand, at the first whiff of smoke, let alone disturbing noise, or actual danger, will head for the nearest exit with a '*Uh-uh, oh, fuck no! Nope, ciao, nada, I'm outta here,*' meow.

Shakespeare reminded us that a coward dies a thousand deaths but a hero only once, and since cats have nine lives, maybe they can afford to lose a few trying to improve and better their reputation and image. But do they? Nope! Those cowards are out the door in an eye blink.

Oh, and it's also possible that the cat, who might even have been high on catnip at the time (just say, no), was the one who knocked over one of your watermelon-scented candles in the bathroom in the first place, and started the house fire.

It doesn't end there. It's also likely that in a house fire your cat will use that expensive little two-way cat flap you had installed in your kitchen door, so that little Mister Wooby-Wooby Whiskers, Chairman Meow, your Kitty Cat Damon, Cat Apillar, Stevens, Mandu, Atonic, or whatever other stupid fucking name you give that arrogant little shit, can come and go as it pleases.

By the way, about that pet door flap of yours, guess what? Raccoons, possum, rats, and other skinny thieves are happy you had it installed, too, for the same reason, easy access. Anyway, it's also the door your cat arsonist will use to make good his or her get-away.

Once outside and clear of the inferno, the mangy mouser will saunter across the street to the safety of your neighbor's house, hop on the warm hood of your neighbor's Prius or Subaru wagon, and curl up inside itself, while you and your loved ones, not to mention that ugly fucking cat calendar, will blister, blacken, and burn away in the flames.

Bottom line: you'll die, your cat shrugs, and then wonders where exactly your neighbors keeps their extra tins of tuna.

Cats aren't heroic. They never have been.

Ever wonder why they're called, pussies?

Just once I'd like humans to be more honest about how cats interact with them, or maybe even settle to have that famous fucking Broadway musical sing about what really goes on in their devious little minds.

"Memmmmmory, turn your face to the mooooon light, let your memory lead you, away from the flames...Tough luck, humans. It was nice to have used you, but a cat never really takes your family's name..."

There's also that whole spooky, evil black magic, and *double, double, toil and trouble*, wart-chinned witches chant that goes along with black cats, and more importantly, bad Halloween candy. So yeah, I'm not a fan of cats; so don't get my hackles up.

Think I sound cynical, do you? Well, there's good reason. The word cynic comes from two words of the ancient Greeks; *Kynikos*, meaning dog like, and *Kyon*, meaning dog. The word was coined for Diogenes, the famed Greek philosopher, who not only went in search of an honest man, but helped spread the philosophy of Cynicism, the school of thought that said the purpose of life is to live in virtue.

Virtuous? Yep, that's us, and we're hip, too. In fact, K-9s are the real snoop dogs so don't give us a bad rap. Like I said, we're good at what we do, and Max and me can hold our own when we're running with the big dogs. Together we've had earned;

A) Two Bronze Stars for Heroism, for finding two hidden IEDs, that somebody higher up in rank, and who was riding in a convoy we were accompanying, figured we'd earned by saving a few lives since the IEDs exploded before they, or any one besides us, were wounded.

B) Two Army Commendation medals for valor, because a few other somebodies saw us find a few more IEDs that they were convinced were meant for them but, hey, there were no explosions, so all was good, thanks to us.

C) Two Purple Hearts (see A, because we got the snot knocked out of us in those two IED blasts), and,

D) A fistful of assorted Atta-boy award certificates and unit challenge coins because a bunch of other higher ups thought we did good, just not good enough to earn a brightly colored medal and accompanying uniform ribbon.

The medals, certificates, and 'atta-boys' give us some serious military cache and Hooah street cred, yo.

All that stuff is nice, but here's the thing, you can't eat it. Me? I get a few yummy beef, chicken, or better yet, bacon-flavored treats that Max carries in a plastic bag in his rucksack and gives me every time I find an IED, a suicide vest, explosives or weapons hidden beneath floorboards or behind false walls. The pats on the head and belly rubs that go along with the doggie treats for a job well done aren't bad either.

Max is a good handler. He's as good-natured as a Golden Retriever, only smarter, which should go without saying, but seldom does. More importantly, he's good at his job. To get the job as a K-9 handler, he took a six-year enlistment, earning a promotion to Sergeant E-5 after our second deployment. He's up for a promotion to Staff Sergeant in June, if he reenlists, which might not happen, depending upon whether or not he gets hired by the Seattle Fire Department.

We've been together now for nearly four years, ever since we were partnered up shortly after my eighteen-weeks of basic K-9 training at the Department of Defense's Military Working Dog training program at Joint Base San Antonio-Lackland Air Force Base, deep in the heart of Texas.

The K-9 training was intense, and while I may not remember the Alamo or San Antonio, I do remember Lackland. It's where they turn tubby, 'I don't know squat' dogs into lean, mean, Hooah working military dog team machines. Can I get a *Rhurr-rah*?

Rhurr-rah!

There you go.

Upon graduation I was introduced to Max when we were both sent to Yuma, Arizona, for three weeks of desert indoctrination training in preparation for our first deployment to Iraq, where we would begin the serious work. In Yuma, there would be additional scent work.

It didn't always work like this with the canine program. Usually after the handlers were trained they were assigned dogs at their duty station. But the wars in Iraq and Afghanistan were flaring up, and more Military Police K-9 dog teams were needed for the fight. Policies and procedures adapted and changed to meet the needs of the service, and we soon learned to adapt and change with them.

In Afghanistan, the Taliban learned early on that they couldn't take the fight to the Americans and ISAF Coalition forces head on and win major battles. It seldom turned out well for them when they did, so instead, they concentrated their focus on another easier tactic. They upped their game and began utilizing more effective IEDs.

Ambush was their tried and true fallback staple for the last few thousand years, and they still used it well. However, in more recent times it was the IEDs that became their most effective combat tactic. IEDs have done the most damage to the ISAF forces and the local populace over the last forty years.

In the last year or so, they have accounted for more battlefield casualties than enemy bullets, Rocket Propelled Grenades, or incoming mortar rounds. Because of the increase in the use of IEDs, and the shortage of dog teams, our services were at a premium. After all, we were dog stars. The trouble with that is that everybody expects you to get a hit every time at bat. I wish it were that simple.

Ty Cobb, Babe Ruth, Ted Williams, and Miguel Cabrera had some of the best averages in major league baseball. They're listed as All-Stars for .300 plus averages, which means three out of every ten times up at bat they got hits. Three or four out of ten put them in some rare company and made them Hall of Fame legends. Keep in mind, the majority of the time, they didn't get a hit, occasionally got beaned by the ball, got walked, or they struck out.

Here in the 'Stan, getting beaned or striking out could get you killed. Maybe like baseball's All-Stars, being at our peak left only one other direction to go. Still, we stepped up to the plate, gave it our best, and swung towards the stars. But the bottom line, we're still in the game.

Various military or government organizations and agencies were yelping and clamoring for bomb dog or drug sniffing teams to accompany them on their tasks or patrol. When their own organizations or agencies didn't have a team available then we were called out. So, it wasn't uncommon to find us working with Marines on a road clearing operation one week, assigned to Army CAV's Scouts the next, joining Special Forces teams for an outing or two, or taking part in U.S. or ISAF Military Police raids or actions. Occasionally, we'll also find ourselves being an adjunct to the State Department team missions, or running tasks for special VIP visits.

That's right, I said *adjunct;* something I picked up when Lieutenant Kelly used it to say that Max and me would be attached to another unit. Actually, the first term he used was *detailed,* only there isn't a dog alive that doesn't cringe when it hears that word.

We're not fond of the word, *neutered,* either. It's like saying, '*You're getting a forced vasectomy*' to a man and while some may argue that there's a vas deference between the two, those, who are on the ball, will tell you there's no difference at all.

Well, they would if they had any balls.

CHAPTER

II

Our small, Combined Canine Detachment compound area here at Camp Phoenix, rests behind its own eight-foot-high wall of Hesco bastions that, from the air, looks like an abandoned giant Lego project in a fucked up playground.

Camp Phoenix, for all practical purposes, is an ever-evolving frontier military boom town. Surrounded by explosive-proof walls and razor wire, its perimeter is protected by guard towers and gates, and the latest in high tech security systems. Inside the walls, what started with tents and frustration has changed to significantly more comfortable surroundings, courtesy of the always busy, civilian contractors and the wants and needs of the various military units that come and go.

K-9 Detachment Sirius (Provisional), as we are officially designated, is a temporary detachment, independent from the primary Military Police Company that patrols and guards the base. We're also independent of our true service organizations since we're an odd mix and thrown together hodge-podge unit of active duty Army, Reserve, and National Guard K-9 teams, serving the higher military bosses at headquarters in Kabul, hence the term (Provisional).

With no rhyme or reason that we can see, but with a winning argument that someone in the NATO-ISAF Supreme Allied Command headquarters envisioned and eloquently convinced the joint military command was necessary, we became an 'on loan,' multi-service, K-9 detachment. We're told we 'serve a greater good.'

Just as in the movie, *Gettysburg* that Max had tossed in and we both watched on his laptop one night, where some character with a bugle on his cap and talking through a droopy mustache pointed out that, '*There is nothing so much like a god on earth, than a General on a battlefield,*' there's was no difference on today's battlefields. Generals hold amazing power.

And although I later saw that same guy do some really stupid things in *Dumb and Dumber,* he well understood the power Generals in combat have to suit their immediate needs. Now, whether or not, it was the four-star General in charge of the NATO-ISAF command that made the decision to create the Detachment, or if it was one of his lesser shooting stars, the Detachment came into operational being and serve who we're told to serve. The simple fact is: when a big dog barks, little dogs listen.

Who knows? Maybe the underlying logic in the decision is that our combined pool might better serve a wider variety of units in temporary need of canine support, or we were, in fact, someone's pet project. Regardless, we had our independence and temporary status.

It's unconventional, sure, but in case you've never been in the military, or aren't familiar with how they operate in times like these, one of the first things you need to know is that everything in the proverbial realm under the top dog's stars is subject to change. That particular change, of course, was also accompanied by the Pentagon's official unofficial budgetary policy of, '*Do more with less.*' Ours is not to reason why or contemplate the wry of it, either. So, for the now, we're here and we're operational. The unit was provided with the basics but anything more, we had to scrounge.

Our Detachment area is laid out in the shape of a horseshoe. Forming the left side of the U-shape lay out are three air-conditioned CHUs, the trailer-like Combat Housing Units. Each of the CHU's, that were pronounced *chews*, held three, ten-by-twelve foot separate living quarters for the handlers.

Each of the living quarters came with a single bed, a small dresser, and a desk. Depending upon Army regulations and the moods of the Commanding Officer and First Sergeant, the GIs housed in the CHUs could modify them within limits with TVs, Play Stations, X-Boxes, books, family photos, state flags, Laptop computers, or posters to help make their personal time reasonably more comfortable.

Forming the right of the horseshoe is a fourth CHU that is fitted with showers and flush toilets. A fifth CHU serves as a supply and weapons room. At the bottom of the horseshoe configuration another CHU serves as a kennel and canine examination/treatment room. Next to it, a final CHU, serves as the Detachment's Orderly room and Detachment Commander's quarters.

We have our own, small, makeshift motor pool on site, which is really only a canvas awning covered portable garage for the Detachment's two, count 'em, two, Humvees. In the center courtyard of the compound we have an outdoor canine obstacle course and an open area we use for bite suit or the bite wrap, arm sleeve training.

On paper Detachment Sirius, (Provisional), has ten to twelve working teams. In reality, we, maybe, can field eight or nine teams. Illness, injuries from training, and war wounds, have all taken their toll on the dogs and their handlers. Add to that the rotating deployments, with dog teams, coming and going, then you'd think it would be enough to drive those in charge here barking mad. Still, Lieutenant Kelly and First Sergeant Hallatt somehow managed to keep it all together.

In his civilian life, the big and burly Hallatt, who had been called up for service in Afghanistan with the Montana National Guard, is a police canine officer from Billings, Montana. He had been a cop for twenty-three years and in the Guard for twenty-two. A career professional, he's good at his job, he's reliable, and he doesn't ruffle easily. As a civilian K-9 officer, military Canine trainer, and Kennel Master, there are few better.

The long and short of it, he loved dogs, and the framed picture he kept on his desk of his wife and two kids laughing as their dumbass, grizzled faced, Golden Lab, named Rowdy, photo-bombed the family photo said as much. Next to that photo was another of Hallatt, the Policeman, with his K-9 partner, a thinner Rowdy in earlier times. He was probably a good dog but in the photo, Rowdy didn't look all that much brighter.

What can I say? He's a Lab. Yeah, I know. They're adorable, but hey, let's be honest, you and I both know they have the IQs of tree stumps.

Because the Detachment is short-handed, the tasks and mission requests are rotated through the working teams, unless a unit, or say, a high-ranking individual, requested a specific team. Then, of course, Lieutenant Kelly and First Sergeant Hallatt are made well aware that rank has its privileges, and act accordingly. Generals, Full Bird Colonels, and Command Sergeant Majors don't like to be told 'no.'

With our twenty-seven and two record, Max and me are considered one of the top teams in the area, which means we have status. We're a known commodity. However, that notoriety has its drawbacks. We receive the most mission requests because when someone from headquarters says, '*We want your best dog team on this,*' they go with the numbers.

Lieutenant Kelly and the First Sergeant are tasked with juggling the requests and making sure that they work all of the teams, evenly. That too, though, is subject to change, as we all would soon learn with Kelly's deployment.

His annoying little bug bite turned out to be a deadly poisonous spider bite. The spider's toxins left a huge pus-filled hole that had begun to eat away a large amount of muscle tissue in his leg surrounding the bite.

Late, one afternoon, the Detachment's First Sergeant and Kennel Master, Master Sergeant Hallatt, called a formation to inform us that Kelly had been evacuated to the military hospital in Landstuhl, Germany. He wouldn't be returning.

And, just like that he was gone.

Kelly was replaced by twenty-three-year-old Second Lieutenant, Dimmer, John Falstaff. One each. Dimmer, of average height and slight paunch, would become our new and temporarily assigned Officer-in-Charge.

Command Sergeant Major Nunez at Headquarters called First Sergeant Hallatt on his satellite phone to say that an OIC for the Detachment should be arriving on or about 1000 hours.

"Should?"

"He left with the morning convoy at 0900, but he seemed anxious to know if Camp Phoenix had a good PX."

"A shopper's paradise, if you have low expectations," said Hallatt as Nunez chuckled.

"Keep in mind, he's only temporary."

"May I ask why he is only temporary, Sergeant Major?"

"Yes, you may. He's awaiting discharge."

"Poor performance?"

"Well, he is a Second Lieutenant, so that's always a tough call to make. Actually, it's for a medical issue."

"Combat wounds?"

"No, other injuries," Command Sergeant Major Nunez said and left it at that. "Command says every unit or Detachment will have an OIC and he's the only junior officer the Colonel had available, and how do I delicately say this…"

"Go ahead."

"Shit rolls downhill."

"And we're level ground?"

"At this moment, decidedly flush, yes."

"Is he Canine qualified?"

"No."

"Military Police trained?"

There was a pause on the other end of the line. "No, he is not," said the Command Sergeant Major. "He is a Quartermaster Corps Officer, and I say again, the only available junior officer on hand and available."

"But can you tell me if he knows, say, I dunno, how to recognize a dog?"

Nunez chuckled. "He's a Second Lieutenant, so you can count that as a maybe," he said. "We're expecting a permanent and more qualified OIC to take Lieutenant Kelly's place, but until then, Second Lieutenant Dimmer, John Falstaff, one each, will have to be your fill in."

"Falstaff, huh?"

"Yes, and again, he's only temporary. I'm sorry."

It was the 'I'm sorry' part that had Hallatt wondering what the Command Sergeant Major was leaving out.

"If it helps any, I overheard Colonel Reese, the General's Chief of Staff, who assigned the Lieutenant to the Detachment, tell him that the General thinks very highly of his K-9 Detachment and not to fuck it up. It's possible he might've told him not to run with scissors, too."

"Enough said," said Hallatt. "I appreciate the heads-up."

"No worries…well, besides the one we just laid on you," said the Command Sergeant Major. "And I say again, I'm sorry. We'll have a permanent OIC in place as soon as we have one available. As the Lieutenant was leaving the Colonel's office I advised him to listen to you and take any advice you offered."

"Thank you. That's appreciated."

"It was the least I could do. Talk to you soon."

"Roger. Out."

At 1210, when a Humvee drove into the Detachment and dropped off the new and temporary Officer-in-Charge, First Sergeant Hallatt, went out to help him with his personal effects and gear, including the shopping bags filled with things the Lieutenant thought he needed for his new command. One shopping bag was overflowing with corn chips, several large size bags of Gummi Bears, three five ounce packages of Red Vine licorice, and a grease stained box of glazed donuts. A second bag held two six-packs of 20-ounce plastic bottles of Mountain Dew.

Dimmer stood five-nine, had late on-set acne, and something of a paunch. Both he and his BDUs looked perpetually rumpled. The Army had physical fitness standards and weight requirements, but since he had an injury to his knee and because he would soon be leaving the Army, he couldn't be held to the same physical fitness requirements or appearance standards.

The manipulative squint to his darting brown eyes should've given the First Sergeant and the others an initial clue to his inner workings, but the human side to the Detachment were a more trusting and inclusive group, while we canines were infinitely better at sniffing out demeanor and deception.

Like all new ROTC or Officer's Candidate graduates he had the official rank and an affectation of leadership. Time, at least for the First

Sergeant and our Detachment, would tell whether he was truly a leader or whether he was someone who was merely filling a temporary slot. At first glance, though, Hallatt wasn't impressed.

"I'm Lieutenant Dimmer, your temporary Company Commander," Dimmer said to the First Sergeant, not holding out his hand but instead reaching back and grabbing a Sony Play Station. The young officer also brought along some attitude.

"Actually, we're a Detachment, sir. We've been expecting you."

"I had the driver stop at the PX to pick up a few things," he replied. "Can the Company Clerk get my duffle bag?"

"I'll get it," Hallatt said, grabbing it from the Humvee, and then leading the Lieutenant towards the CHU that doubled as the Detachment's Orderly Room with attached living quarters.

Lieutenant Dimmer wasn't impressed.

The office was small, sparse with a gunmetal gray government desk, with matching stacked In/Out boxes, three-drawer filing, and several swivel chairs. A three-month, hanging wall calendar hung just below a round, black and white wall clock on one wall of the small office while the opposite wall held a window-mounted air conditioner rattling its way to coolness. A small, three-by-five area rug sported the black and gold logo for West Point's Black Knights, the previous Commander's Alma Mater.

Dimmer's face showed disappointment at what was there, and maybe more so, at what wasn't.

"This is it?" he said, frowning.

"Yes sir. This is your Orderly Room, Lieutenant with your living quarters through the door, there," the First Sergeant, said pointing towards a door left of the desk.

Dimmer set down the shopping bags, walked over to the door, and cracked it open to check out his living quarters. He frowned again. There was a bed, a nightstand, a wall locker, small desk, and a small refrigerator. That was it and for the young officer, the cramped office and living space wasn't enough. Turning back to the First Sergeant he sighed.

"It's not very big."

"The Detachment isn't all that big, sir."

"Then, I'm glad I'm only temporary. Somehow, I was expecting more."

Hallatt didn't respond, thinking that maybe saying he was expecting more, too, might not go over so well.

"Where's the company clerk's desk, or the Company clerk for that matter?" asked Lieutenant Dimmer.

"As I said, we're not a company, Lieutenant. We're a Detachment, so we don't have a fulltime clerk. If we have a handler on stand-down, or whose dog is sick or injured, then that handler will fill in, temporarily, as a runner."

"Out of this office? It's too small!"

"No sir, out of the kennel office. When Lieutenant Kelly was medevac'd to Germany, I moved the bulk of the operations from here to the kennel office. It's a quasi-Orderly Room."

"But there's a clerk, right?"

"Well, up until yesterday it was Specialist Petit's temporary position. His dog, Buster, chipped a tooth last week, so he was filling in. The visiting Vet fixed Buster up, so he and Petit are back in the rotation."

"The rotation?"

"We rotate the assignments when requests come down from command for a K-9 team for a field assignment."

"From your kennel office?"

"Yes sir. With Lieutenant Kelly gone I moved the rotation and assignment chart to the kennel. I've been handling the bulk of the Detachment Operations from my office, however, if you like, I can move it back."

"No, there's no hurry in that regard," Dimmer said, glancing again around the small office. "I mean, you're the First Sergeant and what, the kennel guy..."

"Kennel Master."

Dimmer nodded, noting the distinction, but really understanding it. "Ah, right, right," he said. "And since we don't have a Company clerk..."

"Detachment, but you're right, Lieutenant. There's no full-time clerk, just the occasional, temporary one."

"Then I think it's best if we leave things as they are, for now, anyway."

The First Sergeant nodded and said, "I'll give you some time to settle in and then I'll come back and show you around the Detachment, show you the kennels and examination room, and introduce you to our Vet Tech before you address the troops."

At that, Dimmer frowned.

"Actually, I need to get back to the PX to get a few things," he said, sheepishly. "You know, for my living quarters."

It wasn't an unreasonable request and Hallatt figured the new acting Officer-in-Charge probably needed the time to settle in, anyway. The tour could wait.

"No problem, Lieutenant," he said. "We'll do the grand tour when you get back."

"Oh, and can we find someone to drive me to the PX, First Sergeant."

"No need for a driver, sir. It's just a five-minute walk from here."

"Bad knee," he said, pointing to his left knee and sighed. "It's why I'm only temporary here. I'm in the process of getting a medical discharge."

"Ah."

"So, since I'm moving a little slowly, what say you give me the *grand tour*, as you call it, tomorrow, maybe?"

"Tomorrow?"

"Uh-huh, I hear there's a coffee shop at a food court near the PX, and I could use a mocha right about now."

Hallatt stared at the Acting Officer-in-Charge, unsure of what to make of him, but getting a good working idea. "I'll find someone to drive you, Lieutenant. But I'll need you back for the 1300 formation. You can address the handlers, then."

The Lieutenant checked his watch. "But it's 1220 now," protested the young officer.

"Which should give you plenty of time to make it back by 1300, Lieutenant. We have an operational Detachment to run."

Dimmer frowned and sighed again. The First Sergeant left the temporary Officer-in-Charge to get settled as he went to find him someone to run the Lieutenant on his errands. Walking back to the kennel office he couldn't help thinking that perhaps it wasn't so bad that this new Detachment Commander was only temporary.

Dimmer, Hallatt hoped, wouldn't live up to his name.

At 1300, the six teams of K-9 handlers and dogs that were not in the field on missions, were standing in the sweltering heat in the afternoon formation with an annoyed First Sergeant, whose eyes kept shifting from his wrist watch to the closed Orderly Room door, and then back again to his watch.

At 1310 the new and temporary Officer-in-Charge came out of the Orderly Room and walked towards the First Sergeant with the over-confident strut of a cocky pug.

"Detachment...AH-TEN-SHUN!" said First Sergeant Hallatt.

The Lieutenant dutifully took his place in front of the First Sergeant, the two saluted, and Lieutenant gave the command for us to stand at ease.

"My name is Lieutenant Dimmer and I have been assigned to serve as your acting Com... eh, Detachment Commander. It is very likely that my command here will be short term and temporary. That being said, I will keep out of your way as much as possible, let you do your doggie thing, and leave the 'what all' to the First Sergeant here."

Dimmer turned, smiled, and gave a brief nod to the First Sergeant, who didn't return the smile or the nod. His workload was busy enough and he didn't appreciate the 'what all' hand-off. Temporary and short term, the Acting Officer-in-Charge would still need to carry his own weight.

"To tell the truth," added the new Officer-in-Charge, "I'm not really a dog person, never have been, which you have to admit is somewhat ironic. Funny too, when you think about it."

Lieutenant Dimmer chuckled but the chuckle soon died when he noticed that his admission didn't bring on the smiles or laughter he had expected. The admission, in fact, drew mostly bewildered looks from some of the handlers, and a few frowns from others as well as the First

Sergeant. Even a few of we canines in formation gave him woof-what the fuck, canted-head stares. Everybody loves dogs, or should. We're wonderful!

Looking a little uncomfortable, the Lieutenant went on.

"What's more, I'm not really sure what you do, and it's possible I may not be here long enough to become fully up to speed on your roles, let alone, personally get to know each and every one of you or your dogs. However, I know that as professional K-9 operators..."

"Handlers, sir," said the First Sergeant, correcting him in a low whisper.

"Handlers?"

"They're not operators."

"Okay, K-9 Handlers, then. Anyway, you and your guard dogs..."

"Detection dogs, sir."

This time Dimmer didn't respond to First Sergeant Hallatt's remark and seemed somewhat embarrassed and annoyed by the interruptions. "What I do know is that as professional K-9 *handlers* you will continue to do the good work that you have been trained to do. So, keep it up. The First Sergeant will see your mission assignments and what-all during my short tenure here. First Sergeant, they're all yours."

"Hooah," Hallatt said offering a salute that our new and temporary Officer-in-Charge returned with a haphazard one of his own before turning and making his way back to the Orderly Room and his temporary quarters. Dimmer, apparently, didn't Hooah.

Like the rest of us handlers and canines standing there watching him walk away, Hallatt stared after him for a bit as he did his best not to shake his head in disappointment and frustration, at least in front of the rest of us.

He was, also, flared nostril fuming thinking that he would have a 'Come to Jesus' talk with the Lieutenant later about his less than satisfactory welcome speech and repeated *what-all* remarks. But that would be later and in private, and out of hearing distance from the rest of us in the Detachment.

Doing an about face the First Sergeant addressed our small formation. "Those of you who are not tasked with other assignments will report back here at 1330 for odor detection proficiency training," he said. "Bring your First Aid Kits and extra leashes for inspection. FALL OUT!"

Not all skirmishes or small battles begin with shouted cries, clashing swords, or gunfire. Sometimes they just begin with a frustrated First Sergeant staring at the back of a less than stellar leader and muttering, "You have got to be fucking kidding me" as that less than stellar leader is walking back to his quarters.

Later, in the Orderly Room, Hallatt had his talk with the new and temporary Officer-in-Charge, not that it seemed to do much good. In the days and weeks that followed, Dimmer did leave *what all* to the First Sergeant, passing on the bulk of the workload, and command responsibilities to the Senior NCO.

After the first three weeks of officially being in charge, it appeared that the new Lieutenant was a token figurehead and wasn't about to do anything more that he absolutely didn't have to do. Even then, what he did seemed more for show and self-serving, including having the unit's Dog Star patch sewed on his BDUs so he'd look the part, even if he actually didn't know or appreciate his role. When he couldn't be found at the Camp's Coffee stand at the food court, then he could be found at Camp Eggers checking in on the status of his discharge date, while taking advantage of the Camp's better PX.

While Dimmer seemed pleased with how things were working out, Hallatt was not.

The First Sergeant was growing increasingly frustrated with him, as were some of the handlers who began muttering that the Lieutenant was the *'less'* that the Army was asking them to do more with.

The Lieutenant wasn't a Military Police Officer, he had no experience with Working Military Dogs, nor did he show any genuine interest in doing his job, let alone in learning or even leading the Detachment. And because he was waiting to be discharged from the Army, he said he didn't feel the need to learn more about who we were or what we did.

Not necessarily a good leader or even adequate for the Detachment, the new Lieutenant was, however, proving to be good at mainly just looking out for his own best interests, something not lost on the First Sergeant or the rest of us.

One morning after formation, and after the rest of the K-9 teams had their daily assignments, First Sergeant Hallatt had Max and me hold up for a moment.

"Sergeant Ritchie? I need you and your dog to run a demo for several VIPs this afternoon at 1330."

"Demo, First Sergeant?"

"That's affirmative. The Lieutenant is coordinating it now with some higher-highers at Camp Eggers. Seems he volunteered us for the Dog without a Pony Show."

"Any idea who the VIPs are, Top?"

"Some news people who want to see who we are and what we do, I suppose. Anyway, we'll show them a few inert IED mock-ups and run some training aids. I imagine they'll pet the dog, even when we tell them not to, before we'll send them on their way. Put on a clean uniform while you're at it."

"No problem, First Sergeant."

"My guess is that the Lieutenant is trying to score some points with Command to push along his medical discharge. Small things make base men proud, but you didn't hear me say that about our beloved acting Officer-in-Charge now, did you, young Sergeant Ritchie?"

"No, First Sergeant. Residual hearing damage and all."

Hallatt nodded. "And possibly some heat stroke in this ninety-plus degree heat, as well, seeing how he set this up during the worst part of the day. I'll talk with him afterwards but for now it's a done deal. Be ready to go by 1325."

If First Sergeant Hallatt's facial expression was anything to go by lately, then perhaps Dimmer being temporary wasn't necessarily a bad thing.

CHAPTER

12

The VIP 'reporters' turned out to be a two-man film television crew from a weekly entertainment program out of Hollywood, and a young, good looking female newspaper reporter who wrote for a Scottish Daily in Glasgow.

Their military escort was a young and peppy Public Affairs Officer from Camp Eggers, who seemed happy to be visiting the Canine Detachment, happy to be at Camp Phoenix, and happy to be in Afghanistan. Happy, happy, happy. The only thing that seemed to be missing was his cheerleading pom-poms.

Go team, go. We'll be on the sidelines. Rah.

The PAO introduced the young, willowy, dark-haired Scottish woman as, Stephanie Reid. Reid smiled, said, "Hello, pleased to meet ya," as she shook our hands, and was smart enough not to try to pet me without first asking. I got a smiling nod instead.

Stephanie Reid was outfitted in baggy, khaki-colored cargo pants, with matching long sleeve shirt, sturdy work boots, and red-framed sunglasses. A floppy hat shielded her neck and face from the glaring Afghan sun. She had an expensive Nikon D-7100 digital camera hanging from a strap around her neck, which freed up her hands for the reporter's notebook and ballpoint pen she quickly retrieved.

Of the two-man television crew, one was a semi-familiar, late thirty-something former child star whose career never quite took off, but who maintained a certain degree of celebrity by interviewing and hyping other celebrities more famous or the young stars and starlets on their way up. He had fashionably styled spiked hair, expensively purchased, shiny veneer enameled teeth, a tattered cloth bracelet on his right wrist to show he nominally believed in some cause or another, and an expensive Breitling watch on the other that showed whatever he believed in had nothing to do with poverty. He was also wearing a fake tan that reminded me of a water puddle that was just as shallow.

The former child star blew past the PAO Officer and introduced himself by saying, "Yo, what's-sup?" his catch phrase from his television series. He didn't offer his first name or his hand, and instead adjusted his sunglasses as he stared at us waiting to be fawned over, which no one did except for the Public Affairs Officer, whose mother watched him on the Entertainment program right after Wheel of Fortune.

'Pat, I'd like to solve the puzzle. Is it, 'IT'S POSSIBLE HE'S A POMPOUS TV ASSHOLE?'

"Why, yes it is!" Applause sign prompt for the audience to clap. "Congratulations! You're going to the bonus round!"

The semi-celebrity, who had co-starred in a teen comedy that had aired for several seasons back in the proverbial day, and now was relegated to nostalgia cable and modest residuals, was dressed ine woreH designer desert cargo pants with a matching long sleeve shirt that had both sleeves rolled up to the elbows and locked in place by stylish buttons. His hiking boots were fine leather that had probably never been used on a decent hike, and his Serengeti sunglasses had simulated, but still pricey, faux sea turtle colored frames. Microphone in hand, he was now the talking head with a well-practiced smile that dropped a little in disappointment when we didn't seem to recognize him or be all that impressed, if we did. I sniffed concealed annoyance.

"Anyone here from L.A.?" he asked and when Lieutenant Dimmer, The First Sergeant, and Max shook their heads, he turned his cameraman.

"I'm miked up, Bob. Give me a sound check."

The second half of the TV news crew, Bob, his photographer, nodded, turned some knobs, pressed some buttons, and gave the Entertainment Reporter his sound check.

Bob was a short, fifty-something-year-old with a scruffy salt and pepper beard and a slight paunch. Dressed in old jeans, a Rolling Stones tee shirt, grubby trainers, and a weathered LA Dodgers ball cap, Bob, the veteran cameraman was there to get some useable footage and do his job. He wasn't out to impress anyone.

Shouldering a camera that must've weighed thirty-pounds or more, and judging from his sardonic expression, Bob seemed to hold a little disdain for the entertainment reporter he accompanied and would be filming. I had the feeling I was going to like Bob.

Lieutenant Dimmer enthusiastically welcomed the visitors, but it became obvious that he welcomed the Scottish journalist with more than casual interest. Our new Officer-in-Charge seemed very bent on impressing the young woman, if, of course, your notion of the word, *impressing* meant, shagging her until she squeaked like a happy chipmunk. Fancying himself as a player he was, hopelessly, out of his league, but he was trying to work his way into the majors, regardless.

After the Lieutenant introduced himself, the First Sergeant, and Max and me to the visitors, he turned the demonstration over to First Sergeant Hallatt. Dimmer then sidled up next to the Scottish reporter as the First Sergeant welcomed them to the Detachment and offered up a detailed explanation of who we were and what functions we served in the war zone. He followed this by saying there would be a 'Show and Tell' with some of the training aids and dummy IEDs that we would use today in the demonstration as he pointed to a cardboard box and other items resting atop a folding table behind him.

"The training aids will provide you with a better visual and tactile understanding of what we typically encounter on the job," he said, motioning them towards the table as he removed several items from the cardboard box and laid them out on display.

With the exception of the working photographer who was filming it all, the VIPs, the happy Public Affairs Officer, and Lieutenant Dimmer gathered around Hallatt who began passing around or pointing to several of the heavier types of IEDs while identifying each.

All of the IED props were diffused and made inert, which made for good 'Show and Tell.' As he was passing over a modified pressure cooker, Hallatt offered an explanation on how each was made and how they were employed against the ISAF soldiers and vehicles, as well as against the local populace.

When most of the telling was over, he moved on to the better part of the show with a loud, "Any questions?"

"I thought the Taliban only used them against you and others in the ISAF," said Reid.

"Some Shia use them against Sunni targets and vice-versa, some of the various Taliban factions target local police, schools, foreign charity workers, and some in Al Qaeda seem to go after everyone who they disagree with, at times, including the Taliban," said Hallatt.

The Scottish reporter had several more questions that were surprisingly well thought-out with follow-up queries about the dogs, the handlers, the training we go through, and the very real dangers we face or have faced doing our jobs. The girl was good.

Hallatt patiently listened and then answered each question she had in a clear and concise, 'Just the facts, Ma'am' manner. Unlike the acting Officer-in-Charge, Hallatt represented the true, quiet professional. As he spoke, Stephanie Reid, was scribbling a flurry of notes, occasionally asking for clarification on some of the military terms and jargon he used, or with additional questions brought up by his answers. She was setting the foundation for her article with pages of facts, explained military terminology, and background material that would she would build on, and add in color, depth, and tone from there.

Without a teleprompter, though, the Entertainment TV reporter, the semi-celebrity, seemed at a loss for words, let alone, adequate questions to ask. He wasn't taking notes, nor did he intend to for what would be his 'On Air' interview.

Used to the cameraman capturing the bulk of the visual content for him, he'd later come up with clever copy in the editing process, or simply record what his Director would have his Copy Editors provide for him. For now, though, he stuck with the basic of basics.

"So where are you from, Sergeant?" he asked, sticking his microphone closer to Hallatt. That was followed up with, 'How do you like it here?" and, the all-important, "Hot enough for you? Ha, ha."

With that last question and obligatory echoed laugh from the Public Affairs Officer, he was done. He turned back to the Scottish reporter, who had a few more follow-up questions and was eager to ask them.

As she continued with her interview, the TV talking head nodded along, looking almost thoughtfully at the new round of questions. He nodded again at the responses she received as though he had truly understood all that was being asked and answered, as did Lieutenant Dimmer.

From time to time he smiled his trademark smile- a smile, that at times, threatened to blind us with the reflection off of his perfectly enameled teeth when he turned into the sunlight at just the right angle. However, it was more than the glow off of his teeth that was annoying.

"Yeah, wow, no, that's great! Good stuff! Super!" he said, when they looked to him for his follow-up questions. Turning to his cameraman, he said, "Get some good film, Bob! We'll do some fill-in later, but hey, what say we get a few close ups of the dog and me right now? Is that okay? Can we shoot some set up shots, right now with the dog? The mommy audience will eat it up!"

"No problem," Lieutenant Dimmer said. "Let's do the set ups with Teddy-Thor."

"Just Thor," Hallatt said, correcting Dimmer.

The Lieutenant shot his First Sergeant a confused look but his attention was immediately drawn back to the VIPs.

"So, Thor, huh? Is that short for anything?" asked the Entertainment Reporter.

"No," said Hallatt, not adding anything more to relieve the man's momentary bewilderment, let alone Dimmer's.

It was the peppy Public Affairs Officer who stepped in to move it along.

"The set-ups shots, with Thor, the god of Thunder, sound like a great idea before we move along to the demo."

Dimmer agreed, the peppy Public Affairs Officer smiled, and after the TV Entertainment reporter with the shiny, enameled teeth got his close-ups with me, the Lieutenant took over the talk.

"You ready to see him work?" he asked.

"That'd be great," said the TV Entertainment reporter.

"Marvelous," replied the Scottish newspaper reporter.

"First Sergeant?" Dimmer said turning it over to Hallatt.

"We have a P-bied training aid…"

"P-bied?"

"A Person-borne IED, what you probably know better as a suicide vest," he said, pulling out the training vest out of the cardboard box of warzone wonders.

"Any volunteers?" asked Dimmer, eyeing the two VIPs.

The TV reporter shook his head, no, as he held up a cautionary finger to the rest of us. His attention was focused on the small screen of his cell phone. "Gotta check my work messages, sorry," he said, and stepped away.

That left the Scottish journalist who said she'd do it, but before First Sergeant Hallatt could fit her with the simulated suicide vest, Dimmer stepped in and took it from his hands.

"Here! Hold her camera," he said to Hallatt removing the camera and strap from Stephanie Reid's neck. "I'll do the honors."

Slipping the dummy suicide vest through her arms, he chuckled as he buttoned up the front. "You da bomb," he said, awkwardly rearranging some of the wires on the vest on the dummy explosives.

"I'm guessing that's bomb dog humor," she said, smiling more at his obvious and fumbling advances but not smiling for the reasons he believed.

"Not to worry," Dimmer said, still holding onto the vest's zipper. "These aren't real explosives."

"Well, I *fecking* hope not, for God's sake, Leftenant!"

There were four plastic pipes in separate pouches on each side of the front of the vest that were used to simulate explosives. The pipes were inter-connected with red and green wires and connected to a thumb pressure ignition switch that ran down the right shoulder of the vest, down her arm, and stopped at her right hand.

"Lieutenant," said Dimmer as she moved his hand away from the vest. Dimmer looked back to the First Sergeant and held out an empty hand to take back the camera. "Let me take a picture of you as the dog does his thing."

To Hallatt he said, "We good to go, Top?"

"Not quite, sir. Here you go."

Hallatt handed her a jacket to cover the vest.

"There you go," Hallatt said. "Now, we'll have..."

"Fuck me! Do you believe this shit? I only have one bar here!" yelled the TV Entertainment reporter, interrupting Hallatt and the demo. "I bought a fucking international Sim card at the airport and I still don't have any service!"

"The cell service can be sketchy outside of the larger cities," said the peppy Public Affairs Officer. "But I imagine they have a phone bank set up here at Camp Phoenix you can use."

"There is," said Lieutenant Dimmer. "A few minutes drive from here.'

"Phone bank? Like what? I can get a new Sim card there?"

"No. Actually, it's a hut or tent that provides a common area for the soldiers to call home," explained the Public Affairs Officer.

"A common area?" the TV reporter said, scoffing at the idea of having to use a plebeian mode in a tent for his personal calls. "Uh no, I don't think so."

"Or I can let you use my laptop so you can check your e-mails. How's that sound?"

"Once we get back to your Camp in Kabul, you mean?"

The Public Affairs Officer who was losing some of his pep, nodded. "We can also check on that Sim card of yours while we're at it."

"How much longer do you think we're going to be?" asked the TV reporter seemingly more annoyed that the rest of us weren't annoyed along with him at the inconvenience. He went back to checking his cell phone again.

It was First Sergeant Hallatt who answered him. "Not much longer, Gentlemen," he said, "Once we're ready to continue," Hallatt said annoyed for reasons of his own.

The Public Affairs Officer was back to being happy again. "You bet, Sergeant. No problem!"

With the jacket on over the mock suicide vest and the Scottish newspaper reporter beginning to look a little uncomfortable with the bulky gear in the afternoon heat, Hallatt explained her role in the exercise. Ours was a given.

"Ma'am, I need you to walk over there, about ten yards. Sergeant Ritchie and his dog, Thor, will head over here about the same distance. You'll face each other and on my command, I want you to casually begin to walk by him at your normal pace."

"Okay.

"Don't acknowledge him or Thor, in fact, don't even look at them. Just pretend you're going about your everyday business and keep on walking."

"Is that all?"

"Yes, ma'am, it is."

She nodded to Hallatt and Hallatt said, "Sergeant Ritchie, if you and Thor will take your place."

Max nodded and gave a curt, *Hooah*. In the meantime, the Lieutenant was snapping a few pictures on her camera as Max led me ten-to-fifteen yards away, turned, and faced the Scottish reporter like jousters.

"Ready?" Hallatt called out.

The Scottish reporter nodded as did Max.

"Begin!" said the First Sergeant, well aware that action is eloquence.

We started the demo by walking towards each other, as though we were strangers who were casually passing each other on the street. Max was working me on the six-foot leash. As she went by I caught a whiff of the suicide vest training aid, did a hard head turn, and then pulled Max over to her.

Once at her side, I sat. My head went from the woman, back to Max, and then back to the woman, again. My part in this exercise was done. I had a bingo!

"GOOD BOY!" Max yelled, pulling me away, giving me high praise as he vigorously patted my side. "GOOD DOG!"

"Would you mind if we get a few more shots of the exercise from another angle?" said Bob, the television cameraman, apologetically, to Dimmer, Hallatt, Max, and the Scottish reporter.

"No problem," she said, and everyone smiled, or at least didn't whine as we ran it again just as Bob suggested, with efficient close-ups and several new set-up shots.

"We good?" said the TV Entertainment reporter, momentarily looking up from the cell phone screen, checking his watch for the time, and moving around the compound area, holding the phone up, and still hoping to find service.

Bob, the cameraman nodded. "We're good," he replied, giving the TV reporter a thumb's up.

"Swell," said the TV reporter. To Dimmer, he asked, "Do you, like, have any handouts or something about who you are, and like, what you do? I believe your Public Affairs people said you have some press kits for us and some giveaways?"

The Public Affairs officer looked hopeful, Dimmer looked confused, and the First Sergeant said, yes, they did have some handouts for them in the Orderly Room.

"You want to fetch a few for our guests, First Sergeant?" said Dimmer.

Hallatt was blowing air through his clenched teeth at Dimmer's *fetch* remark as he turned towards the Orderly Room.

"Mind if I go with you?" asked the TV reporter, eyeing the air-conditioned unit on the side of the Orderly Room's north facing wall and not waiting for an answer. "It's hot as fuck out here."

"Sure, go ahead," replied Dimmer. "And get us all a few bottles of cold water while you're at it, too, Top?"

"You got Wi-Fi in the bungalow?" asked the TV Entertainment reporter.

"Orderly Room, and no. No public Wi-Fi access. Just government secured systems."

It wasn't true. International Sim cards worked well on the south side of the kennel, only Hallatt saw no need to tell that to the silly bastard, let alone the temporary Officer-in-Charge. Hallatt figured that the time Dimmer spent at the phone bank, and away from the Detachment, was quality time.

"Don't suppose you have a cold beer in there, do you?"

"Muslim country, sir. No alcohol allowed."

"You kidding me?"

"No sir, I'm not."

That wasn't quite true, either. Thanks to some civilian construction contractors who had access to sealed containers, Hallatt had a cold six-pack of Corona Beer in the mini-fridge in his CHU and a half-filled bottle of Jack in his footlocker. But he'd be damned if this pretentious poodle was getting any of it.

"Keep filming, Bob," the TV Entertainment reporter said over his shoulder to his cameraman. "Get some good shit we can use."

"Well now, he's a proper little cunt, isn't he?" said the Scottish reporter staring after him as he and Hallatt walked off.

The remark was loud enough for all to hear, although, the Entertainment reporter might've missed it as he was still all consumed in trying to find service of his cellphone.

Both the Public Affairs Officer and Dimmer hadn't missed it and were visibly startled by the comment while Max studied his boot tops trying his best not to laugh. Over his shoulder Hallatt gave the Scottish reporter an almost imperceptible smile as Bob, the television cameraman chuckled at the remark, as well, thinking he very much liked the young woman.

Bob, the cameraman gave a quick nod to Hallatt who returned it. They were, after all, kindred spirits. No words needed to be spoken. The nods said it clearly; 'I see you have one of these Yahoos as well,' said the first nod, followed by the second nod that implied, 'why, yes, I do!'

A few minutes later the First Sergeant returned with the much-appreciated bottled water. The TV Entertainment reporter, though, wasn't with him. He was standing in the open doorway of the air-conditioned Orderly Room, taking sips from his water bottle, studying his watch, and letting the cooler air out of the office.

"You joining us, sir?" shouted Dimmer.

"No, I'm good," the TV reporter said, waving him off. "I'll watch from here."

"As you like it."

The K-9 demo continued. We ran several more training aid scenarios with closed boxes, buckets, and bags. The demo seemed to impress the Scottish journalist who snapped a series of photos, and peppered us with a few more questions as she had removed the stifling jacket and vest.

Reid was wiping her sweaty brow as she began asking about us and some of the things we'd found during what her accent came across as, our *tiers of dootie*. Max downplayed the dangerous aspects of it while the First Sergeant provided a more honest appraisal.

"We have two handlers in Walter Reed recovering from several serious wounds. One lost both legs and one arm in a triggered detonation while another, who'd only been working here in Afghanistan for less that thirty-days, lost an eye and several fingers. Over the last nine months we've also lost two military working dogs. And we have one working team that have been caught up in two troubling detonations, suffered concussions and wounds, but who are now here back on the job."

"Still working? Even after being caught up in the two explosions?"

"Yes Ma'am."

"The man has got to be *fecking* daft."

"Feel free to ask him," said Hallatt, stepping aside and turning towards Max and me. "That team is Sergeant Ritchie here and his dog, Thor. He won't tell you what big brass balls he has, but I will."

The reporter's face went visibly pale as she lowered her gaze to Max's groin.

"Sweet Jesus, prosthetics! Are they?"

"No, no!" said the Public Affairs Officer stepping in quick to clarify the remark. "It's an American slang expression. It means they're both brave."

"Well, I should say so. Two explosions. It must've been *fecking* horrible even without losing your bollocks?"

"We're good, now, Ma'am," Max said, once again downplaying the previous injuries and wounds and smiling at her colorful choice of words. She was right, it was *fecking* horrible, and if anyone was shocked by the phrase she used then they didn't fully grasp the nature of the job when things all went south in a hurry.

"Well, you have my respect," she said. "And so does this wonderful little fellow. Okay to pet him my thanks?"

Because she had asked and waited for his answer, Max gave her the go-ahead. Her purple painted fingernails made for a nice colorful round of scratching behind my ears.

"Oh, what a good doggie!" she said, running her wonderful fingernails along my flanks and ears and smiling at Max. The woman gave damn good scratch.

And because she was smiling at Max and me but not him, the Lieutenant stepped in to move the demo along. Max didn't know it but apparently he was cutting into Dimmer's game.

"Why don't you run Tedd-Thor..."

"Thor," said Hallatt, confusing Dimmer once again.

"Okay sure, why don't you run your dog through the obstacle course, Sergeant Ritchie?"

"Now, sir?"

"Yes, Sergeant."

The sun was at its zenith and the peak heat was in the high 80s and climbing and baking the already dried, hard-packed ground. Further along in the dry season and there would be no way that the First Sergeant would let the demo to go on. Even so, he let it be known where he stood.

"And this will conclude the demonstration," he said, staring at Dimmer as he said it.

"Yes, of course," sniffed Dimmer, moving back in next to the woman. "When you're ready, Sergeant."

Max walked me over to the start of the course, gave me the command to sit and unhooked the leash from my collar. With his next command, which, by the way, wasn't *havoc*, we took off in a sprint. Soon we were racing up a leaning ladder, leaping several small hurdles and obstacles, dodging around a series of poles, and crawling through a six-foot section of tunnel to finish the course. Max was running alongside me, all the while, loudly encouraging me as I went.

"Atta-boy, Thor. Atta-boy buddy! Go! Go! Go!"

We ran it like we normally ran it, all out and in sweat-dripping record time. But here's the thing; dogs don't sweat like humans. We regulate our body temperature by panting and sweating through our paws and I was regulating like a faucet.

What's it like running the obstacle course in this heat? Well, try putting on a fur coat and then run in place in a sauna for a bit and you'll get the gist of it. Max and me were overheated and sweating in our same, but different ways after running through the course in the high heat. The exertion was taking its toll. Max was feeding me water from a water bottle he pulled out his cargo pants pocket to cool me down before a sip or two of his own.

The reporter snapped several pictures of that as well, checked the small screen on her camera to make sure she had the photos she needed for her article, and thanked us. The TV Entertainment reporter with the shiny enameled teeth had another approach.

"We almost done here?" he asked, yelling from the Orderly Room doorway.

"Yes, sir, we are!" said the peppy Public Affairs Officer walking over to join him. "Oh, and we have an ISAF hat, patch, and challenge coin for each of you!"

The glare from the TV Entertainment reporter's shiny teeth smile threatened to blind us again.

"Great!" he said, high beaming. "Hey Bob, when you're done with them, get a shot of me with the hat on, interviewing their boss here."

"Believe it or not," Bob, the cameraman said to Hallatt and Max, "Once upon a time I use to work in real news. Thanks for reminding what I've missed."

His admission was followed with a heavy sigh. Hallatt gave a sad smile of understanding.

"Will you make sure he shows my people in a good light?"

"Will do," said the veteran cameraman. "I'm also his film editor and besides that, my son's a Marine."

"Is he over here?"

"Not yet, but probably will be, soon."

"Our dogs and handlers work with Marines from time-to-time."

"Then, on behalf of a worried mother, and a father who pretends he isn't, we thank you for the difficult job you do."

Bob held his hand and Hallatt shook it.

"On behalf of the young soldiers that actually do the work, you're welcome."

"Stay safe."

Hallatt nodded.

Lieutenant Dimmer, who was still hitting on the Scottish newspaper reporter as they walked towards the Orderly Room, turned back to us.

"I've enjoyed this tremendously," she said to Hallatt and Max, and then grinned at me. "It was *fecking* brilliant! I'm very pleased to have this opportunity to get a glimpse at all the crazy shite you do. Cheers, and I mean it when I say, take good care, yeah."

She offered her hand to Hallatt and Max and they shook it.

"Yeah, thank you, Sergeant Hallatt," Dimmer said to Max. "You and the handler are dismissed."

As Lieutenant Dimmer led the reporter to his office to join the others, he was overheard saying, "I was injured in an explosion as well, you know."

"Your head, was it?"

"Eh, no," said a vexed Dimmer. "My knee."

"Ahhh," said Stephanie Reid.

The talk continued as they walked, as did Dimmer's hopes for something more. The conversation, though, looked to be all one sided as Stephanie Reid didn't seem impressed with his charm.

The Lieutenant found us in the kennel a few hours later. Max was brushing down my coat while Hallatt was going over the Canine health records in preparation for the Army Veterinarian's monthly health and welfare visit.

"Ah, there you are," the Lieutenant said, coming through the swinging door from the examination room. "Nice job on the demo."

"Thank you, sir."

"Both the PAO and the television people are very happy and the newspaper reporter says she's going to do a nice write up on all of the good work we're doing here. Said she'd send us the link once the article is published and mail us some copies of the paper, too."

Max nodded while First Sergeant Hallatt, who seemed to be shouldering the bulk of the actual burden for any of the actual command work, done in the Detachment, looked very much like he wanted to piss on the Lieutenant's boots when Dimmer included himself in with the Detachment's, *good work*.

"He's a German shepherd Mal-a-noise, right, Sergeant?" Dimmer asked, while the First Sergeant sighed and slowly shook his head. Hallatt left it to Max to set Dimmer straight.

"He's a Mal-en-nhaw, sir," replied Max, "the *noise* is silent."

"Mmm, but he's a German shepherd, right? Just a small one?"

"Belgian Malinois."

"Same-same, though, right?"

"Different breed, sir."

"Oh," replied Dimmer, sucking air in through his teeth and looking momentarily troubled.

Max stared at the officer, saw that he still didn't get it, and changed the subject. "Where you from, L-T?"

"Chicago."

I could see that Max was tempted to ask him if he pronounced his home state as '*Ill–eh-noise*,' but he let it go.

Instead he asked, "Are you a 31-Kilo, sir?"

"A what?" said Dimmer and there it was, we had our answer. A 31-Kilo was the Army's Military Occupational Skill designation for a Military Police dog handler.

"Oh, my branch, you mean?" said Lieutenant Dimmer. "No Sergeant, I'm a Quartermaster Corps trained. I was with an S-1 supply unit in Kandahar before I got injured in a mortar attack."

"Shrapnel, sir?"

"Eh, no," he answered and left it at that. "Anyway, the K-9 Detachment needed an Officer-In-Charge, so headquarters sent me here to temporarily fill in for a while until they can find another officer to take over, or until I'm medically discharged. So, First Sergeant,"

Dimmer said turning back to Hallatt, "I'll need you to watch over things till I get back…"

"Get back, sir?"

"Yes," said Dimmer. "I need to head back over to Camp Eggers and let the reporter know that the dog isn't a German shepherd but a Mal-in…"

"…Malinois."

"Yes, exactly. How do you spell that?" asked Dimmer retrieving a small notebook and pen from his uniform shirt pocket readying to write.

Hallatt told him and Dimmer wrote it down, so he'd remember.

"That sounds like French?"

"Belgian, sir."

The officer nodded and then gave us the command to "carry on" and we did. Well, Max and the First Sergeant did. Me? My hackles were hackled. I was pissed.

Mal-a-noise? Seriously?

Oh, and by the way, Lieutenant, fuck German shepherds! They look like they've had one too many helpings of dumplings and schnitzel, and skipped more than a few Nazi Weight Watchers meetings.

We Malinois are trim and fit, like fine, world-class athletes. We work harder, smarter, and with more heart and enthusiasm than any other breed on the proverbial block.

And better yet, we're the best-looking working canines in the world and, I might add, sexier than all get out, so Bonejour Ladies. Nice to sniff you. Mind if I nuzzle my way into your heart via your nice warm lap?

Oh, and please feel free to scratch my ears and belly as we snuggle. That's right. "Who's your doggie?"

CHAPTER

13

Because Camp Phoenix doesn't have an on-site Veterinarian, twice a month or so, an Army doggie doc made the trip from Camp Eggers in Kabul to conduct routine checks on the working dogs here in the Detachment.

Due to a change over of Veterinarians, the schedule was off, but word had come down that it was soon to be resumed by the incoming doggie doc. That allowed for Lieutenant Dimmer to go over, and familiarize himself with the Detachment's medical records, training records, and evaluation reports. The review of the medical and training records, and the evaluations reports, was a necessary, and even critical, function for the unit's overall effectiveness.

It insured that the dogs were physically up to the tasks and that the handlers were putting the working dogs through the required training in detection, obedience, and bite work. It was a necessary and critical task.

It was something, too, that the ever increasingly annoyed First Sergeant pointed out was the Detachment's Commander's responsibility. The clerical work needed to be done before the Vet from Kabul arrived and went over the files. Also, it was something that Lieutenant Dimmer had avoided, and didn't seem much interested in doing.

"Sir, you have the reports and the evaluations to go over before the Veterinarian shows up to review them," Hallatt said, while Dimmer dismissed them with a wave of his hand.

"Sure, sure," he said. "Sooner or later, I'll see to it."

"Sooner or later?"

"But you know, since I'm new at this, eh, wouldn't it be better for you to handle it for me? You knowing what to look for and all? I'll just sign off on them once you're done."

"I can help, Sir. But, if you're going to sign off on them then it would be best if you were at least familiar with what you're signing."

"Right, right. How about we look at it all later?"

"Later?"

"Yes, I have a lot of things on my mind right now, First Sergeant. I mean, because of my injury and all. How about we talk about it later?"

"Sooner would be better, Lieutenant."

"Sure, sure, soon, but it'll have to be later."

But the later wasn't sooner nor did it appear at any time to be later, either. And that presented a problem for the Detachment's Senior NCO.

He knew that besides checking on the health of the canines, the Vet, would inspect the kennel, go over the training and utilization records, and the evaluation reports, and then pass along the findings up through the chain of command.

Given that it cost anywhere from $20,000 to $40,000 to train a military working dog, plus the additional costs to feed, house, and care for the dogs in the Detachment, the findings were also about accountability for the program's expended dollars and cents.

The First Sergeant's growing frustration with Lieutenant Dimmer for ignoring his responsibilities and passing off the bulk of the work to him was not only beginning to show, it was coming to a head. Ordinarily, it was a First Sergeant's job to remain calm as he listened to whatever inane prattle or stupid shit his new or inexperienced Detachment or Company Commander spouted off, as long as didn't it negatively affect the mission or the men, and in our case, the canines under his or her command. But when the talk or inaction began to hurt the unit or its efficiency, a competent First Sergeant would step in and put a stop to it. Hallatt is a competent First Sergeant, a very competent one, as the Lieutenant was about to find out.

When he brought up the matter of the records and files again, Dimmer shrugged it off and started in on his fall back excuse.

"As I am just a temporary fix here, I'm delegating you to see that it all gets done, First Sergeant," he said, flippantly, only to have Hallatt eye him like an annoying bug that needed to be swatted.

When Hallatt held his stare, the Lieutenant began to get the hint that his response wasn't good enough.

"You know what the life span of a house fly is, Lieutenant?"

"What?"

Dimmer was muddled by the question, let alone its relevance. He stared at his First Sergeant trying to figure out the line of questioning.

"The life span of a house fly," Hallatt said, again.

The Lieutenant wasn't quite sure what the First Sergeant was getting at, but played along, still convinced that he could talk his way out of whatever this was.

"What? I dunno…a day or two?"

"Fifteen to twenty days from the time it shows up till the time it's gone."

"Okay," Dimmer said, warily.

"During that short period of time it can step into a lot of crap."

"I don't see…" Dimmer started to speak only to have the First Sergeant cut him off.

"Temporary or not, the Detachment is your obligation and responsibility," Hallatt said, matter of fact, and not holding back on what was required of the Lieutenant. "You're the Officer-in-Charge here, not me. You copy?"

"I'm well aware of that, First Sergeant," Dimmer said, defensively. He was pissed off at the First Sergeant's tenor and tone and his clenched jaw and narrowed brow said as much. "I copy."

"Good! Because let me tell you here and now that there will be no excuse for your failing to adequately train and evaluate the working canines, or to properly utilize the handlers under your command."

"I…"

"I'm not done, Lieutenant," Hallatt said, cutting him off a second time.

"Excuse me?"

"No sir, not yet, so listen up."

The First Sergeant's bold and blunt talk had two immediate effects. It forced the Acting Officer-in-Charge to hear him out, and it rattled John Falstaff Dimmer. While the Lieutenant held his tongue, his anger still found a way out through his glare. He stared at the Senior NCO, quietly fuming, and very much wanting to take him to task, but knowing he wouldn't. The fact is he couldn't, for a few very good reasons.

The first being, that at six-three and two-hundred-and-thirty solid pounds, with a bent nose broken from an obvious scuffle or two in the past, Hallatt was physically intimidating. He looked like he could handle himself and had without tapping out. The second reason the Lieutenant held his tongue with the First Sergeant had to do with a follow-up visit to headquarters Dimmer made to the full-bird Colonel in Kabul when he ostensibly went there to present a case for having and needing a full-time Unit Clerk.

In reality, Dimmer was there to check on the status of his medical discharge and presumed he could secure a Unit Clerk for the Detachment, if he pitched the necessity to the Colonel. During this second meeting the Colonel asked him how things were going with the new job.

"There were a few rough spots, initially," replied the Lieutenant, "but, I believe, it's all coming along reasonably well."

"Reasonably, huh?" said the Colonel and Dimmer nodded.

"Yes sir, with me being new and all, and the Detachment being understaffed."

"Understaffed?"

The Lieutenant nodded again. "I don't have a full-time unit clerk."

"That a problem, is it?"

"Yes, sir. I believe it is."

Colonel Reese, listened and, for the moment, held his judgment. "I understand that an assignment like this can be challenging at times, but keep in mind, you're a temporary fix until your discharge comes through, Lieutenant," he said. "I'm told it's moving along, so you just need to be patient."

"Yes, sir."

"As for the Detachment, it's a relatively easy assignment, so you shouldn't have any real problems during your short tenure. The dog teams know what they're doing and they're doing it well. More importantly, the K-9 Detachment is the also the General's pet project, so to speak," said the Colonel. "I strongly advise you to heed the counsel of your First Sergeant, do what is expected of you, and, basically, not interfere with the operational aspects of the K-9 Detachment."

"Yes sir," said a dejected Dimmer.

"So, what's the bottom line, Lieutenant? Tell it back to me so I know that you're getting the message."

"Not to fuck it up, Colonel."

"There you go!"

"Yes, sir."

"Good. And as for your request to have a full-time Unit Clerk assigned to the Detachment, the answer is, no."

"Sir?"

"The Detachment has what, a dozen people, at best?"

"Fifteen, sir."

"Fifteen, when you add in the First Sergeant, the Vet Tech, and yourself to the count."

"Yes sir."

"And Lieutenant Kelly, the Officer who preceded you, and his more than capable First Sergeant, and the assigned Vet Tech, handled all clerical functions previously without incident or difficulty for the dozen or so dog handlers in the unit, so I don't see an overwhelming requirement or pressing need at this time for an additional staffing."

"But, Colonel. I'm new to this."

"Then I suggest you learn, Lieutenant. It's like Braille. You'll run into some bumps but before you know it, it all makes sense. That is all. You're dismissed."

He was dismissed then, and dismissed once more by this unflinching First Sergeant who stood toe-to-toe in front of him like a better boxer who was schooling him with hard jabs on what was expected of him. The verbal beat down wasn't over. The First Sergeant was floating like a butterfly and stinging like a bee.

"Kabul might see any operational neglect as dereliction of duty, well, no might about it. They would, and that would lead to some serious charges against you…"

"Charges?"

This was a solid jab and it set the young officer back on his heels as Hallatt did a follow-up with another one-two combination.

"Roger that, Lieutenant. Charges that, even if you could somehow mitigate and lessen, would certainly hold up your medical discharge papers during an always lengthy criminal investigation."

"Criminal?" Dimmer felt the ground shake beneath him only it wasn't moving.

"Yes sir, dereliction of duty falls under that heading."

This combination had the young officer up against the proverbial ropes, the jab at charges, followed by the hard, straight hit of holding up his medical discharge had him dazed. Any anger that the Lieutenant had was quickly replaced with stunned confusion of a standing eight count.

"Hold up my discharge papers?" he muttered.

"Yes sir, and, I suspect you wouldn't want that, now would you, Lieutenant?"

"Eh…no," Dimmer said, finding new clarity in a small voice.

"Good," said the First Sergeant. "Then, I'll help you get started with the paperwork and then have you take a few of the teams through their training exercises for familiarization."

"And that'll do it?"

"That'll at least show the visiting Veterinarian and the higher-highers you're aware of your responsibilities and that you're taking a serious and active role in carrying them out, which shouldn't affect or hold up your medical discharge, once it's approved. Hooah, Lieutenant?"

"Hooah," came Dimmer's flat response.

"We'll both go over the records and as for the training familiarization, you can begin with Sergeant Ritchie and his dog, Thor."

"Thor?"

"Yes sir, Sergeant Ritchie's dog."

Hallatt was happy with the mild panic that had been in Dimmer's eyes, but there was also the confusion there as well that troubled him. The Lieutenant had something more on his mind.

"Thor's what, his nickname, right?"

"What?"

"It's what you and the handler call him? His official name is Ted, though, isn't it?"

"Ted?"

"Yeah, but the Sergeant just calls him, Thor, or T-Dogg, like you did with the VIPs in the demo," said Dimmer, trying to show his First Sergeant that he had paid some attention to what was going on in the Detachment, after all.

"Ted?"

"Uh-huh. It's on the assignment board in the kennel. I saw it when you showed me around. Ted with two Ds."

Hallatt squinted and pursed his lips like a bright light just pierced his eyes and stabbed the sockets. Hallatt sighed, rubbed his eyes, and said, "T-E-double D stands for Tactical Explosives Detection Dog, sir. The dog's name *is* Thor."

"Oh."

"And besides the paperwork you have to do, Lieutenant, you'll need to run a few iterations of training exercises to get you up to snuff, so Thor's a good one to help get you started."

Hallatt was throwing him a bone because when it comes to odor detection, I can knock it out of the park. Same-same with bite work, something that Lieutenant Dimmer discovered when he volunteered to take part in a training exercise that afternoon after Hallatt's pep talk; a training exercise that the Lieutenant was just supposed to just evaluate. The talk about holding up his discharge papers might've had something to do with his new found canine training interest.

"You ever do this before, L-T?" Max asked when Lieutenant Dimmer said he wanted to give it a try.

"No, I haven't," he said.

The answer drew a concerned look from Max who turned to the First Sergeant to see how he would handle it.

"It can be a little intense," Hallatt added. "You sure you're up for it, sir?"

Hallatt apparently had touched a nerve with the comment and certainly ruffled some feathers. The Lieutenant's ego was now at stake, which was something the First Sergeant was hoping to tweak. Montanans had their own unique way of getting a point across at times.

"Of course, I am," said the officer, somewhat indignantly. "Let's do this, Sergeant."

Hallatt had Max haul out the K-9 training bite suit and bite sleeve equipment, and once he had it ready, offered the suit to the Lieutenant. Dimmer, though, balked with good reason. The temperature was pushing into the low nineties and the full body suit would make it a sweatbox, so he settled for another option.

"How about that arm sleeve thingy?"

"The bite wrap?"

"Yeah," he said. "How about that? I mean, his dog's just going for my arm, the sleeve arm, right?"

Max started to say something, but First Sergeant Hallatt cut him off.

"That's affirmative, sir," Hallatt said, nodding to Max that he had this. "The dog will attack the sleeve."

There was more to it, of course, something that Max understood, but that the First Sergeant figured the Lieutenant needed to learn for himself.

"Make sure you get it all the way up to your shoulder, Lieutenant," the First Sergeant advised Dimmer, who was working at pulling the bite sleeve in place on his right arm and having trouble with it. Hallatt stepped in and assisted him until it was properly in place.

"There you go, Lieutenant!" he said.

The bite sleeve that fit like a long, thick glove over one arm was heavily padded and bore the marks of determined use and training. Designed to protect the canine trainer's arm when a working dog was given the command to attack, it still had a year or two of life left in it.

"Okay, so what now?" asked Dimmer.

"You walk up to Sergeant Ritchie and his dog, you talk a bit, then you turn, and run away in that direction," Hallatt said, pointing to the open ground in the Detachment training area.

"How about I just walk fast? My knee, you know."

"Walking's fine, too, Lieutenant. Just keep in mind the dog will be coming after you to stop you, so you'll need to brace yourself. If you want to pump up the dog your can yell, *Hot Sauce.*"

"Hot sauce?"

"To fire him up, if you think he needs it."

"That's it?"

"More or less," said Hallatt.

There was indeed more, but Hallatt made it sound like less. He smiled a deceptively innocent smile at the Lieutenant and Dimmer nodded, and gave a cocky, no sweat smile in return.

"Sergeant Ritchie?" Hallatt said to Max. "You, and your Malligator can take your position."

"Hooah!" said Max.

"Malligator? That's funny," laughed the Lieutenant.

"Hooah," replied the First Sergeant.

Max led me out to the open area where we waited until the First Sergeant gave a nod to the Lieutenant.

"Anytime you're ready, sir," he said, "you can begin."

As he had been instructed, Dimmer walked over to us, he and Max exchanged words, and then the officer did an about face, and took off at a quick walk. He was, perhaps, fifteen yards out when Max unhooked my leash, and gave me the command to attack.

Ah, play time!

I took off in a Usain Bolt Olympic Gold Medal winning, teeth-bared sprint. The Lieutenant was still moving at a good pace when I hit him with a frenzied, flying tackle that sent us both tumbling.

Still clamped down on the sleeve, I was quickly back up on my feet, yanking, twisting, and pulling on the bite sleeve in any and every direction. I was biting, releasing, and biting the sleeve over and over again and soon had the Lieutenant's arm flapping like a windshield wiper on steroids. The Lieutenant was screaming for me to stop, only that's not how the game is played. He doesn't get a say.

"OUT!" yelled Max giving me the command to release, only I didn't immediately do it. I was having way too much fun with this game to stop, and besides, Max didn't really sound all that serious with the command.

"OUT!" he yelled again. "OUT!"

It probably dropped me a few points in the obedience training category when Max had to give me the command two or three more times and yanked on my collar before I finally relaxed my jaws from the bite sleeve and spit it out. Sitting obediently at his side I left the stunned Officer flat on his ass in the dirt.

"Your...your dog needs more work on his verbal commands," Dimmer said, shaken by the ordeal, covered in dirt, and more than a little angry. Struggling to pull off the bite sleeve, the Lieutenant stood, and did a few large airplane twirls with his right arm. Tilting his neck from side to side and rolling his shoulders in obvious discomfort, he glared at me. He was hurting while I sat there giving him my best Malligator smile.

"If you're not satisfied, sir," Hallatt said, breaking into the conversation. "We can run the exercise again, if you like?"

Hallatt waited patiently for the answer he knew would soon follow.

"No, First Sergeant, that won't be necessary," Lieutenant Dimmer said, rubbing his right shoulder and then changing the subject. "There's a new Veterinarian, a Captain Larson, I'm told, coming in from Kabul to look over the dogs..."

"Today?"

"Yes. I sent our Vet Tech, what's her name..."

"Gabrielle," replied Hallatt.

"Yes, I sent Specialist Gabrielle to pick him up at the helipad, so you should head on over to the kennel once you're done here. He'll need to check out your dog."

"Thor."

"Yeah, your dog," he said, still not understanding the difference.

"Yes, sir."

"First Sergeant, make sure we get copies of the paperwork for our records."

"Yes, sir," said the First Sergeant. "But aren't you going to be here when the new Vet shows up?"

"No, I think I just hurt my shoulder and elbow. I'm going to go to the Aid Station and get it checked out. Oh, and that's another thing…"

"Sir?"

"I'll need a witness statement from the two of you later about the training incident. I think there might be some permanent damage."

Max and the First Sergeant nodded to the Lieutenant.

To Max he said, "You and your dog need to work on that obedience training, especially with those verbal commands. I'll be noting that in your training file, Sergeant."

"Yes, sir."

"And while we're at it, First Sergeant, you need to talk to Allan about properly marking his equipment assigned to him."

"Sir?"

"It's unprofessional for the soldier not to mark the equipment he's responsible for in that manner. I see he took the time to put his name on the equipment but not his rank. That is not acceptable."

"Say again, Lieutenant?"

Dimmer pointed to the bite suit where the name, *Ray Allan*, was painted on the chest protector in bold print. "His equipment. Talk to the soldier and make a counseling notation in his training file. See to it!"

Hallatt and Max looked at the bite suit, then back at the Lieutenant, and stood silent for a four count. Dimmer was pissed off for looking foolish in the comedy of errors and was now flexing some muscle of authority, or trying to. Bless his heart.

"Ray Allan is not in our command, Lieutenant," said the First Sergeant said, wearily.

"What?"

"Fact is, Ray Allan isn't a soldier at all. Ray Allan the name of the civilian company that manufactures a long line of canine training equipment, including the bite sleeve we just used."

Dimmer looked at him briefly for an awkward and uncomfortable moment fighting embarrassment before settling his gaze on the training equipment, as Hallatt and Max waited to see how he was going to respond. My money was on Dimmer, yapping.

"Then... then, make sure the equipment is properly cleaned and put away before the Vet from Kabul gets here. That's...that's government property. You copy?"

"Yes, sir. I copy," said Hallatt.

"Good," Dimmer said and stormed off towards the Aid Station.

And there it was. The First Sergeant stared after him for a moment or two and turned back to us.

"Sergeant Ritchie?"

"Yes, First Sergeant?"

"You will be more forceful with your verbal commands in the future. You copy?"

"I copy, First Sergeant."

"Oh, and Thor," Hallatt said, patting my head and smiling. "Good dog."

We would learn that there was more to Lieutenant Dimmer's mortar attack injuries that had landed him here at the Detachment, and it wasn't necessarily Purple Heart material like he had implied to the reporter.

A buddy of Gabby's had been working in the same Supply Office in Kandahar with Dimmer when the Taliban hit the air base with three mortar rounds. The Taliban, though, weren't targeting the supply office.

They weren't after shelves of blankets, body armor, and bayonets. They were targeting the parked aircraft on the flight line. A $47, bulk purchased Russian mortar round taking out a multi-million dollar Blackhawk helicopter and another military aircraft just made good fiscal and tactical sense.

Dimmer was what some GIs call a *fobbit*, which is GI slang for someone who seldom left the Forward Operating Base, let alone a larger Camp. The dig was usually reserved for someone whose comfy job was other than in actual combat.

During the Vietnam War, and for a long time afterwards, the term REMF was used to describe rear area personnel. But new wars altered the definition while the sentiment or resentment remained the same.

While he was called a *fobbit* behind his back by most of the other handlers, I thought of him more as a prissy, little, show dog, something that proved to be the case when it came to his 'combat sustained injuries.'

Apparently, Gabby's friend, who witnessed the incident, told her how it, and he, went down. Dimmer had his boots off and his feet propped up on his desk in his office, and he was dozing.

When the *Big Voice*, the loud speakers and siren warning system activated by the radar site that incoming rounds were on the way began broadcasting the loud warning, a suddenly wide awake, and panicked Dimmer, leapt from the chair, slipped and skidded along the highly polished floor in his socks, and crashed into the corner of a three-drawer, heavy steel filing cabinet.

The three explosions from the Taliban mortars were followed by a loud crack from the Lieutenant's left knee and a loud series of groans. When the Vet Tech's buddy found him, the Lieutenant was laid out on the office floor, cradling his knee, and weeping in pain. Mewing, actually, with ample reason, as his knee immediately began swelling up to the size of a warped soft ball.

Several X-rays views revealed that the Lieutenant had chipped off more than a few bone fragments in the knee in the fall, and that he had torn his ACL. A follow-up MRI that took a closer look at the damage, also showed that the ACL would need to be surgically repaired, and that the functional aspects of the junior Officer's knee would be permanently limited.

There would be no more running, jumping, or any other strenuous exercises or activity. He was placed on light and limited duty until a medical board of doctors and surgeons convened, studied the X-rays and MRIs, and recommended that Second Lieutenant John Falstaff Dimmer, be medically discharged with approved disability compensation.

Initially, Dimmer was all for it, since he would receive tax-free, monthly disability checks for the rest of his life from the Veterans Administration.

When Colonel Reese informed Dimmer of the decision at Camp Eggers, Dimmer gave a head down and dejected, "Yes sir." He tried to sound sincere about it, as the 'WOO-HOO!' that he was actually shouting inside his head might not have gone over as well.

The joy, though, was short-lived when he heard that the medical board was only recommending a thirty-percent disability rating for the slight limp and future knee operations. There was also some uncertainty about whether or not he might have to repay the Army for the cost of his ROTC college education.

Dimmer appealed the rating decision, and had his Congressman, who was up for re-election, looking into it as well as having his ROTC contract voided because of the war related injury, which he maintained, was through no fault on his own. That he had his boots off, his feet, and he was dozing somehow didn't make it into the incident report.

The Congressman was confident that the Lieutenant wouldn't have to reimburse the army for the cost of his college education, but was less confident about the disability rating, which relied upon a complicated system in the VA's Schedule of Rating Disabilities. That was beyond his political reach.

Thirty-percent was okay, but Dimmer was holding out for more. Because he was awaiting the outcome of both actions, his exact release date was put on hold, which was why he had been transferred to the K-9 Detachment. The bite-sleeve training incident appeared to be his trump card.

When he returned from the medical dispensary with his arm in a sling, he was smiling, but it wasn't just from the painkillers. He was smiling because he would be submitting additional disability compensation paperwork to tag along with his earlier knee injury.

There was little doubt, too, that we would find him in his office, at his desk, his boots on and firmly planted on the floor, calculating just how much the new percentage would translate into a tax-free dollars and cents.

Dimmer, apparently, wasn't so dim when it came to basic economics, even if he didn't seem to understand what actual military service was about, which is why I suppose, the First Sergeant enjoyed that little training exercise we had with him.

"Come on, buddy," Max said, leading me towards the examination room and kennel. "Let's go get you looked over by the doggie doc."

CHAPTER

14

The new Veterinarian wasn't a 'him.'

Captain Larson turned out to be Doctor Deborah Larson; a mid-sized, twenty-something, lithe bodied, fresh faced, round rumped female Army Officer with dark Chocolate Labradoodle hair, and a short, up-turned nose. Her hair was twisted back in a tight bun beneath her BDU cap that sported the black cloth twin railroad tracks of her rank as an Army Captain. By human standards she was good looking. By Army standards, she was a proven professional.

However, I thought she had the same cold, calculating, and ice-blue eyes of a deranged Siberian husky and that initially troubled me. What's more, one sniff and I could tell she was trouble. Dressed in her newly issued BDUs meant that she was new to Afghanistan, which any veteran will tell you made her a Noobie, an FNG for the Fucking New Guy, or in this case, the Gal, she was.

FNGs, or Noobies, if you were being kind, were always trouble. They said stupid things, they did stupid things, and they were trouble with a T, and that rhymes with D, and that stands for Dumbass. Well, at least, I thought so at first sniff, until she bent down, smiled warmly at me, and said, "This handsome guy must be the famous Thor I've heard so much about!"

"Yes, Ma'am, for the god of thunder," said Max, reaching down and patting my ribs.

"Which is probably an appropriate name given the job he does, and you too, for that matter."

The Captain gave me a brief, but brisk rubdown running magic fingers down my back against the grain.

"Nice coat!" she said, admiring my grooming standards.

Perhaps I was a little too hasty in my first sniff assessment. Obviously, she's a very perceptive human blessed with good vision and keen judgment.

Going down on both knees she held out her right hand for me to sniff. The hand smelled wonderful. When she turned the hand over and opened it, a meat-flavored doggie treat miraculously appeared.

Whoa!

"Okay to give it to him, Sergeant?" she asked while I looked back at Max pleadingly and then back at the proffered treat.

"Yes, Ma'am."

I scarfed up the treat and was happily chewing as she pulled me into her lap, where she gave both sides of my ears and the nape of my neck a few vigorous rubs and back leg twitching scratches.

"Well, aren't you a sweet, sweet boy," she cooed. "Yes, you are. Oh yes, you are!"

Okay, okay, maybe the F in FNG, in her case, meant Fabulous.

After she had reached back into one of the cargo pockets of her BDUs and retrieved another doggie treat, it suddenly occurred to me that I had badly misjudged her. She wasn't trouble at all.

In fact, I was now thinking that if she had a few more doggie treats for me in that magical pocket of hers, and rubbed my neck and ears a few more times cooing, then it was possible that she might even be too good for Max.

I waited for another treat, but instead she only comfortably cupped my chin while she scratched my ears. The jury was still out on her, the verdict not yet decided.

"I'm Captain Larson, your new Vet," she said, getting to her feet and straightening her BDU uniform as she rose. "New to Afghanistan, too. And you, I take it are Sergeant Ritchie?"

"Yes, Ma'am," Max said introducing himself and then did something

I hadn't seen him do for quite a while. He smiled a genuinely satisfied smile.

"I've heard a lot about you from Captain Goldfarb. Pleased to meet you," she said. Goldfarb was the outgoing Vet.

Captain Larson returned Max's smile with a better one. There was something chemically interesting happening between them; something immediate and scent worthy.

Uh-oh!

There was no denying the wafting odor of their instant, mutual attraction. And like a lightning strike, no one is certain where or when it'll hit, but where and when it does, Boom! Instant Ozone.

As they made small talk they both began the butt-sniffing dance we dogs do when we're looking to hump, only they did it with hair flips, best of breed muscle flexes, hip shifts, and obvious odor changes to testosterone and estrogen levels.

"Ritchie? As in Lionel Ritchie, like *All Night Long*?"

"As in Max, but we all have our hopes and aspirations, Ma'am."

Quick wit in the military isn't always appreciated from the ranks, and Max's comment brought a quick halt to the conversation.

"Yes, well…"

For an uncomfortable moment she blushed, he squirmed, and they both were staring at everything other than each other before the conversation picked up again as to why they were actually standing there.

"I'm told that you two are one of the top K-9 teams in the Kabul area, and the province too, for that matter," she said, in a tone that said she was trying to be an Army Captain and having a difficult time at it. She was taken with him and Max was equally infatuated. The two were doing their best to remain professional and failing, miserably.

"Thank you, Ma'am, but it's all him," Max said, rubbing my head. "He does the real work, I just get the pay check."

"You're being too modest, Sergeant," Captain Larson said, pushing a lock of hair behind her right ear. She paused with the gesture just long enough to show the tall Sergeant with the raven black hair and bright blue eyes that there was no ring on her left ring finger and hoped he had caught it.

He had, I had, and Gabby, the Vet Tech, who had joined us from the examination room, noticed their dance, too.

Army Specialist Anna Maria Lucia Gabrielle was a proud New Yorker from Brooklyn, an even more proud Puerto Rican, and someone I loved like my big, latte colored, Lesbian sister. If she had any interest in the new Captain, then it was too late.

"Ah, Specialist Gabrielle! Would you get Thor started on his checkup in the examination room while I finish up with some paperwork with his handler. I'll be along shortly."

This first visit was to get a look around and look over a few of the dogs, check out the conditions of the kennel, and to get a working understanding of the Detachment. A later visit would be to go over the records and evaluation reports, as well as to thoroughly examine each dog, individually. For now, though, she would begin by taking a look at me with Gabby since I was the dog in the Detachment with the most Purple Hearts.

"Yes Ma'am," Gabby said.

Max handed the Vet Tech my leash without taking his eyes off of Captain Larson. Gabby took the leash, glanced at the Captain who was wearing a goofy schoolgirl grin, then checked out Max who shared a similar expression, and then turned her attention back to me.

"Come on, T-Dogg," Gabby said, realizing that the music no one else could hear was still playing on between them.

In the adjoining room, Gabby had me hop up on the examination table where she began peering into my ears and pulling back my muzzle to check out my teeth and gums.

"My, oh my, oh my," she said, slowly shaking her head at what we both had just witnessed in the office. "I think they're both in heat."

When I let out a "*Rhurr-rah*" she gave me a funny look and chuckled before going over my paws, the pads on the paws, and checking for any foreign debris, or cuts or abrasions.

"If I didn't know any better I'd say you understood that, didn't you, my little Malligator?"

I smiled my best toothy Malinois smile as she brushed loose swatches of my fur back checking for fleas and more worrisome ticks before examining the scar tissue from the old wounds. She seemed satisfied that they had healed properly as she put on some rubber gloves and then lifted my tail and began feeling around my scrotum and butt, all the while making notations in my health records as she examined me.

"Well, this country has a serious shortage of love, let alone like," she said, "so who knows, maybe it ain't none of anybody's business 'cept their own. He is one good- looking Ricky Martin/Bruno Mars lookalike, and if I weren't a Lesbian, I'd be all over him like spicy salsa on corn chips. But my blinker don't turn in the direction. However, let me say this; from what I seen of it over here in the Stan, fraternization between officers and enlisted can be a real pain in the ass for the rest of us. And speaking of that, I'm sorry buddy, but I need to squeeze and drain your anal glands. Don't move. Stay."

CHAPTER

15

The new Vet was back less than a week later. When she showed up at the Orderly Room, she informed Lieutenant Dimmer she was there to evaluate the working military dogs in the Detachment that she had missed on her last visit because the K-9 teams were carrying out missions in the field.

"If it's all right with you, I'd like to get started as soon as possible," she said.

"Yes Ma'am, sure, sure, no problem," Dimmer replied, but the unannounced visit had the Lieutenant rattled.

When he walked her over to the Kennel Office and let the First Sergeant know why she was there and what was about to happen, Hallatt, though, didn't seem all that worried about it.

"No problem, Ma'am," he said and then showed her where the kennel records and files were kept, both in the kennel office and the examination room. Specialist Gabrielle, the Detachment's Vet Tech joined them in the kennel office as Hallatt briefed Captain Larson.

"What working dogs are here, are in the kennel, and if you need any assistance or have any questions, then myself and Specialist Gabrielle, our Vet Tech, will make ourselves available to you. Your call, Captain."

"Yes, my people are here to help," Lieutenant Dimmer said, chiming in. "And let me be up front about this, too. I'm not K-9 qualified and I'm only here temporarily. First Sergeant Hallatt here has had me going over the records and files with him and I've relied on his expertise in the matter. The records, he said, are good, and I want you to know that I trust and rely heavily upon his judgment."

Hallatt sighed. It was a backhanded compliment and one that set him up to be thrown under the proverbial bus that, so far, didn't have an actual route.

"Everything's there, Ma'am and should be in fine order," said Hallatt staring at the Lieutenant, who wouldn't look at him, but seemed to be favoring his arm in the olive drab colored sling. "And as I said, I'm more than happy to assist in the process."

"Thank you, First Sergeant, and you too, Lieutenant," Captain Larson said, nodding to each one in turn. "I appreciate the offer, but I'll start off reviewing the records and files and then have Specialist Gabrielle assist me with the physical exams shortly afterwards. Say, in about thirty-minutes or there-abouts, Specialist Gabrielle?"

"Yes, Ma'am," said the Vet Tech.

"Good," replied Larson. "I'll close out after lunch with one-on-one interviews with the handlers…"

"The handlers?" asked Dimmer.

"Yes, to get a better understanding about what is or is not in the files. The handlers know their dogs and can tell me about how they're doing and any quirks they may have. Does that work for you, Lieutenant?"

"It does," he said. "The First Sergeant will have them ready."

Hallatt nodded and said, "There are five dog teams here on site with the rest in the field on missions. I'll have the dogs and their handlers lined up and ready at 1300."

The Veterinarian nodded and they all missed Specialist Gabrielle's small smile regarding the one-on-one interviews.

"Anything else, Ma'am?" asked the First Sergeant.

Larson shook her head. "I should be fine on my own for now," she said, checking the wall clock. It was 1037 hours.

"Then my desk is all yours. Help yourself to the coffee brewer. It's a Keurig," he said pointing to the coffee machine on the table beside the filing cabinet. "Clean coffee cups there, however, I suspect there might be the occasional stray dog hair. There's a dozen or so separate flavored coffee pods cups in the Tupperware container, sugar in the smaller one, napkins, and plastic spoons. Oh, and bottled water in the mini-fridge, and French vanilla coffee creamer, if you need it."

"Thank you."

"Again, no problem. Let me get the health records and files of the working dogs that are here today," said Hallatt walking over to the filing cabinet, opening the third drawer of the three-drawer cabinet and retrieving a stack of files. "Those records and files you checked on with your last visit are in the two top drawers, if you need to go over those as well. The top drawer sticks a little."

"Thank you, Sergeant."

Hallatt placed the files on the desk.

"Once I'm done here, I'll stop by the Orderly Room and we'll discuss my findings, along with any recommendations I might have," said Captain Larson, smiling and staring up at them from behind the desk. It was the signal for them to leave her to her work. Hallatt got the message, even if Dimmer hadn't.

"Come on, sir. We'll leave her to do her thing," said the First Sergeant, ushering a still unsettled Lieutenant Dimmer out the door. Hallatt took the visit in stride. The Lieutenant did not.

"Why is she back so soon? What's she really doing here, you think?" Dimmer said as he and Hallatt headed towards the Orderly Room.

"Her job, Lieutenant," said Hallatt and left it at that.

Hallatt's previous 'Come-to-Jesus' talk about things going wrong and holding up his medical discharge had him rattled, and now this unannounced visit didn't do much to ease his anxiety.

They checked in on her just prior to noon and found her leaning over the desk in her chair, scribbling notes. Having gone over the canine X-rays in the files, physically checking over the scars or previous fractures or injuries suffered by the working canines, she then adding her findings to the records and her notes. The open spiral bound notebook she had brought with her, had a few pages of notations as well, attesting to thoroughness.

"Just checking in to see if you need anything, Ma'am?" Hallatt said. An all too quiet and nervous looking Lieutenant Dimmer was standing behind the First Sergeant, staring over his shoulder.

"No, I'm good. I'm fine," she said. "Thank you."

"Any…any problems?" blurted Dimmer.

Larson shrugged. "A few small things, but nothing earth shattering. We'll go over my findings once I'm done."

"Sure, sure. Whatever it is, my people can fix it!"

"Not much to fix, actually. But as I've said, we'll talk once I'm done here. I do have a question, though, specifically about how the records and files are kept…"

"Yes, well that would be the First Sergeant's doing. I'm afraid I'm still somewhat new to all this."

Hallatt lowered his head, slowly shook it, and stifled another sigh. Even with his bum arm Dimmer was still trying to push him under the goddamn bus.

"Well then, First Sergeant, your canine health and training records are looking good. In fact, they're very good. You're to be commended on what you're doing here. I really like the way you color-coded the differences when it came to injuries and wounds in the medical records. In fact, I plan on recommending it for other working canine units. The kennel is one of the cleanest and most orderly I've seen as well."

"Thank you, Ma'am," said the First Sergeant, breaking into a smile.

"You have a top-notch Kennel Master here, Lieutenant," Larson said to Dimmer, who gave a quick, albeit, reluctant nod. He'd lost a little face and was quick to try to get some back. True to form, he didn't seem below assigning blame, nor above in taking credit for anything the *team* did.

"He certainly is," he said, patting Hallatt's shoulder with his good arm. "I'm proud to have him on my team!"

The First Sergeant held his tongue thinking it was possible Dimmer couldn't manage a toddlers' T-ball team, let alone any event involving actual grown-ups. Instead, he decided to move the conversation onto other matters.

Checking his watch, Hallatt said, "I'm not sure what you're planning for lunch, Ma'am. But the Camp has a pretty decent Barbeque tent here, if you're hungry?"

"Yes, really good Barbeque!" said the Lieutenant. "It's only a few minutes away. The First Sergeant can drive us."

Hallatt sighed, again. The Barbeque tent was, at best a five-minute walk. The drive was unnecessary unless, of course, you felt privileged or were being somewhat lazy. He'd need to find the Lieutenant a Company Clerk before he choked the crap out of the conniving little shit.

"No problem at all in picking something up for you, Captain," added Hallatt.

Larson waved off the offer and held up an apple and protein bar. "No, thank you. I have these. I'm fine. Really."

Really or not, the Lieutenant was disappointed. He was still hoping to curry favor with the Captain who could hold up his military discharge if anything went wrong with her findings.

"You two can go eat. I'm fine," she said. "I still need to go over my notes before the interviews."

"If you'd like, I can start lining up the handlers a little early for the one-on-ones," offered Hallatt, trying to save her some time.

"That would be fine. Thank you, First Sergeant."

"No problem at all, Captain," said the Lieutenant.

Captain Larson nodded and Lieutenant Dimmer and First Sergeant Hallatt were dismissed a second time.

The one-on-one interviews began promptly at 1300 hours. Meeting with the handlers, she was, for the most part, efficient, thorough, and professional. However, when Max and me reported to her for the final interview of the day, a noticeable scent change occurred, and I sniffed that there was possibly something more to this one-on-one than was officially announced.

There was. Their flirting continued, even after this latest visit. Captain Larson would find reasons to return to the Detachment. There were plenty of valid ones to be found in the Afghan war zone, injuries to the working dogs from sprains, fractures, shrapnel wounds, heat stroke or dehydration in the summer months, to frost bite in the winter.

You could include Cobra snake or poisonous spider bites, scorpion stings, rabies, or something as deadly as Hyalomma, the Crimean-Congo hemorrhagic fever or any of its mutated variants from the small, but well-travelled busy brown kennel tick that had worked its way to, and settled, in this part of the world via goats, sheep, dogs, jackals and hyenas. There were also fleas to worry about as well since we were in a country where Bubonic Plague still could found out in the distant provinces. One dog I know, Duke, had been kicked by a camel in passing and suffered a broken jaw. Another, a happy little Chocolate Lab named, Sweetie, had her back left leg broken in a helicopter crash.

So with all of what could befall us in the combat zone, no one would question the frequency of her visits, or her tenacity and professionalism in providing the best possible canine care or treatment for the working dogs. That there was another more specific and personal reason for the increased visits wasn't necessarily apparent.

Initially, or at least early on, First Sergeant Hallatt and Gabby hung around the kennel office to observe and help out with the checkups and evaluations. But when it became ho-hum routine, and it became clear that they weren't really needed for the bulk of the time she was there performing her duties, they both found other things they needed to do, especially when Captain Larson seemed to be taking an inordinate amount of time with her one-on-one-and-one interviews with Max and me.

Because the Captain didn't seem to be taking any interest in him, Lieutenant Dimmer assumed, just as he had attributed to all women that didn't take a personal interest in him, that she was a lesbian.

So as time went on, and she and Sergeant Ritchie spent more time together, he hadn't caught on to what was happening between them, although Hallatt and Gabby had. Not that I was complaining because with each 'evaluation' visit the doggie treats flowed from the magical BDU cargo pant pocket like the sweet, sweet nectar of Hecate, the Greek goddess of the wild places, and, of course, magic.

With each subsequent visit, they delved deeper into the depth of their smiles, exploring whatever else this was becoming. One month on, when no one else was around, and when it was just the three of us, they dropped the pretext of rank, and spoke plainly like real people and not army types.

Captain Larson became Doctor Deb, and Max, well, he became putty. It was obvious she was enamored. I would've said 'smitten,' but that sounds too much like kitten, and I didn't want to hack up a hairball.

Each new visit and get-together took them further into their journey of discovery as they worked on the social building blocks familiar to all new relationships under construction. The conversations subtly flowed from the trivial to the more substantial.

She was from Woodbridge, Virginia. He was from Seattle. She had a younger sister, Christina, while Max was an only child. Her father was an Analyst for the Department of Commerce, her mom a schoolteacher. Max's father was a retired Chief Warrant Officer who served twenty-five years with the Coast Guard who now worked in the Planning Office for the King County Department of Transportation. His mother was a Registered Nurse.

Doctor Deb said she was a Leo and Max nodded and said he was an Aquarius, which pleased her for some reason I could not fathom other than the obvious stars and moon beams dancing behind their happy eyes.

She said she did Yoga three times a week in the morning, and Max said he would be more than happy to watch her do her yoga, if he could sit back, drink coffee, and grin.

"Thor does a very good Downward Dog."

"I'm sure he does," she said, smiling. "So, what kind of music are you into? Who do you listen to? What do you like?"

"Country, mostly."

That answer surprised her; baffled her, actually. She sat up straight and gave him a confused look.

"Country music? Seriously?"

"Yes Ma'am," he said. "Garth Brooks, Alan Jackson, George Strait…Metallica."

"Metallica?"

"It's complicated. And you?"

Michael Bolton, Air Supply… AC/DC."

"AC/DC? Oh, thank God!" Max said, chuckling. "For a moment I wasn't sure if there was any hope for you."

But there was and he knew it, and so did she.

With time and inevitably, the talk turned to the always touchy subject of, relationships; old or existing flames, and to what more was igniting the kindling between them. For her, there was no present relationship. She had dated and broken up with a Mortgage Loan Officer named, Victor. The break-up apparently hadn't been amiable.

"Victor was an asshole," she said, finally, dismissing him to the past.

"Ah, but at least he had good taste in women," replied Max. "Well, one in particular, anyway."

That earned him a smile and, of course, the obvious question.

"And you, anyone back home, patiently waiting?"

"There was... once," he said, with a shrug. "Michelle. She's...well, how do I put this? She's a frustrated Princess in search of a Kingdom and apparently, I was no longer Prince Charming, so she de-moated me, which is total bullshit! I mean, look at me. I'm charming as all get out."

"De-moated? Clever."

Max shrugged. "I try."

"Well, you, at least, have a lovable dog."

"Oh, and that's another big reason why it ended. She didn't like dogs."

That admission actually shocked her and Doctor Deb reeled back in her chair and visibly blanched. "How's that possible?"

Max shrugged, again.

"Then she's an idiot for several reasons."

Now it was Max's turn to smile.

With that pressing issue out of the way the conversation turned back to the trivial. Doctor Deb admitted that she was a big time *Buffy, the Vampire Slayer* fan while Max wasn't, but said that Joss Whedon redeemed himself with *Firefly*.

"Shiny!" she said, and Max knew that this was indeed true love.

Two months on, and after one of their one-on-one 'interviews' without me behind closed doors, I caught her scent on him, and his on her, when they came to get me out of my cage in the kennel for a physical exam. You didn't have to be Deputy Dog to figure out that when they were behind closed doors there had been some frolicking and, I suspect, a little mutual belly-rubbing going on.

Fraternization, too, was an F word, especially in the military. There were rules that prohibited Officers and Enlisted men and women from having personal relationships. The gist of it was that they were two households, both alike in dignity, and both far apart in practice. Career wise, it could lead to problems for both of them, but I sniffed the passion that overtook their reason. It was new, illicit, and exciting, and they were overcome with desire. While they acted on it, in secret, it wasn't necessarily secret to all.

In an age-old congress they wore mischievous smiles as shields to deflect suspicion.

As Max took me from my cage and hooked me up to my leash, they were both giggling and smiling stupidly at each other. They didn't seem to notice that her Tee shirt was on inside out. If I had a hose I would've sprayed them down with cold water and smacked Max on the nose with a rolled-up newspaper.

When I briefly stuck my nose in Captain Larson's crotch and her hand carefully guided it away, I gave Max a smiling, 'I know what you two are up to' look. I was just about to go back in for a second confirming sniff when Max yanked up hard on my leash and nudged me away with a knee.

"Leave it, Romeo," he said, shooting me a glare. "Leave it."

The Romeo quip was, of course, a sarcastic crack at me for a recent rendezvous with my own in-country jihadi Juliet. It came about two days earlier when we took part in a combined U.S. and Afghan Military Police raid on a small, but active Quetta Shura Taliban operation in Kabul. The Quetta Shura, based out of Quetta, Pakistan, are *the* leading fighting faction of the Taliban. They control nearly every aspect of Taliban operations in Afghanistan, including the small, day-to-day doings in Kabul.

The mission today was targeting stolen ISAF weapons and military equipment that a local faction of the Quetta Shura had snatched up and stored in an inconspicuous looking little flower shop on the western outskirts of the city.

There was good Intel that the flower shop held a cache of stolen handguns, Assault rifles, body armor, night vision goggles, and rations that were stored in a locked backroom of the shop and were being readied to be smuggled out of the city to Taliban fighters in the field.

The flower shop, stash house operation had only come to light when someone at the shop sold one of the stolen Assault rifles to a local Al Qaeda wannabee, who gave up the shop after he was arrested.

The combined Military Police and local Police Op was executed just after sunrise. The early morning raid on the flower shop was designed to keep Lookie-loos and rubberneckers at a minimum. The sun was just breaking over the horizon as we rolled up on the flower shop. When we came bursting through the shop's front door, the still sleepy, but wiry Ali Baba, who ran the flower shop, bowled over an Afghan policeman as he leapt out a side window, and then sprinted down a long, thin alley.

"Got a runner!" yelled the Military Police team leader.

"On it!" yelled Max, unhooking me and I was off-leash, out the window, and chasing down one of Ali Baba's more athletic 40-thieves.

Max and another MP in the raid party were climbing out of the window and following. With me fast on his heels, the Ali Baba knocked over some buckets and trash containers in the alley trying to slow me down and make good his get-away.

I made a tumbling leap over the makeshift hurdles, but was quickly back up on my feet, and back in pursuit and in the race. I was quickly closing the gap and was just about on him, ready to chomp down on his ass in a small courtyard when he made a sudden ninety-degree turn and bolted through an open doorway, slamming a large iron metal gate shut behind him.

I was up and bouncing against the closed gate barking like a mad dog as he ran out into the main street only to be blind side tackled by an Afghan policeman and another MP. The chase was over.

"WE GOT HIM!" came the call from the street and Max began whistling and calling me back the way I had come.

I was on my way back to him when something in the courtyard caught my eye that stopped me mid-stride. A beautiful Afghan honey of a hound that was chained in a corner of the courtyard was checking me out. She was long and sleek, with an auburn coat, warm brown eyes, and a body that was something to yelp about.

"Well, hellooo… you saucy little vixen," I barked as she batted her lovely eye lashes at me and presented herself with a 'come hither to my withers' smile over her dusky shoulders. Grrrrr, momma.

We were well into improved U.S. and Afghan doggie-style relations when Max stepped into the courtyard from the alley and found us happily copulating.

"THOR! NO!!" Max yelled, disgustedly running towards, we two star-crossed lovers, trying to stop the act of two households, both alike in dignity. "BAD DOG! NO! BAD DOG! HEEL!"

"Is sokay…sokay," said the dog's owner, stopping Max before he reached us with a calming upraised open hand and nod as he watched on from a nearby doorway. The short, squat man in his late forties, smoking a morning cigarette, calmly shrugged off what was happening. "They make beautiful, strong babies. Is sokay. Sokay."

Max wasn't happy with me, but after another 'Is sokay' from the man in the doorway, he relented with a shrug of his own.

The raid had been a success, the stolen weapons and equipment had been recovered, and, the man responsible for operating the shop was in custody, so maybe Max figured this mission deserved a happy ending.

"You got two minutes, Romeo."

Two minutes, ha! I was done in one!

Parting was sweet sorrow, but on the short ride back to Camp Phoenix Max gave me a doggie treat, alleviating some of the feral farewell. A cigarette, though, might've been more appropriate to go along with the Sean Connery, ala James Bond, satisfied smirk I was wearing after my time with Miss Moneypuppy.

What? I like most of the early James Bond DVDs and even the Daniel Craig versions that Max watches on his laptop on our downtime in between missions. The Roger Moore ones, not so much. Climbing up onto his bunk and watching at his side, I appreciated that Connery seldom seemed to be shaken or stirred.

Whoa! Let me guess? You didn't know that dogs watched movies? Yeah well, we do. We listen to your books on tape and your CDs, too. However, we really enjoy movies, whether it's on your laptops and, better yet, your big screen TVs that give us a pixelled view to the world and everything broadcasted through that amazing fifty-inch window. However, and this really grinds my gears, I don't much care for that MGM growling lion in the opening credits in some of the movies.

I growl and work myself in a frenzy every time that lion comes within inches of us, angrily roars, and I find myself protecting Max from the imminent attack while he just laughs until the lion retreats back into the darkness as the movie begins. For some reason Max seems to think it's as funny as all get out. He calls me an idiot every time that lion sneaks up and threatens to attack us.

But, here's the thing, he hasn't been attacked by the lion yet, and he safely gets to watch his movies while I watch on and keep a wary lookout for that damn big cat, Simba. That's me, the ever-vigilant watchdog.

Idiot, my ass.

Now, as for movies, besides the old and the new Bond films, some of my all-time favorites, are *Homeward Bound, All Dogs Go to Heaven* and *Lady and the Tramp*. I actually enjoyed most of what that old Texas mutt, *Old Yeller*, is up to, too... well, I mean, all except for the whole rabies thing. That bothered me until Max pressed a button and *Old Yeller*, magically appeared as a puppy again.

He chuckled at that and was chuckling on the Humvee ride back to the Detachment after finding me locked in my intimate embrace with my Afghan beauty in the courtyard.

"You really are a dog, aren't you, buddy?" Max said, scratching my neck and smoothing down my ears. "My little Romeo, my T-Dogg."

Okay, so maybe I couldn't judge him about his canoodling with his Veterinarian Labradoodle. The warzone, however, wasn't the time or place for any serious relationship, but whatever it was, it was rapidly moving in that direction as their latest talk turned to post-deployment.

"You have, what, five months left on your deployment?" Doctor Deb asked, wondering about more than what the days, weeks and months showed on his calendar.

"Five months and eleven days, but who's counting."

I was lying down at his feet, head up, and staring intently at her magical doggie treat pocket, again. The treats are there. I know they are. Tasty treats. Tasty, tasty treats.

"Then it's back to Fort Gordon?"

Max brightened considerably, but then, he had reason to be happy. "Seattle," he said. "I'm getting out of the Army."

"Out of the Army?" His answer surprised her.

"That's affirmative. When I was home on my last leave, I took both the written and physical tests for the Fire Department."

"Really? The Fire Department."

"Uh-huh. I got an e-mail from them last month saying I placed in the top ten and that they're hiring twelve new people in the coming year. No more fire fights. I'm actually going to fight fires instead."

"Well then, I'm looking forward to buying one or two of their fund raising shirtless firefighter calendars, possibly three."

"Three, huh?"

"Well, one for my sister, and my best friend, Diana," she said. "They have a thing for hunky Firefighters."

"And you?"

"I just think it's important to support the crucial work that those brave Firefighters do."

"By buying calendars of them, shirtless?"

"Not to forget dressed in suspenders with glistening shoulders and abs."

Doctor Deb smiled wickedly and Max just slowly shook his head and chuckled.

"You know, I don't think first year rookies are allowed to be in the calendars."

"Oh, no problem," she said. "I'll still take three calendars. Maybe even four!"

She was smiling wickedly as she said it and Max slowly shook his head and reluctantly gave in.

"Then, I'll see if I can get you a bulk discount."

"Super! That would be nice," she said and then changed the subject. "As I recall, Jimi Hendrix was from Seattle, wasn't he?"

"He was. Nirvana and Soundgarden too! Seattle's the home of Grunge Rock, rain, the Space Needle, more rain, Starbucks, and a cold, misty drizzle that passes for early summer. By August we can usually remove the windshield wipers from our sunglasses."

"I take it, it rains there a lot?"

"It does. In fact, in the summer we don't tan, we rust."

"That bad, huh?"

Max shook his head and smiled. "Naw, not really, but my dad was friends with a Seattle newspaper guy named, Emmett Watson, who back in the day when the city had two newspapers, ran a Lesser Seattle campaign."

"Lesser Seattle? Like what, to keep people away?"

"Yep, to keep Seattle small so that it didn't lose its original character and flavor."

"Did it work?"

"Nope, more people moving in every day, in fact, a ton of new folks who love everything about the city, and now can't wait to change it."

"Well, I heard the Pike Place Market is worth seeing."

"It is, especially in the morning before it gets too crowded," he said. "I know a nice little bakery nearby that serves great coffee and some tasty scones and cinnamon rolls."

"I'd like that."

Max smiled. "You'd like the Market, I think. Flying salmon fish throwers, some good, and not so good buskers, lots of interesting little shops and stalls selling everything from nice art, hand-made jewelry, colorful flowers and vegetables, crafty knick-knacks to cringingly bad schlock, but always worth a look-see. I think you would like it."

"I think I would, too," she said with demure smile that was an easy read. Max returned the smile while Doctor Deb brought the conversation went back to his new career choice.

"Don't take this wrong, but won't the Fire Department take you from the proverbial frying pan into the literal fire?"

"Maybe," Max said, with a half shrug, "but it's a whole lot safer than working as a bomb dog handler in a war zone. I just wish I could take Thor with me. He's been through more than enough and deserves an actual backyard."

"No kidding. I've found more than eight shrapnel scars and a few missing patches of fur from the two previous IED detonations in Iraq! Did you know either of his previous handlers?"

Max gave another slow smile as he began smoothing down my ears. "He hasn't had any other handlers. This is our third deployment together. Isn't it, buddy?"

"Third deployment?" Doctor Deb said, momentarily stunned by the admission. "I... I thought this was your first deployment."

"It feels like it at times."

"But you...you work Thor on leash!"

"Mostly."

"Which means you were caught up in the IED detonations, too!" Her eyes went wide as her mouth dropped open in shock. Max gave shrugged that off as well.

"Which also makes the Fire department and its better benefits seem like a much wiser career choice," he said.

"I suppose it does," she reluctantly admitted. "But it's another dangerous profession."

"True, if you're talking about the Firefighter calendars, again? You women can be brutal. I would hope that, perhaps one day you women would learn to appreciate we men for our minds?"

"When you start using them, sure," she said. "Seriously though, aren't you a little worried about it?"

"Nope, I bear a charmed life," he said, and then asked about her plans.

"How about you? Are you staying in the Army or will you one day give it up and go into private practice?"

Doctor Deb leaned back in her chair, took in a deep breath, and then slowly exhaled. "The Army paid for my schooling. I'm afraid I still have a few more years to go on my commitment," she said. "After that, I don't know, maybe go into private practice."

"Back east?"

"Virginia, yes."

"Woodbridge?"

"No, Manassas, actually. I like it out there."

"Lots of bulls running free, I hear?"

Doctor Deb's face twisted as though she'd sucked on a lemon at the pun. "Ooh, that's bad," she groaned.

"Then you probably won't like it either when I say that it seems, at least, for now, our careers have literally gone to the dogs."

"Now that I don't mind," she said, looking directly at him and holding the stare. "I love my job."

"Me too, well, most of the time and especially when things are exploding. So, what and who are you reading, young Army Captain?" Max asked pointing to the paperback book that was partially peeking out of one of the other pockets in Doctor Deb's BDUs.

This?" she said, retrieving the book and holding it up. "Poetry. Theodore Roethke."

"Ah," Max said and then surprised both her and me. "*I wake to sleep and take my waking slow and feel my fate in what I cannot fear and learn by going where I have to go,*" he said, reciting a line of the poem from memory.

The look on her face was one of genuine surprise. Max, the dog handler was more than he appeared. Doctor Deb was impressed.

"You've read Roethke?"

"Some," Max said with a shrug. "And for some reason that's all I remember of the poem from college. Most likely so I could sound smart to somebody I was trying to impress, a waitress in a bar, I think."

"Did it work?"

"Not at all. Nor did my singing Garth Brooks', *I Got Friends in Low Places* off-key while I was wolfing down some spicy chicken wings. I thought I was hot, but it turns out it was just the habanero sauce."

"No appreciation for a man for all seasonings."

"None," he said. "I also memorized part of Coleridge's *Kubla Khan*, but the 'Stan ain't exactly Xanadu, so Roethke seems to take on more meaning here. Well, at least until they build a damn pleasure dome."

Doctor Deb chuckled and asked, "Where did you go to school?"

"Wazoo."

"Wazoo?"

"Washington State University. Go Cougars! And You? University of Virginia at Charlottesville, I take it?"

"Nope. University of Maryland- College Park. Go Terrapins…only slower…"

"Because they're turtles."

"Exactly. I take it with all of that poetry you say you almost remembered, but recall quite well, that you majored in English Lit?"

"Minored. Had a Business Marketing major, and when neither one didn't get me a good job after I graduated, an Army Recruiter told me that business in this part of the world was booming, so I enlisted. Apparently, I didn't ask enough of the right questions. I was sadly misinformed."

"I believe that's a line from, *Casablanca*."

Max nodded, pursed his lips, and tried his best Bogart. "It is, and so is, I think this is the beginning of a beautiful friendship. Thank you, Netflix."

He smiled, she smiled, and they were doing their figurative butt-sniffing dance again that was taking them well beyond friendship.

The dance, though, was interrupted when Lieutenant Dimmer came barging into the examination room and abruptly stopped when he saw Doctor Deb. The junior officer came to the position of attention before the more senior officer.

"Captain," he said to Larson, saluting.

"Stand at ease, Lieutenant," she replied. "We don't salute indoors."

Dimmer stood 'at ease,' but not really with ease.

"I'm about finished with my examination of Sergeant Ritchie's dog, Thor," she said to Dimmer. "And I think you and I will need to sit down with First Sergeant Hallatt one of these days and discuss retiring him."

"Now, Ma'am?"

"No, not now, but soon, and based upon the number and nature of the injuries that I'm sure you're aware of from his health records, I'd say we have a good case here for his retirement. Wouldn't you agree, Lieutenant?"

He might have, if he had actually read the medical records.

"I do," Dimmer said, pretending he had. "And we will, at your convenience, Ma'am. However, I just received a request for a K-9 team for a convoy mission later this evening. Sergeant Ritchie and his dog have been requested by the higher-highers."

"Thor," she said.

"Yes, Ma'am, his dog."

Both Captain Larson and Max just stared at him. Lieutenant Dimmer still didn't get it and probably never would.

"No problem, L-T," said Max, breaking the momentary silence. Back to Doctor Deb he said, "Thanks for looking after him, Ma'am."

"That's why I'm here, Sergeant. Stay safe out there, the both of you," she said, scratching me behind my ear in just that right spot before reaching back into that magic pocket of hers and coming out with a doggie treat.

DAMN! HOW DOES SHE DO THAT?

CHAPTER

16

This latest mission was no big thing, but what was going on between Max and Doctor Deb definitely was. As time went on, the Doctor Deb's Vet visits and check-ups went hand-in-hand with carefully timed, frenzied, and sweaty fraternization between the two of them. The puppy love matured. They were both downright frisky.

Their liaisons continued, usually when Lieutenant Dimmer was at Camp Eggers in Kabul trying to get the Medical Board to increase his disability percentage rating, and when First Sergeant Hallatt and Gabby rode along with him to pick up supplies for the Detachment.

The trip to Eggers also allowed Dimmer, Hallatt, and Gabby time to kick back and relax at the on-base Coffee Shop over a better cup of coffee, before they picked up some local souvenirs and gifts for their family and friends at the Camp's on-base Bazaar. The Camp Egger's Bazaar allowed local vendors to sell their wares in a controlled, secure environment, thus avoiding any nasty suicide vest cleanups on aisle five at the local Stallmart.

Dimmer may not have been any the wiser as to what was going on, but Hallatt and Gabby had it all figured out and began taking their time on the equipment and supply runs to Kabul. Anyone with a good nose, though, could tell you from their scents that Max and Doctor Deb were fixated on formulating their own pack, making a litter of puppies, and happily frolicking in a flowery field chasing colorful butterflies.

I liked that. I also like that Max had promised that he would figure out a way to adopt me when my Army time was done and I was officially retired. Prior to the passage of what became known as *Robby's Law* by Congress in 2000, and as a cost-cutting measure, the government hired private civilian contractors to take possession of the military dogs once our usefulness and careers were literally at an end.

Military Working Dogs, who had faithfully served the military, and who were at the end of our service, were being put to sleep, euthanized, and put down out of convenience to the government. It was a *'Thank you, you saved a lot of lives. Now hold still while we stick this needle in you and send you to that nice make-believe farm upstate'* fuck you.

WTF Woof?

For working military dogs, *Robby's Law* was the last minute reprieve from the Governor, a life saving call in the form of a Congressional Law that allowed for the retired military canines to be brought back to the U.S. so they could be adopted out to enjoy a well-deserved better life.

The trouble with the adoption process was that it was slow and cumbersome. Worse still, it hadn't given any of the dogs' former handlers any priority in the adoption process, many of whom desperately wanted to adopt the dogs they'd worked with during their deployments.

This didn't sit well with Hallatt, Max, Pete Kannemeyer, or many of the other handlers, former handlers, and supporters who lobbied for the important change. The lobbying efforts paid off and the K-9 handlers and former handlers were finally bumped up to the front of the line when it came to the adoptions.

However, adopting a retired military working dog still took dedicated time, focus, and effort. Those who intended to adopt their dogs had to get the necessary paperwork ready to submit long before any official retirement order by the military. Max had my packet ready, and he had a fallback plan in place as well, just in case.

"You're coming home with me, Buddy, even if I have to shove you in a FED EX box and declare you as *'Smelly, Old Household Goods'* on the customs form," he promised after another successful mission where we found a nasty little IED buried on the road to Kabul.

The promise was made all the more credible with Doctor Deb saying that from my injuries over the years, sustained in combat, my retirement was both justified and warranted. And she told Max that she wouldn't have to pull some strings to make it happen, because everything was there in the health records. Few would challenge her professional prognosis, let alone the official nod from the Senior Veterinarian at Headquarters after she had showed him my file.

The sit down with Lieutenant Dimmer and First Sergeant Hallatt involved going over the health and training records, pointing out the shrapnel still embedded inside me that was prominent in the X-rays, and discussing the arthritic changes in the right hip socket that was courting Dysplasia that would sooner or later require surgery.

"Based upon these findings, my suggestion is that he be medically retired within the next six months, unless either of you, can convince me otherwise," Doctor Deb said to the temporary Detachment Commander and the Kennel Master.

Dimmer was out of his depth and looked to Hallatt for an answer that he could echo. Hallatt, who had listened to her reasoning, and was leafing through my health records, reached over and took a sip from his coffee cup as he weighed what he was about to say.

"Thor is an outstanding working dog and has been a valuable asset to the Army, and our unit, in particular, " he said. "He's one of our top dogs, if not THE top dog we have. Quite frankly, we need him," he added, presenting his case to keep me on. What's more, he wasn't done. "With that being said, with the noted shrapnel damage, other sustained injuries, and the hip dysplasia, I will, reluctantly, have to agree with you, Captain. That'll still put us down one working dog and will put a strain on others in the rotation."

Doctor Deb and Hallatt looked to Lieutenant Dimmer, who nodded along.

"It will," he said, settling on what the First Sergeant had said rather than a working solution.

"Then we'll need to have command looking into replacing him within that six month time frame," added Hallatt.

"That will be my recommendation as well," said Doctor Deb.

The two turned towards the Lieutenant awaiting his response. Dimmer, doing what he did best, kept nodding.

"Good. Then, it's settled," Doctor Deb, said.

And it was and all was good and all was right with this end of the world, if you didn't count the ambushes and fire fights with screaming Jihadis who desperately wanted to kill you, incoming rocket or mortar rounds, occasional sniper fire, or random things exploding as you walked or drove by them.

Any one of these things, or any in combination of them occurring between our next mission and the time I was officially retired, was entirely possible. I wasn't alone. This was the case for every dog and working K-9 team in country.

I, at least, was close to a retirement date and was looking forward to getting comfy and curling up in Max's favorite plush easy chair back home. The chair even has a built-in heated massage unit.

"You're going to love it, T-Dogg!" he said. And I knew I would since I heard him say it was a Bark-o-Lounger.

CHAPTER

17

The war in Afghanistan, literally and figuratively, droned on. By the end of August, Lieutenant Dimmer's medical discharge was finally approved. Although, the actual discharge date was still a few months off, he wasn't complaining.

Word had come down, too, that he would not have to repay the government for his ROTC college-based education, and because of the latest 'service related injury,' the disability rating from the Veteran's Administration for both his knee and shoulder totaled 60%. Dimmer was positively buoyant.

His shoulder sling was still firmly in place when he came searching for Max and me for yet another mission. As he entered the Kennel Office, the First Sergeant nodded to Dimmer, but scowled at the sling. I wasn't alone in thinking the sling was a prop that would likely stay in place, right up until the time he walked away from the army as a civilian, at which time, he would toss it aside in the nearest trash bin. His BDU blouse sported one of the Sirius Dog Star patches Lieutenant had ordered.

"Sergeant Ritchie here?"

Hallatt nodded towards the kennel. "He is," he said to the Lieutenant, and then bellowed, "RITCHIE!"

Max made his was through the examination room from the kennel where he'd been hosing down my cage. His brown military tee shirt, boots and trousers showed dark blotches where the water from the hose had splashed him.

"Yes, First Sergeant?" he said to Hallatt who nodded to the Lieutenant who was standing in the doorway, frowning. The notion of cleaning out a dog cage wasn't just foreign to him, but displeasing as well.

"Sir?"

"A Special Forces team needs a bomb dog for the next two days," Dimmer said. "You're up."

"Two days?"

"That's affirmative," Dimmer said, and then filled Max in on the where and when. *Why* never seemed to hold much sway on the Army's list of important, or even relevant questions, well at least at our level. "You're to report to a Captain King."

"Yes sir, Captain King," echoed Max. "Hooah."

"I'm betting it's a Tier-1, Spec Ops thing," Dimmer said, his fan boy buoyancy happily bobbing in his stream of thought. "How cool is that? Hey, maybe they'll give you a challenge coin for working with them. See if you can pick one up for me, while you're at it, Sergeant. Okay?"

Max replied with a chin-up nod and a small Hooah while Hallatt wore a fixed scowl. Quid pro quo generally required a quo in return and so far the Lieutenant wasn't offering anything of substance, let alone value.

"Did I tell you that my medical discharge had been approved?" the Lieutenant said, smiling to the First Sergeant and Max.

"Yes sir, you did," said the First Sergeant, hoping to shorten the conversation.

"No date yet, but soon."

"That's good news, Lieutenant," said Hallatt, only not in the same context or with the same meaning Dimmer had provided.

"It is, indeed. Anyway," Dimmer said back to Max, "you'll need to report to base operations by 1700 tomorrow and they'll hook you up with the Spec Ops people. I'll get one of the other handlers to drop you off."

Dimmer held up his arm in the sling to show he was incapable of driving the Humvee.

"I'll take you," said Hallatt, thinking that the Lieutenant couldn't be gone soon enough.

Max gave a nod to the First Sergeant. "Hooah!" he said and the First Sergeant returned it.

"Hooah."

"Yeah, hooah," echoed the uninspired Lieutenant a half-beat later. "Oh, and like I said, see if you can score me a challenge coin."

The following afternoon, just after 1400, the First Sergeant dropped us off at the security gate of base operations for the mission.

"You sure you want to be dropped off this early?"

"Better too soon than a minute too late," Max said hooking up my leash and grabbing his G-Bag.

Hallatt smiled. "Eager to shake a spear at the Taliban, soldier?"

"Hopefully, they'll get the point."

The bulk of the handlers Hallatt had supervised over the years, were generally young, and, who, for the most part soon became competent professionals. Some were more competent than others and Hallatt viewed Max as was one of the better ones.

The kid didn't bitch or whine, and never turned down an assignment. He would make a good MP Canine instructor or even a good police K-9 officer, if so inclined. And, if he ever wanted to go into Law Enforcement, Hallatt would be happy to write him a letter of recommendation. He was glad to have him in the Detachment and wished he had more soldiers like him.

"See you two when you get back," he said. "Oh, and don't do any stupid shit."

"Roger that, Top."

"If you can't get a ride back when you're done, have the Ops Center call the Detachment, and I'll send someone to come and get you or I'll do it myself."

"Hooah."

As Hallatt drove off Max turned and checked in with the armed guard at the Operations Center security gate. There, we waited around for a few minutes at the locked entrance before a sturdy, resolute looking Korean-American Captain came out to greet us. The nametag on his uniform read: Kang, not King.

Kang was accompanied by a tall and lean Warrant Officer, who had the world wise, 'been there, done that a few times' cynical look of a veteran NCO that had come up through the ranks, and, more than likely, had. His nametag read: DAVIES.

"All right, K-9!" said the Captain grinning through the fencing and a much too sparse beard. Max started to salute only to have the Captain wave it off, as the armed guard unlocked the gate and let us in.

"We'll dispense with that while we're operational, Sergeant," he said and then grinned at me. "I'm Captain Kang, this is my Alpha, Mister Davies. My assistant team leader."

Mister Davies nodded and Max returned it.

"Gentlemen," Max said only to have Davies, chuckle.

"Not hardly, Sergeant," he said, "But we do hold the rank. What's your dog's name?"

"Thor."

Kang and Davies nodded, approvingly. Neither one leaned over to pet me which told me that they worked with K-9 teams before and were wise enough to understand the protocol.

"Great name for this line of work," Kang said and turned away from the security gate. "Glad to have you and your Malligator along on this little outing, Sergeant Ritchie. I've heard good things about you two. Word has it you're very good at what you do."

It was a 'walk and talk' as we headed towards a nearby Quonset hut, adjacent to the secured Ops Center, saying he wanted to introduce us to some of 'his people' we'd be working with on the mission. 'His people' were his team. With Special Operations teams; Delta Force, Navy SEAL, Para-Jumpers, Rangers, Marine Raiders, or Green berets and there was no mistaking the special delineation and admission reference.

"My Detachment Commander, Lieutenant Dimmer, said this would be a Tier-1 operation. Is that right, sir?"

"Naw, Tier-1 is for the knuckle-dragging, Buick bench-pressing, Ninja Delta Force or Seal Team Neander-short and Tals. We're Special Forces," he said, beaming. "We actually know who are fathers are, passed our IQ and psychological tests, and are greatly encouraged by beautiful women the world over to frequently procreate. It's a burden, at times."

"And yet, we somehow manage," added Davies.

"We do indeed!"

Max chuckled at their exchange. While these officers were highly skilled professionals, *Operators,* in the Spec Ops lingo, they were also laid back with the typical biting sense of humor and relaxed '*nothing to prove*' big dog confidence that even a dog like me could appreciate. I liked them immediately and I sensed Max did as well.

Davies was pushing forty while the Captain was in his mid-to-late twenties, at best. Because Special Forces Warrant Officers, who weren't pilots, rose up through the ranks, they tended to be older and experienced, they brought with them a wealth of practical knowledge and hard earned lessons learned that the younger officers didn't have. The pairing insured for a good leadership platform, one that whoever implemented the program realized could be tactically beneficial to everyone on the team.

"As for our little outing, it's not a Tier-1, more like a little SWAT-type raid with some local Police, more like a Tier 1.5 upgrade with better looking people. Ah, here we are. Our makeshift team room! Think of it as day care center for disturbed children with guns and knives as crayons."

CHAPTER

18

As we stepped inside the team room a tall and rugged looking Master Sergeant, who I took to be the Team Sergeant let out a loud, *ATTENTION*, only to have Kang give a quick *AT EASE* settling things down in the room.

The Master Sergeant, whose nametag read: MOBSBY, had the look of a veteran soccer goalie who well understood the game and the strengths and weaknesses of all of the players on the field and what was actually in play. He also looked like he might head butt you, if you got in his face, or tried to go around him.

The Quonset hut and temporary team room was a large, open, air-conditioned room, filled with chairs, cots, and several benches and folding tables. A blank white board the size of a big screen TV was ready to serve as a screen for a laptop and projector that rested on a nearby table. An empty cork bulletin board stood to the right of the white board. Their positioning and purpose would become clear later with the team briefing, but for now they remained a mystery.

"Listen up, people!" said the Special Forces Captain calling for their attention. "We've invited a few guests to join us on our task."

Heads turned and eyed us with curiosity and mild disdain. Max and me were, after all, outsiders. This we expected. It was a given. As the Captain made the introductions, we initially received a few howdy nods and one or two 'who the fuck are you?' looks in return until he went over our bona fide credentials.

The nods returned, along with a few barks and growls. Our record erased some of the doubts and skepticism, but not all. We were still the 'unknown commodity' with this mangy looking, furry-faced lot. And the dozen or so Operation Detachment team members were, indeed, mangy looking.

Several looked like they were Cosplay Orcs on their way to a Terminator event while the rest could've easily been extras in a ZZ-TOP video. It's possible one or two might've had more fleas in their beards than I had on my butt and tail. This pack was of a breed I hadn't encountered before. This was a team of all alpha dogs.

"We need him and his dog on this one," Kang said, looking around the room. "So play nice, you filthy animals. No offense to your dog, since I'm sure he has better grooming habits, and is not likely to shit where he sleeps, unlike some of these scoundrels and brigands," he said back to Max.

"You left out we ne'er do wells, Captain!" said a thin, but wiry black soldier, looking up over the top of an Ace Atkins paperback novel. The soldier was a Marvin Gaye look-alike and Gaye would've been proud of the soldier's goatee.

"One must be wise when passing judgment, Staff Sergeant Barnes."

"You're a real Judge Judy, Captain."

"Yep, that's me! Tough, but fair," Kang replied. "And without her hefty paycheck. I hear she makes $900,000 per workday, and I make, what, Mister Davies?"

Kang turned to his Assistant Team Leader for the answer.

"Slightly above minimum wage," replied the Warrant Officer, matter of fact.

"And so does the bomb dog team which makes them brothers in arms, with less fleas. Master Sergeant Mobsby..."

"Yes sir?"

"Find them a cot, if you will."

"Hooah," said Mobsby.

"There will be a mission briefing later," said the Captain to Max, giving the officer a *Hooah* before the Team Sergeant led us across the room to the empty cot.

The Captain gave a loud, *CARRY ON* command before both he and his Alpha exited the team room, and the room came back to life.

The team room had the ambience and odor of a low rent, back street gym, and like a gym, music was playing in the background while everyone went about his business. One of the team members, a tall, lanky soldier with sleeve tats and a chip toothed grin was drowning out Tim McGraw singing how he went two-point-six seconds on a bull named, Fu Manchu. McGraw, though, was singing that it was two-point-seven seconds, but maybe the Special Forces soldier was living like he was dying as well, so, all things considered, maybe the one hundredth of a second difference wasn't all that far off.

After the brief interruption the hairy-faced team members went back to doing what they were doing before we came back through the doorway. The ten or so members of the team were playing cards, singing out of tune, cleaning and checking weapons, or honing and sharpening a variety of seemingly already ridiculously sharp knives.

A burly Samoan, the team Sniper, was quietly adjusting the scope on his M24 rifle. The bolt action, .308 long gun had considerable reach and with the precision scope was deadly accurate in a competent sniper's hands. Other team members were busy preparing MRE rations for snacks, sipping on Red Bulls, Gatorade, or from water bottles, or stretched back out on their cots reading dog-eared paperbacks, while two more were mercilessly ragging on each other as they went back to working their way through the video game, HALO-2.

"Bam! Take that, bitch!" said one of the players, wildly pressing buttons on his controller as he twisted and turned in his blue New England Patriots folding chair.

"That's what your momma said when she slapped you up alongside your head for not being potty-trained until you were twelve. BRUTES! BRUTES! BRUTES! Watch your front! Watch your front!"

"No problem. BAM! BAM! BAM!" said the first player pressing buttons with his thumbs and fingers like a mad man. "I am the Master Chief!"

"No, you're a Master wanker!"

"Yeah well, your Momma was always willing to lend a hand and you can tell her I really appreciate the naked selfies she keeps sending me."

"Yeah well, my momma has short standards. STRAFE!"

"Don't you mean, *low* standards?"

"Uh-uh, not when we're talking about your pecker. IT'S RIGHT IN FRONT OF YOU! IT'S RIGHT THERE, YOU IDIOT! HIT IT! HIT IT!"

"That's what she said!"

After Max set down his Go-Bag and gear, he pulled out a collapsible water dish. Pulling out a liter bottle of water he also had in his Go-Bag, he filled the dish.

"There you go, buddy," he said, setting the dish down in front of me.

When I had finished lapping it up, he led me back outside so I could do my business. Later, he'd feed me and we'd take another short walk before calling it a day. Later-later, he might even dig into the small baggie of doggie treats he had brought along in his Go-Bag for a late night snack.

For now, though, Max stuffed the Go-Bag with his things and the all-important doggie treats under the cot. As he led me from the room I suspiciously eyed the Team Members in the room and gave them a stink eye.

Curst be he that moves my bones.

As we came back into the team room, one of the team members, who was cleaning a handgun and had it in parts and pieces on a towel on his cot, was staring down a shiny pistol barrel at us. He was wearing a ratty looking Pearl Jam tee shirt, BDU trousers, flip-flops, and a smirk.

"I ate grilled dog with Bulgogi a few times in Korea," he said, squinting at us over the pistol barrel. "It tasted like shit."

"Sounds like you started at the wrong end," Max said as several of the other team members guffawed and howled in response.

The Special Forces Dog Eater smiled and slowly nodded to Max, who smiled back and returned the nod. It was touché and B.

"Maybe it just needed a little more kimchee, Soju, and hot sauce," the Dog Eater said reassembling the pistol and then checking its action.

"Could be," Max said as he laid down on the cot, crossed his feet, and closed his eyes to nap. "Oh, and Thor," he said as he patted me on my head, "feel free to take a toothy chunk out of the asses of any of these sonsofbitches, if they pull out a cook book or start to fire up the Barbeque. Hooah?"

"*Rhurr-rah*," I said and dropped down on the cool concrete floor beside the cot. The *Rhurr-rah* had them all laughing again, even the Dog Eater, who I eyed like the cannibal he was.

It was an hour later when the Special Forces Team Leader and the Assistant Team Leader returned and began the mission briefing.

"*LISTEN UP!*" barked Master Sergeant Mobsby as the dozen or so team members gave the two their attention.

The mission, the Captain said, would take us to the heart of the Kote Sangi neighborhood in the western and rougher part of Kabul.

He was tacking up photos on the cork bulletin boards and locking the pictures in place with multicolored push-pins as he was speaking. Judging from the groans and dour expressions from the team members when he mentioned Kote Sangi, they were familiar with that part of the city and didn't particularly like it.

After the Team Sergeant gave the others a weary, *AT EASE* command, Kang went on with his briefing. The subdued cloth rank insignia on the front of the Team Sergeant's BDUs showed that he was an E-8 in rank and triple tabbed with Airborne, Ranger, and Special Forces tabs. A smaller patch showed that his blood type was O- Positive.

Kang said that word had come down from a reliable Police informant that Abdul-Mateen, a local biggie in the Haqqani network and high-valued ISAF target, would be joining three or four other insurgents in making IED and suicide vest party favors, at a safe house there just after midnight.

Mateen and his people were planning to carry out a coordinated bomb attack on the ISAF coalition headquarters in the city the following day. The Team Leader thumped an eight by ten photo of a short, chunky-looking and scowling, dark-bearded man in his forties. Mateen was looking over his left shoulder as he was entering the repair shop. A second photo offered a profile shot that could've been Danny DeVito with a jaunty looking pakol hat and salt and pepper beard. A third mug shot showed a younger Mateen, straight on, and wide nostril glaring into the camera. He was dressed in a bright orange Gitmo jump suit.

"Intell has it that Mateen is responsible for masterminding most of the car bomb and suicide attacks in and around Kabul. And here's the kicker," Kang paused for a few beats for effect. "Three years ago he was captured in the Northwest Territory by the Pakistani Special Forces who, in turn, turned him over to the ISI. They identified him as a member of the Haqqani network, who were just as much a pain in the ass to them as they were to the ISAF.

"So they turned him over to one of our secret three-lettered agency types and whisked off to Guantanamo. There, after a year or so in Cuba, with nothing gained from gentler and kinder interrogation methods, and nothing to support the allegation against him that he was connected to Al Qaeda, he was deemed by someone with too much sensitivity, but no actual judicious sense, to be a low-level threat, and released from the U.S. military prison. He was repatriated to a neighboring Arab country after promising and vowing never to return to the fighting, insisting that he intended to carry on his everyday life as a simple mechanic."

"And immediately returned to the fight," said the tall team member that had been singing along with Tim McGraw. "It probably wasn't his fault, though. The wonderfully trusting folks who released him probably didn't know that mechanic is slang for a Hit man."

"Well, you'd at least think they heard that Jason Statham was up for the role in the remake that might've given them a clue?" said the team Sniper, the big Samoan.

"The sensitive ones don't watch those kinds of movies. They think they're filled with too much gratuitous violence."

"So what kind of movies do they watch?"

"Alien versus Predator, Dracula, American Zombie…"

Kang let out a heavy sigh. "Hey, Siskel and Ebert, you done?"

The two soldiers said they were, which was partially true.

"Which one is the fat one, Captain? Siskel or Ebert?"

"Ebert," said the officer.

"So that makes me the other one."

"Fuck you," said the sniper. "I'm pleasantly plump."

"Well, plump. Sure, you big Hawaiian."

"Samoan."

The second soldier smiled. "Oh, and Captain, it's *Rotten Tomatoes* now for movie reviews, just saying."

Kang sighed again. "We done here with the movie reviews and sensitivity training?"

The two soldiers said they were done a second time as Kang stared them down until they actually were done talking.

"Anyway, Mateen's our primary target," he said, regaining their attention and pointing to the first photo and thumping it again for emphasis.

"Did Intell confirm that it is an active bomb factory?" asked the Dog Eater only to have the Team Leader shake his head, no.

Intell, of course, was short for military intelligence, and although some jokingly said it was an oxymoron, most units who operated in the field relied heavily on the critical information and analysis they provided.

Like a jigsaw puzzle, Intell gave us some of the key pieces we needed to make out the picture of what we might be facing on a given mission. The rest we would have to find and figure out for ourselves with boots on the ground. Paws, too, to bring the rest of the puzzle pieces together.

"Actually, the bomb factory this time out is in a motorbike repair shop. To avoid detection Mateen rotates the bomb making business from site to site. The repair shop is his latest build-a-beard bomb store," Kang said.

"Can we expect a few party favors, then?" someone said behind us. "Crock-pot IEDs and shit?"

"It's likely we will a few pressure cooker IEDs and suicide vests," cautioned the Captain. "Although, they might not be in play or ready to go by the time we come knocking. That being said the Entry Team shoots anyone near a button or switch. Clear? Sergeant Price?"

"Clear,' said the Dog Eater, whose name apparently was Price, while I would continue to think of him as the K-9 cannibal.

"Clear?" Kang said looking to the others.

"Clear!" came back the gathered response.

Kang continued. "The building itself is single-storied stand alone, tucked inside a walled courtyard with two, large barn door-like swinging wooden gates as its entrance. During business hours the wide swinging gates would appear to be open to welcome all customers, although, according to the surveillance detail, no one seemed to be allowed in other than Mateen and a few of his nefarious friends. There's one guy who appears to be the gatekeeper. The undercover officer said he caught a glimpse of a wooden stock of an assault rifle next to a bike frame near the man, so he's the sentry. There's a smaller Judas Gate for after-hours that serves as their primary entry and exit point. We can expect it to be guarded as well. There's a heavy metal gate at the rear of the building that the undercover officer said is chain locked and can't be accessed, but we'll cover that, too, just in case."

"Windows?" asked the team sniper.

"One in the front and one in the back, both heavily curtained."

"Of course, they are," grumbled the sniper.

Mister Davies was tacking up several photos as Kang was speaking. The photos showed the repair shop front and rear. The curtained windows were prominent in each. The large courtyard wall that enveloped the shop was maybe ten-to-twelve-feet high, mud bricked, and pitted. Beyond the open barn-like swinging wooden gates revealed motorcycles, scooters, and stripped frames in various stages of repair just inside the small courtyard.

The hard-packed ground inside the courtyard was stained with dark, shimmering blotches of oil. The small Judas Gate that was attached to the left side of the barn door like gates was no bigger than a small closet door that was only fit for a Hobbit.

The photos also showed a lone guard, who was anything but a customer, standing just inside the open main gate. Another eight-by-ten provided a good look at the metal gate in the back of the shop that opened to a thin alley. The chained back door could easily be surveilled from either end of the alley, making for an easy shooting lane against anyone coming or going out of the back.

"The surveillance pictures," Kang said, "were taken that morning by an undercover Afghan police officer, who passed along the memory card to the Police Commander, who in turn, passed it along to our Intell people, who did their thing."

The Captain posted a makeshift map along with several drawings beside the photos, laying out the repair shop, the streets, and alleys surrounding the target site.

"What's their security like? Anything more than just the one guard at the front gate? Watchers in the street or windows?"

"From what we've identified so far, it's just the one sentry, but you can be sure that they'll be watchers so we'll bring a cell phone jammer to fuck up their immediate commo."

The members of the team closed in around the photos, studying the lay out of the street, courtyard, back alley, and most of all, the face and profile of Abdul Mateen.

"Any idea what the inside of the shop looks like?" asked Price, the Dog Eater. "Any photos of that? Naked chick calendars on the walls in nothing but head scarves, or old copies of Better Goats and Gardens magazine in the waiting room? "

"No shots of the interior," replied the Captain, "but I'm told it's one large, open room with benches against the back wall where they work on the engines, or in this case, IEDs and suicide vests. Most likely there'll be bikes in the shop that are being worked on or that they're configuring to use as V-bieds."

Using the white board he picked up a marking pen and drew an approximation of the shop's interior.

"Just the one main room?" asked the Marvin Gay look-alike.

"I'm told there's a smaller room near the back door that serves as a toilet. Could be they'll store the party favors there until they're ready to go."

"Any pics of the surrounding neighborhood? What's across from the shop? Or any other avenues of approach that might be choke-points?"

It was Sergeant Price, the Dog Eater, again, asking more of the necessary questions.

"No," said the Captain, apologetically. "Just a city map showing the roads in and out."

"How old is the city map?"

"Too old. Back when they had a working Tourist Information Center, hippies bought hash for pennies a toke, and one or two of you were conceived in the back of a mini-van to the Commodores singing, *Brickhouse.*"

"I like that song!" said one the video game players.

"And so did your Momma," said the other as the Team Sergeant brought it back to the Captain's original question with a loud, *"SETTLE DOWN!"* and an accompanying scowl.

"The map is old," said the Captain. "But it's all we got to work with at this time. The major boulevards and streets are the same, and our target is just off one of the main streets."

"Any aerials or chance for a ground recon by our people?" asked the Dog Eater, only to have Kang shake his head.

"No," he said, adding, "This is it. We don't want to chance it by sending anyone else in and spooking the bad guys."

He pointed to the photographs and frowned as he did. "Which is why we're going to make a quick in-and-out on the raid. The Entry Team will hit the shop, grab Mateen, any of us people with him, and anything; cell phones, computers, papers, and whatever else there is of Intell value, and scurry the fuck back out. The rest of us will secure the avenues of approach and the alley and provide cover fire. We will not linger any longer than we absolutely have to."

"QRF?"

Kang nodded. "A Quick Reaction Force will be on stand-by at Camp Eggers, if needed."

"And we're sure this bearded Danny DeVito looking motherfucker will be in the shop when we arrive?"

Kang nodded, again. "The Informant says their little party is on tonight, and the Afghan Police Commander believes it to be solid info, and our Intell people trust the Police Commander," said the Captain.

"Local or National Police?"

"Local. The Police Commander and a team of his people will be assisting us."

That admission, too, drew some groans and snarls and earned a momentary frown from Captain Kang, who, started to give them an *AT EASE,* only to be beaten to it by the stern looking Master Sergeant Mobsby. The Team Sergeant's voice boomed across the room, as did the authority it carried.

"AT FUCKING EASE!" growled Mobsby. Soon it was quiet, again. With order restored, Kang continued.

"Word is that he's given us some good, solid leads in the past. One thing that gives some serious weight and gravity is that six months ago, the Police Commander's wife, two sons, and his only daughter were killed in a bomb blast meant for him. Mateen was responsible for the attack, and that means the Police Commander hates Mateen more than we ever will. That being said, it probably wouldn't hurt to keep an eye on his people in case they get any green-on-blue funny ideas."

That green-on-blue tag, where supposedly loyal Afghan or Police forces attacked U.S. or other ISAF soldiers, drew some serious nods from some in the assembled audience. It had happened in the past with ISAF forces with enough troubling frequency to warrant a warning.

"Thatcher?" Kang said to one of the two video game players.

"Boss?"

"You're on it," said the Captain. "You'll have our six on this."

"Roger that, Captain."

Kang's attention turned back to the white board as he went over the plan and fallback plan, one more time. Nothing would be left to chance.

"Our mission is to capture or kill Mateen," Kang said, this time using a red marking pen to circle the bomb maker's photo. Next, he circled the entry and exit points.

"The vehicles will be staged here, a block or so away. When the Entry team is in position here," he added, showing the repair shop's street-facing wall, "I'll radio for the extraction vehicles to race in to the site. By that time, we'll have taken the shop and who and whatever else is in it," he said staring at the Dog Eater while marking the Judas Gate.

"Security teams cover here, here and here." Kang, the Team Leader, marked the roads in the immediate vicinity of the shop and the door in the back that led to the alley.

"Exfil route?"

"Exfiltration is down this side street here and the next road over until we reach the main boulevard and hightail back to here where it's covered by a local police checkpoint. Everybody copy?"

"Hooah," came the group response.

"And the Rules of Engagement on this little outing, Captain?" asked Price, the Dog Eater.

"The R-O-Es are simple enough. It's an in-and-out mission. We hit the safe house, hard and fast. Capture Mateen, if possible. I say again, if possible. He's high-priority. But, if he, or any of his people reach for a weapon, start to press a button or switch, or try to make a run for it, you give them two to the head and one through the ass crack. These are some serious bad guys. We don't let them get away. Period. Hooah?"

"Hooah," came the group response. Max nodded and I used a back leg to scratch my left ear.

"And because things sometimes go boom in the night," said the Team Leader, turning to Max and me, "we've invited this illustrious canine team here to crash the party with us. They'll go in with the Entry Team. You good with that, K-9."

"Yes sir, no problem," replied Max, knowing this was a given. It was why we were here.

Heads turned and nodded, someone barked, the Dog Eater yelled, *Bulgogi*!' and the room erupted in laughter before calm, or what passed for it with this group, was restored by the Team Sergeant, once again with his booming voice and one of his familiar scowls.

Kang identified which of his people would serve as the Entry team which, I suspect was more for us than the team members who knew their jobs. When named, each member of the Entry Team nodded to Max who nodded back. SFC Price and SSG Barnes, the black soldier with the Marvin Gaye goatee, would make the initial entry, with the rest of us in the Entry Team stacked up and moving in immediately behind them.

Captain Kang then identified the others who would provide overwatch and security during the raid, who'd serve as vehicle drivers, those who'd be with him, and where each would be deployed. There was some bitching and name-calling rivalry between those selected for each group, but it was all good-natured, like oversized wolf pups play fighting.

"Kick off time will be Zero-300," said the Captain, "so get some rest and be geared up and ready by Zero 2:45. Any questions?"

His 'Any Questions?' closing remark failed to illicit a single question. The Special Forces team members knew the drill and we were all left to see to our gear and the limited battle rattle we would carry for the mission. Weapons, ammo, body armor, and testosterone only.

Kang turned to his Team Sergeant again. "They're all yours," he said.

Mobsby nodded and gave a CARRY ON command to a much quieter audience. "Study the photos before lights out," he said.

A short time later with nothing more for us to do, Max laid back on the cot for some shuteye. Lying at the foot of the cot and guarding him, I watched as the Special Forces soldiers, checked and re-checked their weapons and gear, before they, too, hit the racks.

After the lights went out I remained awake and on alert for a long while. The Special Forces team members, who were about to bring their own thunder and downpour on the Taliban bomb-maker, were surprisingly serene. All was quiet in the team room. This was the calm before the storm, and the storm was coming.

CHAPTER

19

The glaringly, bright overhead lights that came on in the team room at Zero-2:30 and the shout that accompanied them had the startling impact of someone jumping out of hidey-hole and shouting, BOO!

"Rise and shine, ladies! Gear inspection in two zero mikes," said Master Sergeant Mobsby, sticking his head in the door of the team room before disappearing behind it again as the sounds of grunts, farts, ball scratching, and grumbling filled the room.

Feet hit the floor with decided thumps as we rose, but didn't necessarily shine. When you had half an hour to go from deep sleep to warrior mode, you could easily make the transition with Red Bulls, coffee, or a milk bone or two. Max and me were ready to go in one-five.

At ten minutes to three a battle ready Kang, Davies, and Mobsby returned and began checking out the team's battle rattle equipment, leaving us to make our own K-9 checks after a quick look-see at what we were carrying. There was little talk involved. Kang's people were pros, and little to no real adjustments made to what they wore or were carrying. They were ready.

We followed the Captain, Warrant Officer, and the Team Sergeant outside where three, old and battered looking, engine idling, Toyota Hi-lux King Cab four-by-fours, and one tarp-covered delivery truck were waiting. The vehicles were locally acquired with beefed up engines and suspensions, dark glass, and, at a quick glance, Taliban approved.

The four-by-fours and delivery truck would get us to the target site without necessarily announcing who we were.

There was a 'Lock and load!' from the Team Sergeant as Kang did a commo check into the small microphone on his PNR, the Personal Net Radio, the team would use to communicate during the mission. The PNR's and attaching headsets were small thirteen-ounce radios with a range of maybe a kilometer at best. Each team member had a PNR with the exception of Max and me since we were only tag-alongs.

Master Sergeant Mobsby was the first to charge his weapon at the red safety barrel at the front of the Quonset hut as each one of us in line followed in turn.

Once done Kang yelled, "Mount up!" as one by one we all climbed into the awaiting vehicles.

The pre-dawn dark sky was clear and cloudless under a quarter moon. The mountains brooding over Kabul were barely visible and in deep shadows.

Exactly at Zero-300, Kang gave a 'GO!' into his COMM headset radio and we were rolling. After departing the base, we linked up with the Afghan police at a pre-positioned point along the way, and then sped through the city's darkened streets towards our objective.

The run was made lights out with the drivers using NVGs-Night Vision Goggles- that were attached to their helmets to easily navigate their way in the thin moonlight. Kabul was at rest, or what passed for it in this southwest Asian illusion of serenity.

The ride bumped and bounced us over dimly lit, pot-holed streets towards the repair shop in Kote Sangi neighborhood, with three Afghan police vehicles using running lights in close pursuit. With the on-again, off-again, and then back on-again nighttime curfew in place, there was no other vehicle traffic, let alone foot traffic on the streets. We blew through police sandbagged bunkered checkpoints that were positioned on the main boulevards and passed mile after mile of high walls and closed gates.

What few Afghans we passed in doorways or open windows didn't give the line of speeding vehicles a second glance, much less, closer scrutiny. All across Afghanistan, and especially in the rougher parts of any of the big cities, towns, or villages, closer scrutiny only invited serious problems. Curiosity came at a cost and the surviving populace learned early on to lower their gaze or shift their attention away from those with stern fixed stares and automatic weapons.

Soon, the convoy slowed as it eased into Kote Sangi. One long, run-down, shabby looking block before the designated target, the convoy came to a slow, rolling halt. Quietly exiting the vehicles, the Entry team tactically slipped into the shadows. We made our way on foot forward towards the motorbike repair shop while the remaining members in the raid party took up their designated cover fire positions.

The pre-dawn morning was dark and still, and would be until 4 a.m. when the muezzin in the local mosque would use the loudspeakers, high up on a minaret, to call the faithful to the *farj* morning prayer.

The night vision goggles the Special Forces team members wore attached to their helmets and lowered over their eyes illuminated the darkness with an eerie green glow through the lens. The lime green light bounced back and silhouetted the profiles of the faces of the Entry Team members with a ghostly aura.

Max and me were fast on the heels of SFC Price, the Dog Eater and Staff Sergeant Barnes, until the two quickly came to a halt as Price held us up with an open, up-raised hand. A lone guard was standing in the courtyard just inside the open Judas Gate, his position given away from the pulsating orange glow and pungent aroma of hashish that he was smoking. The Dog Eater smiled. The sentry was toking a bowl.

Both of the Special Forces soldiers had anticipated the sentry and had planned on how to take him out. That the lone guard was getting high just made the task a little easier. With the immediate area and the avenues of approach covered, the two moved in like fleet-footed Dobermans towards the open Judas Gate. The Dog Eater and Barnes worked in a well-practiced and frightening unison.

Hugging the courtyard wall and creeping up to the open gate, the Dog Eater let his M4 long gun drop to his side on its sling as he reached down and grabbed a discarded, half-crushed, liter plastic water bottle from the litter on the street.

With an underhanded toss he flipped the empty plastic bottle to the far side of the gate. The plastic bottle hit with a distinctive, crinkled thump. The noise was enough to draw the lone guard's curiosity.

As the guard leaned out of the Judas Gate with his assault rifle leading the way to see who or what had made the noise, the Dog Eater snuck in behind him, snaked his arms around the sentry's throat in a chokehold, and kicked his legs out from under him, seemingly in one fluid motion. In a panic the guard, who was struggling to breathe, dropped his rifle as he reached up with both hands trying to free his neck, but to no avail. He thrashed briefly and then went limp with little clamor or commotion.

Barnes snatched up the dropped weapon and covered the open gate as the Dog Eater, dragged the unconscious sentry back down the outside wall facing the street. The unconscious sentry was gagged and his hands and feet were tightly bound with plastic zip-tie flex cuffs anchored to his ankles.

Once he had him trussed up, the Dog Eater leaned the sentry against the outside wall and lowered the man's head down into his knees giving him the appearance that he was sleeping.

Another hand signal from the Dog Eater brought the rest of us in the Entry Team into position against the perimeter wall behind them. Max and me took our place in line behind the two Ninja-like operators with the three remaining members of the Entry Team stacking up behind us.

We'd be the third and fourth ones through the door once it was breached. As the accompanying K-9 team our job was to sniff out any explosive devices Mateen and his people were working on. We'd also search for any hidden weapons caches that they might've stashed.

One more hand signal from the Dog Eater and we were through the Judas Gate and snaking our way around a half-dozen motorbikes in the inside courtyard and working our way to the right of the repair shop's scarred wooden door. A dull light from inside the shop showed through a small opening in the curtain-covered front window while muted voices held a spirited conversation.

As the Dog Eater turned and eyed the rest of us in position and waiting, he whispered into his PNR comms and nodded that all was ready. With his left hand upright and his right hand holding a death grip on the business end of an H&K, MP-5 assault rifle, he began a silent countdown from three to zero.

On zero the door would be kicked in and the Dog Eater and Barnes would charge into the shop and get everyone inside to play nice, or be sprayed with well-aimed automatic rifle fire. Those of us behind them would immediately follow.

On the silent zero the Dog Eater heeled kicked the front door. The old wooden door violently splintered as it flew open, banged against the inside wall, and stopped at an awkward, broken angle. The hanging door was held in place by one loosely attached hinge at the top of the doorframe.

Staff Sergeant Barnes was the first man through the door, taking one side of the main room as the SFC Price, the Dog Eater raced in behind him covering the other side.

Now, it was our turn, only as Max urged me forward I came to an immediate, arm twisting stop, and dropped like a stone in place just as I had been trained to do, which caused Max to trip and stumble over me.

He did a two-point face plant with his chin and nose on the empty shop's concrete slab floor, swore and tried to push himself back up. With his ass up and face down like a Downward Dog Yoga pose and me still prone, we were both blocking the doorway. The rest of the Entry Team that were bunched up behind us couldn't get inside the shop, and folded in like an accordion.

"FUCK!" Max yelled on his knees and hands, still trying to stand. The room was empty with the exception of a small cassette tape recorder on the far counter and a small, bare-bulb lamp. The talk we'd heard from the outside came from the recorded conversations.

Behind us another team member was shoving Max's shoulder and back yelling, "MOVE! MOVE! GODDAMNIT! GO! GO!" only Max couldn't move and they couldn't get around him because I didn't budge. Something was wrong. I could smell it.

I held my ground and blocked the doorway. When that wasn't enough to get their attention, I started barking, loudly all the while looking up, because I had sniffed out what the two Green Berets in the lead had missed.

A remote-controlled V-shaped charge, wired with the electrical charge igniter, had been positioned over the shop's doorway. I could smell the electrical switch, too, along with the anxious sweat off of the palms of the man who had placed the device.

When the front door was kicked in, the top of the doorframe gave way, and the deadly, and now dangling, V-shaped explosive device was pointing up towards the ceiling.

The shop was purposely left emptied for a deadly reason. In its original position, the IED that was filled with a block of plastic Semtex explosive, and studded with nails, bolts, and ball bearings, was designed to shred and kill everyone entering the room. Placed where it was, it wasn't immediately visible. No one had seen it. For me, though, the scent was overpowering, as was the immediate threat.

"**I SAID,** *MOVE*!" screamed the soldier behind Max giving him another shove only to have Max shove him back to keep him from entering.

"NO! BACK! GO BACK!" shouted Max, twisting back and warning him off. "MOVE BACK!" He shouted.

I was still blocking the doorway, barking my ass off, and trying to warn the soldiers about the IED. Max had understood, even if the others hadn't. He was back down on his knees, only now with his hands up, blocking the entrance, and yelling at everyone to get back.

"IT'S BOOBY-TRAPPED!" he yelled. "GET OUT!"

Turning back around, he reached out to pull the closest team member to him out of the room when the electrical switch was triggered. Our cell phone jammer would be of little use.

Because the IED had shifted when the doorframe buckled and broke, the main thrust of the blast went into the ceiling. Even so, there was an overpowering blinding flash as the hellish eruption sent a sand-blasting shock wave of searing heat, and a rush of pinballing shrapnel, splintered wood, and broken bits of concrete throughout the room.

The force of the explosion violently slammed us back and down as shrapnel from the shape-charge bounced around the shop until it found purchase.

In the wake of the detonation, the repair shop was a swirling haze of dust. As it began to thin I vaguely began to make out the fate of the others. All four of us that were inside the shop were injured and down.

Blood was spilling out onto the room's concrete slab floor and pooling with dust raining down like dry snowfall. The Dog Eater was crawling over to a nearby corner of the pitted room dragging his weapon behind him. Propping himself up with his back in the corner, he pulled a chem-light glow stick from his vest, bent it to activate it, and tossed it into the center of the room. A pale blue light slowly brought the blast damage into better focus. Price, the Dog Eater, was holding his intestines in with one bloody hand and steadying his rifle in the other for whatever came next. When he tried communicating with his PNR he realized the headset was gone.

Barnes, the black sergeant with the Marvin Gaye goatee, and the one Max had reached for but couldn't grab, was down and writhing in pain in the center of the room. He was desperately trying to stem the heavy flow of blood from what was left of his right leg that had been ripped away just above the splintered and shredded knee.

A dazed and glassy-eyed Max had been blown against the front facing interior wall. Lying on his side he was slowly beginning to stir and having a hard time of it. I was on my side as well, lying just to the left of the doorway, against the broken door a few feet away, staring at him. My lungs were burning and the warmth spilling down my back legs told me that I had pissed myself.

I tried to stand to go to Max, but my right shoulder gave way and I collapsed. When I tried standing a second time, it was the same result. I couldn't get to my feet, let alone walk. When I tried crawling my front legs wouldn't work, either. All I could do was watch on and bleed.

Concussions were a given, and we both had bleeding wounds of one kind or another, but it was the two Special Forces soldiers appeared to be the most seriously wounded.

Max showed a few small cuts on his face with a superficial wound to his scalp just over his right ear. A dime size bruise was forming on his swollen upper lip where he'd been hit by a piece of concrete. He was covered in a layer of fine pale dust and had a small, dark rivulet of blood dripping down his forehead and the right side of his face and neck. That wasn't all.

There was a steady flow of blood seeping from an ugly rip in his left calf muscle and as he started to move I saw a dark and growing rosette of blood on his lower back, where shrapnel had sliced into his BDU uniform shirt, just below the protection of his body armor.

Max, though, was a fighter. Rolling over on all fours, he pushed himself up coughing and spitting out dust and phlegm. He was opening and closing his mouth and working his jaw a few times trying to clear away the ringing in his ears and found some relief. Running a hand over his forehead, he quickly dismissed the small amount of blood he found on his fingers. Even with the painful pound of flesh that was his torn calf and the small hole in his back that he couldn't see, when he heard me whimpering against the door and saw me hurting, he immediately started towards me. But he was stopped by a woeful plea from the Dog Eater.

"Hey, Bulgogi?" said Price in a pain-racked voice pointing to Staff Sergeant Barnes with his rifle. "Can you help him? Can you help my buddy? He's bleeding out."

Max turned and found the Dog Eater holding a pile of steaming intestines in place with one hand and his rifle in the other. He was tilting his head towards his more critically wounded teammate in the center of the room who was holding what was left of his leg and struggling to get a tourniquet in place. Max hesitated, looking to the soldier with the missing leg, over to me, and then finally back at the Dog Eater.

"Christ! What about you? Your guts are hanging out."

"They're not going anywhere. Help him first. I'll cover you," said the Dog Eater. "Go ahead."

The Dog Eater was right. His buddy needed the immediate help. Blood was puddling and the soldier would bleed out in a matter of minutes, if he didn't get the tourniquet on and working.

Max crab-crawled over to the center of the room to the wounded man and patted his shoulder. "I got it," he said as the wild-eyed soldier in the horrible pain nodded. Barnes was doing his best to keep it together and trying not to slip into shock. He was putting up a brave fight, but he was struggling from the blood loss and growing shock.

"It's okay. I got it," Max said, again, taking over the bloodied task. "I got it."

"My...my leg..." only Barnes didn't get a chance to finish as gunfire erupted outside on the street in front of the shop and Mateen and his people sprung the second phase of their planned ambush.

The bitter and violent exchange of machinegun and small arms fire filled the pre-dawn darkness and echoed through the empty streets.

"Barnes! Cover the entrance!" yelled the Dog Eater, more to get the younger soldier's mind off of his lost leg and the shock he was slipping into. He needed a distraction and the Dog Eater had given him one "Cover the doorway!"

"Got...got it," said the black sergeant coming up on his elbows bringing his rifle up and ready. His professionalism kicked in, even when his leg couldn't. You didn't get into the Special Forces without considerable effort and resolve, something both he and the Dog Eater were now showing in strength.

The gunfire on the street was accented by the whooshing rush and explosion from an RPG round. The rocket-propelled-grenade roared towards one of our awaiting vehicles, hit it with a fiery explosion, and set it ablaze.

Kang's driver, who had just exited the truck as he took a defensive position down behind the front wheel well, was wounded in the explosion. Shrapnel had slashed open his left cheek down to the bone but he was returning fire.

The fight outside beyond the courtyard was intense, but short lived. Within minutes the second phase of the ambush and follow-up firefight was over, and the battle noise was replaced with yelling. There was always the yelling, and mixed in with the pitiful moans and cries of the wounded.

"CLEAR!" came the first cry that was echoed by others outside from the remaining members of the Entry and Security teams.

"CLEAR!"

"CLEAR INSIDE!" yelled Max from inside the damaged repair shop, letting those outside that it was safe to enter.

With the tourniquet working, Max crawled over to the Dog Eater to assist him. The Dog Eater was fumbling with a bandage, trying to encase the bloodied and bulging lump of intestines. He was having a difficult time trying to tie the bandage in place around him as he held on his torn abdomen.

"I got it!" Max said, taking over the task, easing the Dog Eater forward, and tying it off around the man's back in a hurried knot. When he had finished he used another bandage that the Dog Eater had out to momentarily cover his own leg wound.

Across the floor, I let out a crying whimper and Max shot me a troubled look over his shoulder.

"You're going to be okay, buddy," he said, to both the wounded Dog Eater and me.

"COMING IN!" came a loud voice from outside the doorway.

"CLEAR!" Max yelled a second time as the Special Forces team medic and the three remaining members of the entry team swarmed through the shop's broken doorway.

"Who needs me most?" yelled the medic coming through the doorway and into the darkened shop. His eyes were slow to adjust to the bloody scene in the blue shadows and when he flipped on a Maglite, it brought us out of the dark and revealed the full extent at what had happened.

"He does," yelled Max, pointing to the soldier on the floor with the missing leg. "I got a tourniquet working. And Sergeant Price here could use some serious attention, too. Abdomen wound, torn intestines."

"I'm literally trying to keep my shit together, Doc," said the Dog Eater, chuckling at his small joke while holding the bandage in his lap. "A shot of morphine might do me wonders."

The Special Forces Medic nodded and tossed a small Syrette to Max, who gave the shot to the wounded NCO. The Medic gave a morphine shot to the soldier on the floor as he checked the tourniquet Max had applied. The Medic nodded to himself as he applied a large bandage over the soldier's bloodied stump.

"Get him to a vehicle!" he said to the first two Entry Team members coming through the door behind him, and they did just that, lifting the man up and carrying from the repair shop.

The Medic then scurried across the floor to help the wounded Dog Eater. The bandage Max applied would do for the moment, but now they needed to get him out of the shop as well.

"How about you? You okay?" the Medic said back to Max, noticing the blood dripping down his left ear from a small cut on his scalp. "You're bleeding, guy."

"Other than a torn calf muscle, some scratches, and a big fucking headache. I'm good-to-go. I need to look after my dog."

Max started towards me only to have the medic hold him back for a moment.

"Hold up! Good-to-go, huh?" the medic said taking in the ugly looking tear on Max's leg and not buying it.

"At least out of here," Max said, dismissing the wound and a handful of small cuts or minor tears that he seemed all too familiar with from previous blasts.

"Yeah, well, let's at least get a better bandage on your calf muscle," said the Medic pulling out several bandage pads and a thick roll of gauze. With the clean pads in placed, he wrapped the gauze around the leg to get a better handle on the bleeding and to keep the hanging flesh in place. As he was reaching for a roll of adhesive tape Max handed him the half roll of sandwich wrap from his pants pocket.

"Yep, that'll work," said the Medic. "You need something for the pain?"

Max shrugged. "Half dose, maybe. I need to look after my dog."

"Yeah well, let me know when you need the other half," said the medic, injecting him with the morphine before wrapping the bandage with the plastic sandwich wrap and smoothing it over in place. It would hold.

Back to the Dog Eater, he said, "You ready?"

He wasn't, but SFC Price, the Dog Eater grunted and said he was anyway.

"Then, let's move."

"You're a good man, Bulgogi," the Dog Eater said to Max as he was being helped up. "So's your dog. Take care of him, man. Seriously. You done good."

Max gave a small nod, anything more and he was afraid his head might fall off.

Shouldering the Dog Eater to his feet and starting towards the doorway, the Medic reached down and retrieved the severed leg as they went.

"You sure you're good?" said the medic over his shoulder to Max, who was already working his way over to me.

"Good enough for now," he said again, as he limped over, sat, and pulled me into his lap where he began checking over my wounds. "Hey buddy, I got you," he said. "Good boy. You're gonna be fine. I got you."

A thumb-size piece of shrapnel, the size of a lug nut, had ripped through my canine harness and shot through my right shoulder like a jagged-edged steel bolt. It was a nasty in and out wound with the finger-size projectile finally lodging into the wooden doorframe behind me. The missing lug nut felt like it was lodged in my chest, but it was only a bad bruise from a piece of broken section of the concrete floor that hit me like a fastball, and made it difficult to breathe.

Shrapnel had sliced open my left hind leg and blood was spilling from the two gaping wounds, so those were the ones Max immediately treated. There were other smaller cuts and rips, but they didn't look to be all that serious. They could wait.

Pulling out the modified K-9 First Aid kit from his left side pants cargo pocket, Max got busy with the bandages, scissors, sandwich wrap, and the small roll of duct tape. Tearing away the wrapping with his teeth he spit out the paper as he began pushing the four-by-four gauze bandages into the hole in the shoulder to stop the bleeding to the entry and exit wounds.

"I got you, buddy," Max said again, rhythmically stuffing the gauze in the open wounds until the bleeding had finally stopped. Satisfied it was working, he then began wrapping the shoulder with the roll of gauze and then covering with the sandwich wrap and strips of duct tape that he cut to fit. Wrapping it all in sandwich wrap Max sealed in the bloodied meat of the major wounds.

When he had finished with me he tried applying a bandage to the small, but bleeding and annoying small wound on his lower back that the medic had missed. Try as he did to reach the wound, he couldn't secure the bandage in place said, "Fuck it!" and gave up.

He packed away the First Aid kit and looked me in the eye. "Not today, buddy. Not today," he said, scooping me up and struggling to get on his feet under our combined weight and our injuries.

Once on his feet, and limping badly, he wobbled us out of the blown-to-shit repair shop's doorway, into the walled off courtyard, and back out towards the street, staggering as we went.

Seeing our struggle, Master Sergeant Mobsby ran in and lent a much-appreciated hand, shouldering us to the working vehicles. In the pulsating glow from the burning vehicle that had been hit and destroyed by the RPG round, we could make out the reason for the earlier battle noise and street mayhem.

Just after the detonation inside the shop, and when the line of vehicles pulled up in front of the Judas Gates, the Afghan policeman who had given us the tip about Mateen being holed up in the repair shop, exited their vehicle, and turned his assault rifle on our raid party. He wasn't alone. Another policeman had joined him.

In the predawn light, they fired on the command vehicles and anyone standing around them. The Afghan Police Commander took a bullet to his upper left arm in the attack, while both the driver and radioman were killed.

Staff Sergeant Thatcher, the Special Forces soldier, whose job it was to watch for a green-on-blue attack, quickly returned fire, foiling their fight before the turncoats could take out any more of us.

Stepping out from behind cover and charging forward, Thatcher dropped one of the two turncoats before taking a round through his throat. It was Captain Kang who took out the second attacker with a well-aimed shot on the run as Mister Davies raced out to pull the wounded soldier back behind cover before the incoming rounds had stopped. Thatcher was dying and there was nothing the frustrated Assistant Team Leader or the Team Medic, could do to stop it. The second phase of the enemy ambush wasn't over.

A Taliban fighter, who had been crouched down on a nearby rooftop and shouldering an RPG, raised up and got off a good shot. The

Rocket Propelled grenade swooshed out of the tube and took out the lead, but now empty, four-by-four.

Kang's Toyota Hi-Lux truck exploded in a fiery ball and sent glass from the windshield flying like shimmering shrapnel. A piece of the flying glass sliced into the Special Forces Captain's left cheekbone looking more like a bad hipster piercing than a combat wound. When Kang plucked out the annoying glass shard, a small channel of blood began dripping down his face as he scanned the rooftops an surroundings for more enemy while his fully engulfed four-by-four lit up the pre-dawn sky. Flames danced in the darkness in a macabre display.

"HIT THE ROOF!" yelled Kang, and the command came just in time.

A second or third RPG round never materialized, because before he could load and loose off more rounds, the big Samoan sniper rose up from his cover and took out the Taliban fighter with a well-aimed shot. The insurgent slumped over on the rooftop as his RPG fell and clattered on the street below. The round exploded in the street, sending shrapnel into the nearby buildings.

Mateen, the bomb-maker, who had planned the ambush and triggered the explosion in the repair shop, was thrown off by the premature gunfire. His opening fire was to signal the second phase of the ambush, only the rogue policemen and the fighter with the RPG had literally, and nervously, jumped the gun.

The flustered bomb maker was left firing his assault rifle well after his targets had taken cover. The thirty rounds he'd fired from a second floor window in a building just opposite the repair shop didn't hit anything more than the line of empty vehicles. The Ak-47 rounds punched holes through the vehicle windows, doors, and side paneling, but did little real damage.

Kang and his people were targeting the window opening, keeping Mateen down, and buying time for Master Sergeant Mobsby to move into position below the window. As Mateen was down and reloading another magazine into the assault rifle, Mobsby was ready.

When Mateen raised up to fire a second time he was greeted by a well-tossed fragmentation grenade from Mobsby, who was hugging the wall directly below the window. The fragmentation grenade landed behind Mateen, exploded, and sent him toppling out of the window and down to the hard, dirt-packed street. His fall from grace included shrapnel from the grenade. He had lost his right thumb, and had a badly wounded and broken left leg.

Mateen wasn't dead and there would be no escaping. Rolling over, he sat up, raised his hands in surrender. He then began laughing at Mobsby and the true Afghan Policemen that were quickly swarming in around him. Thanks to the Americans, Mateen knew the drill.

It was his cynical laughter, the burning vehicle, and the mad scramble to get our wounded in the remaining vehicles, that was the show we saw from our idling vehicle.

Mateen's laughter gave way to angry insults and snarls, and with my ringing ears the only word in English I could clearly make out from him was, 'Gitmo,' something he repeated more than a few times. Gitmo was slang for the military prison in Guantanamo Bay, Cuba, where he knew he'd certainly be sent, again.

The wounded Afghan Police Commander, though, was determined to keep him in Afghanistan. Holding a hand over his shattered shoulder, the wounded police Commander walked over to the bomb maker who had murdered his family and so many other innocent Afghans, including his loyal driver and radioman, and stared down at the insurgent in disgust. Mateen was still laughing and swearing at him, and the rest of us as well.

Leaning down, the Police Commander calmly said something to him in Pashto; something he repeated in English.

"No, no Guantanamo," he said, slowly shaking his head. "No Guantanamo."

In a sudden understanding, the bomb maker realized his fate as the wounded Police Commander dropped his hand from his bloodied shoulder and drew his handgun. Mateen raised his hands to shield his face as the Policeman pulled the trigger and kept pulling the trigger.

The bullets blew off two fingers of the bomb maker's hands before they blew several holes into the right side of Mateen's head a millisecond later. As Mateen's body slumped to the street the Police

Commander emptied what was left of the handgun's magazine into the bomb maker's lifeless body.

When his officers went to retrieve the bodies of Mateen, the dead insurgents, and the turncoat policemen, the Police Commander barked out a command that stopped them in place.

"NO!" he shouted, this time in English. "Leave them to the jackals."

None of us was really sure if there were jackals in the city, but we all understood his meaning. He was making a point to his people and ours. The two loyal Afghan policemen who had died in the shootout were loaded into the back of the delivery truck with Thatcher, the dead American.

"Everyone accounted for?" yelled Kang, wiping the dripping blood from his eyes and watching on.

Mister Davies was getting a head count of all of those in the raid party including our wounded and dead. When he was done, he nodded to the Captain.

"We good to go, Doc?" yelled Kang.

"Hooah!" replied the Team Medic.

"Take Mateen's photo for proof of death, and then saddle up, we're rolling! Keep your eyes out for bad guys!"

As truck doors slammed and the shot up vehicles started to move, there was an awkward stillness in the surrounding neighborhood. Like the aftermath of an inner city neighborhood on the 4th of July where fireworks weren't allowed, but the ground was covered in their debris and the odor of gunpowder filled the air, the streets were awkwardly quiet.

"Get the feeling he's not too thrilled about our Catch and Release program?" said Mobsby, who had climbed in next to us and was seated directly behind the Team Leader. The Team Sergeant had tilted his head towards the dead bomb maker.

"I don't think his dead wife and children were either," said Captain Kang.

"Fuck Mateen," said Mobsby. "Hooah?"

"Hooah," came the response that was echoed by several others in the vehicle, including Max, who had me cradled in his arms.

"Keep an eye out for any more nasty surprises," said Kang into his headset to the team in the trailing vehicles only the cautionary command wasn't needed. The surviving team members were ready for whatever came their way, and given the ambush they'd just endured, they were looking to get more than a little even.

CHAPTER

20

Blood from our wounds was seeping out of the bandages and **down onto the** seat and floorboards as we raced through the still dark, city streets, taking an alternate route back to the base.

This time, though, the small convoy was running with lights on and at Nascar-like speeds.

Kang had radioed ahead our status to the Ops Center, and at the main checkpoint to the military base, the heavily protected guard post by the MPs and guards on duty, waved us through the gate. The Combat Surgical Hospital- the CASH, too, had been alerted to our situation and immediate need for assistance.

As the convoy wheeled into the vacant helipad area adjacent to the designated emergency room, and braked to a jerking, squeaking stop with pinging engines, a team of doctors, nurses, and medics that were standing by, raced over to offload, assess, and treat our wounded.

The medical staff was slicing and dicing away our uniforms, boots, and weeping bandages to get to the wounds. Well before we were brought through the Hospital's emergency room doors, they were inserting IVs, shifting blood pressure cuffs into place, and adding better bandages to those that were soaked in blood and covered in dirt. They worked in teams and they were good, very good. But then, the on-going war had given them much in the way of practice to improve their critical skills.

With no Veterinarian on-site, they even began treating my wounds in the ER until a doggie doc I didn't recognize, and whose uniform smelled awfully new, showed up and took over my treatment.

Being cuddled in the soft, warm bosom of a young nurse that smelled of fragrant Lilac soap beat the hell out of the, 'It's okay, fella' pat on my head from a Veterinarian I didn't know.

"It's okay, fella," the Doggie Doctor said, patting my head over and over, again. "It's okay."

It wasn't okay, and how is it that as a Veterinarian in a combat zone, he doesn't know that the repeated pats on my head felt more like a fucking jackhammer than tender little consolation taps after being caught up in an explosion?

To be fair, judging from the smell of his uniform, this Veterinarian was new in-country, and, perhaps, hadn't caught on yet that explosions are a little different than bumping your head playing, Fetch. He'll learn. We all do. We have to. When I let out a loud yelp after he patted me one too many times as he took in my wounds, he got the message, and stopped after Max growled from a nearby gurney.

"Hey, be careful with him!" he said, watching on. Covered in a ghostly layer of powdered dust and smeared blood, Max looked like one of the walking dead.

"It's okay. He's good," said the Vet, getting the hint, and also getting it from several glares from the surviving wounded team members. I, apparently, had a few new friends.

Pulling back the bandages that Max had applied to my shoulder wound, the Doggie Doctor began probing the rips and tears in me to get a better look at what he would have to deal with and treat. After a few '*hmms*' and worried frowns, he gave me a shot of some good doggie drugs before wheeling me over to a nearby Radiology station set up in another section of the room for a series of X-rays.

After studying the X-rays and going over the troubled areas on a laptop screen, the Doggie Doc had a better idea of what he had to do and quickly went to work. He began by trimming away the blood and dirt matted fur around the more serious shoulder wounds, cleaning out the debris and dirt, and then slathering on an antiseptic wash to slow and stop an infection. Next, he went after the pin cushioning shrapnel in the smaller wounds that had my butt looking like I'd gone a few serious rounds with a feisty porcupine.

As he worked, the administered drugs began kicking in and washing over me in a comforting flow of rolling waves. I soon found myself drawn out to an unseen sea, floating away in the semi-somnambulistic surf. Within minutes I felt like I had washed up on a nice little beach, shook off the water that wasn't there, and then chased after a flight of happy little butterflies.

I followed the fluttering little fellows into a nearby green pasture where I sniffed out a few piles of cow pies and joyfully began rolling in them, all the while, and somehow, still laying on a sheet-covered gurney in the hospital emergency room. Nobody else seemed to notice the large, colorful butterfly that touched down on my nose and smiled as I rolled.

"What say you run through the field and chase us again?" the butterfly said, and it's possible I might've let out a happy *yes* bark in reply.

It's also possible I might even have been humming to myself as I merrily returned to the chase as the new Vet was digging into me and taking out the fragments and slivers of shrapnel.

When the Doggie Doc felt sure that he'd taken care of the serious wounds and had gotten all of the splinters and shards, or at least all of the troublesome pieces that mattered and wouldn't have me pissing blood, he began closing the wounds with heavy stitches. The needle and the sharp tugs from the stitching didn't bother me at all, thanks to the doggie drugs.

When the Doggie Doc started to roll me out of the Emergency Room, Max protested a second time.

"Hey, where you taking him? Where are you taking my dog?" Max said, starting to stand and wobble towards us, only to have the Nurse, who was cleaning out debris from his leg wound, quickly sat him back down. Max was shirtless with a clean bandage and tape wrapped around his stomach and back covering the small wound.

"Whoa! Whoa! Whoa! No, you don't, Sergeant!" she said, firmly, taking him by the arm and sitting him back down on the gurney. "We need to treat that leg wound of yours. Until then you're not going anywhere for the time being."

"But my dog…"

"…Is okay," the nurse said, gently patting his shoulder. "He's in good hands."

"Not to worry," added Doggie Doc offering his own encouragement. "He'll be fine. He just needs to rest, and so do you, Sergeant."

The Doggie Doc nodded to Max and Max reluctantly agreed without a head-aching nod.

"You'll be fine, Thor. You're as good dog, buddy," Max said while I gave him a laid back muffled, 'woof.'

I was smiling and as I did, an avalanche of drool dripped down my tongue that was hanging like out of the left side of my mouth like a bright pink tie that I couldn't seem to reel back in.

"Good dog," Max said. "You're a good boy."

"And you are, too, Max," I said muffling a bark. "Thanks for letting me chase the butterflies. Ain't they pretty?"

Max acted as though he hadn't heard me as I was rolled out of the Emergency Room following the zigzagging flight of happy butterflies down a long, well-lighted corridor to a hospital ward.

With the doggie drugs taking serious hold, sleep was beckoning, and I found myself giving up the chase as my eyelids began to droop. The butterflies were drifting away without me. Their wings waved goodbye as they went.

"Buh-bye," I said, trying to lift a paw to wave goodbye. Maybe it moved, maybe it didn't. It didn't matter. I knew. They knew.

My eyelids felt as heavy as sandbags and just as hard to lift, and I found myself giving in to a much-appreciated slumber. A lifetime, or maybe just a few hours later, I awoke, and started to stir. With half-opened eyes and looking and sniffing around, I found myself in an unfamiliar kennel cage, on my side, woozy, and very much in pulsating pain. The pain was growing with intensity with each waking moment and I could hear a headache coming on like a Scottish Highland drum and bagpipe parade.

The painkillers were wearing off and some very real hurt was setting in. I yelped in a voice I didn't recognize and that brought in a Vet Tech I didn't recognize, either.

"Hey Doc!" yelled the Vet Tech stranger back through the kennel door to the kennel's examination room. "The bomb dog is in pain."

That brought in Doggie Doc, the head patter. When the Vet Tech stranger opened the cage door, they both stepped inside.

"How are you doing, buddy?" Doggie Doc said, taking a knee and holding my head in his hands as I shook and whimpered like a scared-shitless Chihuahua.

Scratching my ears, he gently checked on his handiwork beneath the bandages. The stitched wounds were swollen and weeping, but it wasn't unexpected. Healing took time and this was only Day One. He left the bandages in place.

"Let's see if we can make you a little more comfortable," he said, and ordered up another round of pain medication. After the Vet Tech had retrieved it, and the Doggie Doc stuck the needle in my rump and, once again, I soon found myself drifting off into a current of delightful delirium. The happy butterflies were back and fluttering, leading me to a comfortable field when I could find some restful sleep.

This set the pattern and routine for the long days, and even longer nights that followed; the waking in pain, woozy feeling, and then yelping for a new round of drugs. Time doesn't really mean all that much to dogs, but what there was of it here became an abstract blur with its passing.

The plastic-covered chart, hanging on the nearby wall that tracked my pain medication in hours and days showed that a week had passed before I'd even noticed it was there. It was also about that time when they started to wean me off of the drugs that I gradually began to focus on something more than my cramps, aches, and assorted throbbing pains. My legs were rubbery from inactivity and even standing took some doing. I was tired of being tired. I needed to move. I had seventy-five square feet of space in my cage, and so far, had only utilized the few feet of what I was laying on.

When I finally mustered up enough strength to stand and remain upright for a bit, I got cocky, and tried to take a few steps. On the third step I stumbled and fell hard to the concrete floor, slammed down hard on my hurt shoulder, yelped loudly, and fouled myself as I lay there.

That got me disgusted with myself enough to try standing and walking one more time. Cramped and shaky, I managed a few steps and moved away from my own mess.

"Hey, let's get you cleaned up," said the Vet Tech stranger coming through the swinging doors of the kennel and catching a whiff of both of what was on the floor and still sticking to me. He wasn't Gabby, but he was good at his job.

The Vet Tech stranger led me to another cage, cleaned me up, and then applied fresh bandages before hosing down the kennel cage and laying down a clean rubber mat. It was two days later before I could actually stand and walk, and although I limped when I did, I was happy to be mobile.

Both the Vet Tech, not so much a stranger now, and the begrudgingly good Doggie Doc, seemed pleased with my progress, just as I was pleased a day or so later when I heard a few old, familiar voices on the other side of the kennel's swinging doors, and caught the scents that went along with them.

"Hey Thor! You have some visitors," said the Vet Tech as my nose climbed and pushed through the chain link fencing when I got a whiff of Max, Doctor Deb, the Doggie Doc Vet, First Sergeant Hallatt, and Specialist Gabrielle in the adjoining room. Notably absent was Lieutenant Dimmer.

Sore as I was, I managed a happy yelp with my tail madly swinging back and forth like a runaway metronome. When the door was pushed opened the Doggie Doc led in the parade of visitors. Doctor Deb followed the Doggie Doc and his Vet Tech. Gabby was next carrying what looked to be my lucky chest harness neatly folded in her hands with Hallatt coming in behind her. I could smell Max only he hadn't come through the swinging door, yet. He was taking his time. A healthy chunk of calf muscle had been torn open in the blast, and, like me, he was probably still moving slowly, too, and more than likely, on crutches. Between us we maybe only had four good legs.

"There you are, Thor. Hey buddy," Captain Larson said, unlatching the gate to my cage and stepping inside. As she knelt I managed to falter my way over and slink into her lap as the others watched on.

After a few happy sniffs my eyes went to the swinging door again, back to Captain Larson, and then back to the door that led to the examination room next door. Okay, so where was Max?

It took me a moment to realize that Gabby wasn't holding my chest harness. Max's scent was coming from his folded BDU shirt she had in her hands. My head was up and my eyes followed Gabby as she handed the uniform shirt to Captain Larson, who took it and set it down at my side. When she looked at me again her eyes were a wet and glistening.

"I'm so sorry, Thor," Doctor Deb said as she slowly stroked my head. "So, so sorry."

Sorry? For what, not bringing doggie treats? But when I looked up and saw that her eyes were wet and glistening with tears, I finally understood. Max was gone.

I lowered my head down on Max's shirt, and kept it there.

Doctor Deb pulled her shoulders back, rubbed her eyes, and did her best to remain professional. She wasn't having an easy time of it. She was struggling. When I looked over to Gabby I saw that she was biting her lower lip while Hallatt had lowered his head and was slowly blowing air through his teeth.

"We'll take you back with us," Doctor Deb added, gently scratching me behind my ears. "I've started the paperwork to have him medically retired," she said to Doggie Doc, who was watching on behind her.

The Doggie Doc had no objections and said as much.

"From these new wounds and what I've seen in his health records, I'd say he's earned it," he said.

"If he's ready to travel, I'd like to take him back to Camp Phoenix with us today," Doctor Deb said, giving her eyes time to dry. "I think he'll be more comfortable there."

"No problem," Doggie Doc said with a nod. "A shame about his handler."

She gave a quiet nod as her fingers brushed over Max's folded shirt. She couldn't speak. There were no words. There never are.

CHAPTER

21

At the recommendation of Captain Kang, from the witness statements both he and Mister Davies had taken from Sergeant First Class Price and Staff Sergeant Barnes in the hospital, and by other witnesses from the Entry Team who substantiated the accounts, Max was awarded a posthumous Silver Star for Gallantry.

He was credited with keeping the rest of the Entry Team from entering the shop when he saw it was booby-trapped, and for ignoring his own wounds as he treated several seriously wounded soldiers after the explosion while the fight was still going on.

Gallantry, in the eyes of the military, is rated one step higher than heroism in combat. It is the number three award for valor behind the Medal of Honor. The distinction, though, seldom serves much in the way of actual solace or consolation, for the loss of son or daughter when the medal in the oblong dark blue presentation box is presented to a grieving family.

Thousands of miles, and another world away, Max's family accepted the medal with burdened hearts and an overwhelming sense of palpable grief, just as they accepted the folded American flag at his military funeral from the Officer in charge of the Honor Guard as a lone bugler standing off to the side of the ceremony played, *Taps*.

Not long after I had returned to the Detachment, Captain Kang and his Team Sergeant, Master Sergeant Mobsby, paid a visit to offer their condolences, along with a Special Forces Certificate of Appreciation for our K-9 services to their team.

They also wanted to return my battered chest harness that they had retrieved from the military hospital in Kabul.

Lieutenant Dimmer was practically tripping over himself, giddy with excitement from the VIP visit, and especially the award certificate. The Detachment was being honored by the Special Forces, which as the Officer-in-Charge, he figured, began with him.

When the Lieutenant led the visitors across the compound and into the Kennel Office, they found a stern-faced First Sergeant Hallatt at his desk, looking up as they entered. His coffee cup was well in hand as he was going over a stack of training records. Alan Jackson's back-up band was deep into the steel guitar solo of, *Remember When*, and coming through loud and surprisingly clearly from the small speaker attached to his I-Pod.

Hallatt started to stand, and was halfway out of the chair, and going to the position of attention when the Captain waved him back down and gave him the command, *"AT EASE."*

The First Sergeant sat back down and reached back to pause the music.

"Gentlemen?" he said, wondering what the intrusion was about.

"They presented me with an award!" blurted Dimmer, holding the small, framed certificate out with his good hand.

"A Certificate of Appreciation for the unit," clarified the Special Forces Captain, as Mobsby stared at Dimmer after the outburst trying to get a better read on him and the comment.

"Yes, yes. Of course! Of course! That's what I meant," said the Lieutenant fumbling with his reply only Captain Kang's focus wasn't on him anymore.

"And, we'd like to return this, First Sergeant," the officer said to Hallatt.

Captain Kang was holding out my harness. A Special Forces arrowhead patch and tab were sewn in on the right side of the chest protector next to our Dog Star patch. "We wanted to return it with our condolences and thanks."

"No thanks necessary, sir. It's our job," blurted Dimmer only to have the Green Beret Captain shoot him another hard look that said he was anything but pleased by the interruption. It was the very same look a dog walker would have when he or she reached down with a thin plastic dog poop bag, grabbed up a handful of warm crap from a very large dog, and immediately discovered that there was a gaping hole in the bag.

Kang wasn't alone in this, as the Special Forces Team Sergeant and First Sergeant Hallatt were staring at the junior officer with frustration.

"You get injured working as a dog handler, did you, sir?" Master Sergeant Mobsby asked, pointing to the arm sling, already suspecting the answer, but asking anyway.

"Eh, well, no, Sergeant," replied Dimmer. "I'm not a handler."

"But you were, right?"

"No. I'm just temporarily assigned here."

"Ah, I was confused by the patch," the Special Forces Master Sergeant said pointing to the Dog Star patch on the Lieutenant's pocket.

Dimmer nodded. "It's a unit patch."

"Issued then," said the Team Sergeant disappointedly, with a head bob that said it explained everything.

"Yes," replied Dimmer with a smiling nod.

Mobsby was of the belief that patches or tabs needed to be earned, and his frown said as much. Dimmer, as usual, failed to pick up on the frown or its meaning.

"Gentlemen, Thor's in here," Hallatt said, getting up from his chair, leading them through the examination room, through the swinging doors, and into the kennel proper.

As they came pushed through the swinging doors and came down the hallway to my cage, I sat up and stared vacantly at the visitors.

"You've got some visitors, Thor," he said, opening my cage and scratching me with his left hand behind my ears while he patted my side with his right hand.

"This okay?" asked the Green Beret officer to Hallatt as he started to hang the vest above the door to my cage.

First Sergeant Hallatt said it was and helped the Green Beret officer secure it in place. Dimmer, who was looking on over Hallatt's shoulder, was still grinning and staring at the award certificate.

"Okay to pet him?" asked Kang and Hallatt said it was.

Both Special Forces soldiers leaned in the cage and took over the scratching.

"You're one of us, buddy," the Special Forces officer said, solemnly. "You and your handler always will be."

His Team Sergeant squared his shoulders and gave a respectful nod. I suppose I could've given a *Rhurr-rah*, only I still wasn't up to it yet.

"Can we get some pictures?" Dimmer said, digging his cell phone out of his pocket with his good hand while he held the certificate up with his injured arm. The once confined arm in the sling suddenly found miraculously revived use. "You know, with the two of you presenting the award certificate?"

The Lieutenant wasn't the least bit shy about making the request, nor was the Special Forces Captain shy with his response.

"No, Lieutenant," Kang said. "We're still operational and we're still in a warzone."

"Sure, sure. Got it. Got it!" Dimmer said, putting his cell phone away.

"You the one who put Sergeant Ritchie in for the medal, sir?" Hallatt said to the Special Forces Captain.

"I did," Kang said, turning to Hallatt to get a better read on him, eye to eye. "He saved some of my people's lives at the cost of his own. It was well deserved and the very least I could do."

Hallatt held out his hand to the Captain, who shook it. Hallatt did the same with the Team Sergeant.

"Thank you, Gentlemen," he said, and meant it. "Sergeant Ritchie was a good handler, a good kid."

"Yeah, thanks," echoed Dimmer, happily staring at the certificate and clueless to his half-ass concern.

That proved a little too much for the Special Forces Captain, who now knew all that he needed to know about the temporary Officer-in-Charge, and it was more than enough.

Dimmer, though, would only help him add to the assessment.

"You sure I can't talk you into taking a picture or two. Something just for the Orderly Room?" he said, pushing the issue.

"Lieutenant," said the Special Forces Officer, in a tone that was decidedly pissed. "Anyone ever tell you you're a real dick?"

"Sir?"

But the Captain was no longer talking to the Lieutenant. His respect and attention went back to the Detachment's First Sergeant.

"First Sergeant," Kang said, nodding to Hallatt. Mobsby, the Team Sergeant nodded along, signaling the visit was over. No more words were necessary.

Hallatt nodded back at the two visitors before they turned and walked out of the kennel and back across the compound to their Humvee that was parked in front of the Orderly Room. Watching on from the open doorway of the kennel, Dimmer frowned as they climbed inside the Humvee and fired up the engine.

"What's his problem?" he grumped as they drove away.

"What do you think, Lieutenant?"

"I don't know."

Hallatt sniffed and nodded. "And there it is."

CHAPTER

22

Max's slight head wound wasn't slight, nor was it the simple nick it had initially appeared to be. The scalp wound, above his left ear, and that was partially hidden by his hairline, had seemed small and insignificant at the time. There was minimal bleeding and it had the deceptive look of a scratch. In fact, it was a great deal more.

When we were brought into the Emergency Room, the medical personnel immediately began treating him for the more seriously looking torn and bleeding calf muscle. A concussion was a given so they checked and noted his dilated pupils as well as the blood in his right ear from a battered eardrum. They would monitor him to insure that it wasn't a TBI and they would treat the concussion, regardless.

The smaller, and less serious wound to his lower back, as well as the various cuts and scrapes that he sustained the blast took a back seat to what was driving his pain. Those they would go over and treat, too. The bloodied calf was serious so that's where they spent their focus and time. Max, too, didn't help his cause any by telling them that other than the ripped leg and a screaming headache, he was okay.

He wasn't.

A tiny piece of shrapnel, a fragment no bigger than the head of a ten-penny nail, had pierced through skin, muscle, and bone into his left temple. The shrapnel and splintered pieces of bone that pushed through with it, tore deep into his brain, and slowly began to hemorrhage. There was little to no external bleeding.

The damaging effects, the deadly serious ones weren't immediately noticeable. Max's insistence that he was okay, yet one more time, sent the always understaffed Trauma Team working on the Dog Eater, Staff Sergeant Barnes, and the wounded Afghan policemen. Emergency Rooms are busy places and priority is always given to those most in immediate and urgent need.

When one of the Doctor's came back to check on him a second time, checking his eyes and ears, and asking once again, how he was feeling, Max shrugged off his injuries.

"Tired, sore, and thinking, maybe, my dog and me need a new line of work," Max said to the Doctor. Still seated on the gurney he offered a half smile. "Other than feeling like crap and that maybe the IED extracted a pound of flesh this time out, I'm fine, Doc. I'd like to check on my dog, if that's okay."

"It isn't. Your dog is fine or will be, and me thinks that, maybe, thou doesn't protest enough," said the Doctor, warily. "So Shakespeare, I think we're going to keep an eye on you for a while until we're sure it's nothing more. Hooah, Sergeant?"

The Hooah from the Doctor meant 'no fucking way' to Max's request to check on me, so Max frowned, and gave a "Hooah" in return. One word fits all.

After they closed and bandaged his wounds, and cleaned him up some, Max was moved to a nearby ward. Protest or not, they would keep him under observation and temporarily tend his wounds. The immediate prognosis was that he would be transported to the military hospital in Landstuhl, Germany, where a team of surgeons could better decide what they would need to do about his nearly torn calf muscle and possible Achilles tendon damage. The Emergency Room in the CASH unit was just a quick fix.

His lower leg wound wouldn't immediately be sutured, either. To reduce the likelihood of infection, the Trauma Team cleaned and treated the wound, and later in the ward he was assigned to, the wound would be cleaned again and again until he was flown to Germany.

Sewing the muscle back in place wouldn't be difficult for a team of specialists, and the Military Hospital in Landstuhl had those specialists.

The real problem would be the physical therapy. There would be no easy fix. Getting back in shape would take time. Max promised himself that he would do the physical therapy and necessary work, so he would be ready to be a Firefighter. However, there was little he could do now but rest.

It was maybe an hour later when a medic in the ward noticed that Max's balance was off when he tried to stand, saying he had to go to the latrine.

"Hey Sarge, you okay?"

"Gotta pish, ish shawl."

"No problem," the medic said, handing him a plastic bedpan bottle with a convenient flip lid. "Here you go."

"Naw, its sokay," Max said, waving it off. "I can…I can walk by myshelf…I'm good."

"Take a seat for a moment," said the medic taking Max's arm and sitting him back down and thinking something was off.

"I…I gotta pish."

"Sure, I just need a sec."

The medic called over the night Nurse on duty. "Hey Lieutenant, you got a minute?"

"No problem, what's up?" said the male nurse joining them.

The medic tilted his head towards Max giving the nurse a worried look.

"I gotta…gotta pish," he said again, rubbing his eyes with the back of his knuckles.

"How's your vision?" asked the nurse, checking Max's eyes and not liking the pin-pointed pupils, let alone the garbled and slurred speech.

"Tired ish shawl," Max said, again.

The nurse nodded and looked to the medic. No words were needed for what they were witnessing.

"Go find a Doctor," said the nurse to the medic.

"Yes, sir," said the medic who hurried back to the nearby Emergency Room.

The Emergency Room was no longer caught up in the life or death struggles they'd been fighting. Those critically wounded were in surgery, so for now several doctors, nurses, and medical technicians were cleaning up or taking well deserved breaks.

At the far end of the Emergency Room an American flag was draped over a gurney covering the Special Forces soldier that had died in the fight. The specialist from the hospital morgue would soon be by to collect it.

"Ma'am," the medic said, stepping in and getting the attention of one of the Doctors. "Can I get you to take another look at the dog handler they brought in?"

"Why? What's going on?"

The medic explained what was happening with the soldier and the doctor quickly followed the medic back to the ward where they found Max sitting on the hospital bed cradling his head in his hands. The nurse had a blood pressure cuff on Max's left arm and didn't like the numbers he was getting from the reading.

"180 over 98," the nurse said to the doctor.

"How are you doing, Sergeant?" asked the doctor staring into the young soldier's glazed eyes.

Max managed a weak smile.

"Head hurtsch," he said, trying to stand only to have the doctor sit him back down. "Tire, really tire."

"No, stay seated," she said as she lifted his eyelids and searched Max's eyes before she went over his ears and scalp, revisiting the small scalp wound partially covered by his hairline.

"Tired, huh?"

"Bad headache, too. Hurtsch…"

"Did we get a cranial CT scan?"

"No Ma'am," said the nurse, checking his chart. "No one ordered it."

"Let's do it, now. Let's get him into Radiology, STAT," said the doctor as Max was rushed into another part of the Surgical Hospital where they inserted the contrast dye and began the scan. The contrast dye would show any anomalies, which it did with the scan. The results revealed the full extent of the cerebral damage in stark black and white detail.

Max was immediately wheeled into surgery, but two hours into the operation, and after frantic efforts by the Surgical Team to keep him alive, Sergeant Max Ritchie, the veteran K-9 handler, and soon to be hired rookie firefighter from Seattle, died on the operating table.

A medic carefully covered Max's body with the American flag on the hospital gurney before it was rolled to the morgue. There, the bodies of Sergeant Thatcher and Sergeant Ritchie would be turned over to the Mortuary Affairs Specialists and readied for the cargo hold flight stateside to Dover Air Force Base, Delaware, where they would be autopsied and processed for a military funeral in their respective hometowns.

People always say that all dogs go to heaven and that we'll eventually meet up with our owners, again. In a better world than this, that might be so.

It's a nice thought, really, and one I hope is true, because here's the thing; when the humans we love, die and disappear from our lives, forever, their scents, remain locked in our memories.

Time doesn't lessen the grief of the loss, and we are forever haunted by the loneliness of their passing. So, if, by chance, all dogs do go to heaven and we meet up again, then it's the long wait in between that is very much like our own private Hell.

CHAPTER

23

I **was spared bone damage. Because I had only suffered muscle**
and tendon injuries when I was wounded, '*through and throughs*,' as
they're better known, my recovery only took a month and days. Once
these latest wounds had sufficiently healed, Gabby and First Sergeant
Hallatt had me up and exercising again.

Twelve days into this training, I was doing significantly better. I was
coming along at a decent pace. Despite a slight limp, and more than a few
objections from First Sergeant Hallatt, and because someone higher up in
command determined that the ISAF units in Afghanistan was still critically short on bomb sniffing canines in the war zone, Lieutenant Dimmer
was asked to put me through a short, in-country recertification program.

Upon completion of the training I would be placed back into the
mission rotation schedule. When he was also asked if he had any objections to that plan, Lieutenant Dimmer said he hadn't.

"Yes, sir. Can do!" he told the Colonel who had done the asking.

"Good. Then make it happen."

Lieutenant Dimmer didn't want to disappoint those who controlled his separation papers and pending civilian destiny. The First
Sergeant wasn't happy when he got the news and made a quick road
trip to Kabul to see the Command Sergeant Major to discuss it.

Command Sergeant Major Nunez listened to Hallatt's take on the
decision and said, "But your temporary Detachment Commander said
he had no objections to putting the dog back in the field."

"Of course, he doesn't, Sergeant Major. If you'll excuse my language and critical insight, my Detachment Commander is a fucking idiot. The dog got caught up in a blast that killed his handler and severely wounded two Special Forces soldiers they were accompanying. The dog's wounds have barely healed."

"The Chief Veterinarian-in-charge reviewed his medical records, noted the injuries, and signed off on the training since your Detachment Commander gave the go-ahead."

"Fuck, fuck, fuckitty fuck!" said Hallatt.

"If you like I'll share your concerns with the Colonel," offered Nunez while Hallatt nodded.

"Thank you," he said. "It's appreciated."

When Doctor Deb had returned to Afghanistan, after escorting Max's flag-draped casket back to Seattle and attending his funeral, and had learned of my recertification and Dimmer's role in the decision, she vehemently protested my return to duty, and petitioned for my retirement.

Unwavering in her pursuit, and armed with a thick file of combat injury reports, supporting X-rays, and her own medical findings, and those of the Veterinarian who had treated me in the Emergency Room in Kabul to back it up, she found some minor success and support.

The senior *somebody* in Headquarters at Kabul, who had made the final decision to put me back to work, and who she presented her fact-based petition and accompanying health file to for review, offered one important concession.

"The Working Military Dog," he said, "will be removed from the field and officially retired once a new dog arrived from CONUS, and the new team was in place, up to speed, and available for call outs." CONUS was the military acronym for Contiguous United States.

Doctor Deb wasn't thrilled with the decision, but at least the preliminary approval for my retirement was officially in print, with the final sign off ready to be sanctioned. However, because the NATO ISAF Command needed K-9 teams in the field, and because I had passed the recertification process, there was little she, Gabby, or Master Sergeant Hallatt could do about it. Temporary Officer-in-Charge, Lieutenant

John Falstaff Dimmer, to no one's surprise, was the only dissenting voice.

Of course, he was.

Doctor Deb's plan, she reminded me with each visit after her return, was to adopt me once I was officially retired. She had spent considerable time to make sure that the paperwork packet was ready to go when the official word and date came down that I was retired.

"You're going to be flown to my parent's home in Virginia," she said on a canine health and welfare visit as she and Gabby checked out my scars on the Examination Room's table.

"They're really excited!" she said to Gabby. "My Dad bought a brand new doggie bed for him from Costco, along with a can of tennis balls, and a five-pound box of doggie treats."

"Someone will be a happy dog!" said Gabby. "They have any other pets?"

"My mom has a cat named, *Hello…*"

"Hello, as in Hello Kitty?" Gabby said, staring at her and trying not to laugh.

Doctor Deb gave an embarrassed, 'what can I do?' shrug and said, "She thinks it's funny. I'm hoping they'll get along well, or at least well enough that Thor doesn't eat the cat until I complete my deployment and go to fetch him."

"I'm sure they'll get along, Captain. Thor's a sweetheart."

"He is, isn't he?" Doctor Deb said.

She pulled my head into her hands and vigorously scratched my neck and ears. "Don't eat my Mom's cat, Thor. You hear me? Don't eat the cat."

She smiled and I chuffed. She had nothing to worry about. Any kitty named *Hello* would probably taste like bad sushi anyway, and as long as the little shit kept away from my five-pound bag of doggie treats and didn't take a dump in my doggie bed, then I wouldn't feel any need to turn him into a squeaky chew toy.

Doctor Deb was persistent when it came to checking in on the status with headquarters on the incoming K-9 replacement team and my retirement. She was there at least once a week, and she was also in touch with a doggie doc she knew at the K-9 school in Lackland, to get the latest scheduling updates. Her persistence paid off. A short time later word came down that a new dog team would be arriving within the next few weeks.

Doctor Deb was ecstatic hearing the news and she drove to Camp Phoenix to personally inform Lieutenant Dimmer. Included with the official notification were her increased visits to our Detachment.

Much to Gabby's and First Sergeant Hallatt's satisfaction, and Lieutenant Dimmer's annoyance for the pain in the ass she was becoming to him, she reminded the temporary Detachment Commander of his responsibility when it came to looking out for the best interest of the canine program, and one dog in particular. Me. I was her dog in the fight, and I would be her dog out of the fight as well since the adoption paperwork was approved along with the retirement date.

Already not a fan of the Lieutenant, she let him know, in no uncertain terms, that she would hold up his discharge with a mountain of paperwork, and make his life a '*shit-storm of misery,*' if anything happened to me before I was pulled from the field. She was standing two feet in front of the Lieutenant, the way a Drill Sergeant might do to a less than satisfactory soldier or Marine in Basic Training, when she said it.

"You understand me, Lieutenant? Tell me you do in no uncertain terms."

"I'll do my best, Captain," Dimmer replied, properly intimidated.

"No Lieutenant," Doctor Deb said, clenching her jaw and leaning in to within inches from his face. "You'll do whatever's necessary."

"Yes, Ma'am."

"Because if anything happens to that dog, I'll hold up your discharge papers and have you filling out paperwork and explaining why until your eyes spin. You copy?"

"Yes Ma'am, I...I copy."

"Then, as long as we understand each other, we're good," she said.

Dimmer suspected that things weren't actually *good* good, so he would need to tread lightly, very lightly, and had him thinking that his Medical Discharge couldn't come soon enough.

Doctor Deb went on to deliver the same message to my new handler, Private First Class, Billy Young. When she had finished telling Young what she expected, in the same verbatim talk and tone she gave the Lieutenant, and the Private offered up a blank stare, she wasn't sure he had really gotten the message, so she said it again. This time she said it deliberately slower and with considerably more emphasis.

"You get what I'm saying, Private? You copy?" she added when she was done.

"Yes...yes, Ma'am," he said, uncertain what the Captain meant by the '*shit storm of misery*' threat, or even why she seemed mad at him. He hadn't done anything wrong, but he nodded along anyway.

"Hooah," he said, having learned early on in uniform that even if he didn't really understand something that someone with higher rank had said, Hooah was always the correct response.

CHAPTER

24

Specialist-4 Billy Young is an eighteen-year-old stumbling puppy of a human, who, at best, looks to be about fourteen or fifteen years old, tops. Because of that, and a few other reasons, everyone calls him, 'Young Billy' or 'Oh, Billy.'

When it's '*Oh, Billy,*' the word, '*Oh*' is often muttered with a disappointed sigh and manner of a new mother who finds her toddler in the crib, diaper off, and fingering painting the walls with feces.

Young Billy is a work in progress, with speculation, by some, that like the painting of the Golden Gate Bridge, anything he learns will immediately need to be reapplied over and over again to keep it from flaking.

One morning, shortly after a routine training exercise, and after several of the other handlers had ragged on him for being new and for screwing up a bite training exercise, Billy Young walked me over to the kennel office where he found the First Sergeant entering the results of the exercise into the training records.

At best, Hallatt had only been in his kennel office all of ten minutes or so, when Young Billy knocked on the door. Hallatt yelled, '*ENTER!*' and we stepped inside the CHU as commanded. A necessary mug of coffee from the First Sergeant's overworked Keurig Coffee Maker was lovingly cupped in his left hand as he opened up the first canine file with his right. Toby Keith was singing that he wasn't as good as he once was, and was having fun with a couple of twins named Bobby Jo and

Betty Lou. And like Toby, First Sergeant Hallatt, was the only cowboy in this place.

"Got a moment, First Sergeant?" asked Young Billy standing in front of Hallatt's desk as I dutifully sat at his side.

Hallatt reached over and paused his I-Pod. "Sure, Specialist Young. What's up?" he said, leaning back in his army issued, swivel chair and taking a slow sip of his coffee.

When Specialist-4 Billy Young didn't answer right away and started fidgeting and finding serious interest in the tops of his boots, Hallatt frowned.

"Contrary to popular belief, Specialist Young, I don't have super powers," he said. "I can't read minds, so if you have a problem, spit it out."

Looking up Young sheepishly told First Sergeant Hallatt that the other handlers were ragging on him and calling him, 'Young Billy' and, and…"

"And what?'

"It…it bothers me."

"Bother's you?"

"Yes, First Sergeant."

Hallatt took another sip of his coffee, with the momentary pause providing him time to reflect on the advice that Command Sergeant Major Nunez had offered him in Kabul when it came to counseling those under his command.

"Try to, or appear to be understanding, at least, because telling a soldier who comes to you with a personal problem or issue to '*man the fuck up, soldier,*' just might not be conducive to the modern Army's problem solving process, let alone earning your next promotion to E-9 in today's army," advised Command Sergeant Major Nunez.

"And I suppose a kick in the ass doesn't fit this new kinder and gentler Army format, either?"

Nunez shook his head, woefully. "Not like the good old days, no."

"They were good, weren't they?"

"They were, indeed, but might I suggest a more avuncular approach to counseling your people, even when it comes to the seemingly most unimportant or inane matter?"

"Talk to them like an Uncle?"

"It couldn't hurt unless, say, they had an Uncle who use to lock the soldier up in a car trunk when he or she was a toddler and shoot holes into it so the little rascal could breathe."

"That's wrong, right?"

"Right. That's wrong."

"Shouldn't waste bullets."

"That's one way to look at it, I suppose."

Hallatt thought it over for a second or so, before conceding the point. "I'll give it a try," he said to Nunez, "as long as I don't have to the hug the whiny little shits or have to offer them a bottle of warm milk and burp them when I'm done."

"Oh, and no verbal Shaken Baby Syndrome with your people, and especially with Second Lieutenants, either. They're fragile."

Hallatt gave a heavy sigh as he slowly shook his head, showing that this new approach might take more than a little work.

"This whole promotion to E-9 thing sure seems like a high-wire act."

"It is, and it can be shaky," said Nunez. "So find balance."

Hallatt would now try to find balance with young Specialist-4 Young.

"GI humor can be merciless at times," he said to Young, staring over his coffee cup, "And being new, I'm afraid, is one of those times. But here's the thing- time passes. You know what a *Rite of Passage* is, soldier?"

"Not really, First Sergeant."

Hallatt knew that when a soldier said, 'Not really,' that usually meant, *no*.

"A *Rite of Passage*, at least in the military sense, is a trial or test that you have to face head-on and get through in order to move forward. It's a challenge that will help define who you are and what you are to become."

Hallatt was thinking he was sounding not like a favorite Uncle, but more like Socrates as he took another sip of his non-Hemlock flavored coffee. He knew who Young was, but not what he yet may become. That still remained to be seen, once he stopped being a pussy.

Setting his coffee cup down and steepling his hands in front of his nose and mouth, Hallatt said, "If there's one thing I've learned from my career in the Army about nicknames, it is that the more a GI hates, or complains, about one that some others have given him or her from the get-go, the more it gets used and sticks.

"Besides, it's not really harassment or name-calling either, since, let's face it, the army's method of referring to a soldier is by rank, last name first, and first name last. William Young is your given name, isn't it?"

"Yes, First Sergeant."

"And I imagine your friends and buddies back home call you Bill or Billy, don't they?"

"Billy, First Sergeant."

"Not William?"

"No, First Sergeant."

"Then help me out here…what's the real problem, soldier?"

"It…eh, it doesn't sound right the way they say it."

"The way they say it," echoed Hallatt, thinking that his counseling high-wire act was getting wobbly. "So, what then? You'd like people to call you by what, a nickname? Say something like 'Red,' if you have red hair, which you don't, or 'Shorty,' if you're tall, which you aren't, or something like the hometown or state you come from like; 'Tex,' or 'Chi-town,' or 'Hollywood.' Right?"

PFC Young's eyes dropped back to his boot tops, again. "Well, eh…no, not like where I'm from, First Sergeant. Uh-uh."

"Oh, why is that? Where are you from, Specialist Young? Where's your hometown?"

"It's a small town in Missouri," Young said, his voice losing some its volume.

"I imagine there are a lot small towns in Missouri, so, which one is it?"

"Knob Lick," Young said, in barely a whisper.

"Say again?"

"The town's name is Knob Lick. Knob Lick, Missouri."

"Seriously?" Hallatt said, stifling the urge to laugh and surprising himself by holding it all together.

"Yes, First Sergeant. It's just south of Farmington."

Hallatt nodded, giving Young the impression that he actually knew or cared where Farmington was, thus giving him time to fight another urge to laugh, or tell him to get the fuck out of his office, and not to come back until he grew a set of *cajones*. Instead, he offered what Command Sergeant Major Nunez would consider to be a more acceptable counseling response.

"I'll talk to the handlers, but I also think you need to shake it off for now, Specialist," he said. "Try not to let it show that it bothers you. You copy?"

"Yes, First Sergeant," Young said, reluctantly.

"Once you prove yourself to the others over here in the 'Stan, things will change. It just takes time. You can do it. Besides, we all need a little dose of humility every now and then for what hails us?"

"First Sergeant?" said Young Billy, obviously confused by Hallatt's comment.

"It's eh, a play on words. I was trying to be clever."

"A play?"

"The whole world's a stage and we're all players, but never mind," said Hallatt. "Just keep in mind that you got a great dog to work with. If there's an Audie Murphy who lifts his back leg when he pees, he's it. So, trust your dog and he'll get you through your deployment! Hooah?"

"Hooah," said Young. However, some confusion was still lingering, and so was the soldier.

"Something else on your mind, Young?"

"Yes, First Sergeant. Who's Audie Murphy?"

Running a hand up over his eyes, Hallatt fell back on some Old School Army counseling. "Google it! Now get the fuck out of my office."

Once the soldier was gone Hallatt hit the PLAY button on his I-pod back on and then took another sip of his coffee thinking that maybe being E-9 is probably over-rated anyway before he cranked up the volume on the I-pod and went back to the training files.

Things, though, didn't change for 'Young Billy.' He was still having trouble proving himself, so the nickname stuck, and 'Young Billy' he became. Because 'Young Billy' isn't all that old, I'm hoping he can learn enough to keep us both alive.

'Young Billy' has a keen understanding of the obvious, but not necessarily what might lie beneath, something that became apparent during his mandatory in-country certification training.

After a few seriously dumbass mistakes, with Young Billy rooting around in the simulated piles of garbage and searching for the unseen IEDs, or him trying to disarm a practice suicide vest after I had alerted to it, First Sergeant Hallatt chewed him out, loudly a few times in order to drive home a few critical points.

"Specialist Young, you are not MacGyver, you copy?"

"Yes, First Sergeant!"

"Say it."

"I am not MacGyver..."

"Louder!"

"I AM NOT MACGYVER!"

"Good, so leave the fucking IEDs alone after your dog has made the alert!" yelled the First Sergeant. "You copy?"

"Hooah, First Sergeant."

"If you want to blow yourself up, fine. But you will not purposely injure or murder one of my working dogs. EOD will take care of the IEDs. You just find them, mark them, and move away to a safe distance."

Lieutenant Dimmer had come out to observe the training. He was watching on as Hallatt had Young Billy re-do each of the training scenarios. Dimmer had come out of his office because he'd heard his First Sergeant yelling, "REVERSE!' more than a few times.

Reverse was the training command for the handler to go back over a training aid he or she had missed, and Specialist Young had dragged me away from a few of them even as I had made my alerts, and Young had overlooked them as well. After several rounds of having to do it over and over again, and finally getting it right, the First Sergeant gave Young a reluctant nod upon completion.

"I'll hold you dog here. You put away the training aids," Hallatt said to Young Billy.

"Hooah, First Sergeant!"

As Young was walking off Dimmer asked if the soldier was ready for the field missions. Hallatt shrugged.

"He's adequate, at best, sir."

"But there's no reason why he shouldn't be added into the rotation schedule?"

The First Sergeant knew that the only reason the Lieutenant had been on-hand to observe Young's certification training was because Headquarters wanted to know why a physically fit, school trained dog handler, wasn't on the rotation roster, especially since the Chief Veterinarian had given a thumbs up for his dog to start working again.

"If you want to bring in a third string punter off of the bench in a crucial game when you're second and long on your own twenty yard line, then yeah, he's ready," Hallatt said, offering a more honest assessment.

"I'm informing headquarters that we're adding him into the rotation."

"I said, he's adequate, Lieutenant, but by now I'm sure you know that the job requires more than that," protested Hallatt, knowing his protest was falling on not just deaf ears, but ones that were so filled with bureaucratic static and ear jam that a skeptical and cautious phrase like 'adequate' was as good as 'he's ready to put his life and the lives of others in danger.'

Dimmer shrugged off the First Sergeant's concern. His Medical Discharge had been approved and he had less than a week before he would be leaving Afghanistan and the Army. He would do whatever it took to appease and please Headquarters. He wasn't about to upset the higher ups that had approved his discharge, and who could very well hold it up, if he angered them.

"I'm not about to tell the Colonel that just because you think PFC Young is inexperienced, he isn't ready. He has more experience than I do and I'm in charge of the Detachment."

"Yes sir, it's good that you well understand the problem."

Dimmer wasn't sure if that was an insult or a compliment. Hallatt gave no hint, either way, which left the junior officer somewhat unsettled.

"I'll let Kabul know PFC Young has passed his training and that he's in the rotation," said the Lieutenant heading back to the Orderly Room.

Hallatt stared after him slowly shaking his head. "Of course, you will," he said.

CHAPTER

25

O ur first mission assignment came the following afternoon.
In eighteen hours we would be accompanying an ISAF/NATO
Forces element on a weeklong road clearing operation down in the
always-troublesome Wardak Province.

The mission would take the convoy past '*The Bloody Hump*,' a
culvert patched portion of the always troubled road just outside of
the village of Sayad Abad. It was a known stretch of the highway that
the Taliban had frequently used for ambush. Had Lieutenant Dimmer
read the daily Intell reports he might've been aware of that. He hadn't.
Instead, he gave the go-ahead for the mision.

We had less than a day to make ready.

It is 'Young Billy's' first combat patrol and he's excited about it because he's young and because he has no real idea what to expect or fear.
His Go-bag was ready, even if he wasn't.

"Hey! Hey! Malligator!!" he said, kneeling at my side and scratching the ruff of my neck as he slipped on my leash in the kennel. At
First Sergeant Hallatt's insistence, we would be going through one final
training exercise in preparation to the upcoming mission. "We're going
to take it to these raghead, mother fuckers! We're going to kick some
Tali-butt on the mission, D-dogg! It's gonna be fun! So let's go have a
good training day!"

I stared at him like the puppy that he was, and is. I didn't wag my
tail or offer up a '*Rhurr-rah*' because I don't have the heart, let alone the

voice to tell him that we're not always the ones who do the kicking, and that the notion of fun in this profession in a warzone wears off quickly. Few die well that die in battle. He's young, and maybe he'll learn that too, if there's time.

Yeah, there's always that.

"Let's do this, buddy!" Young Billy said jumping to his feet only as he did he accidentally stomped down on my left front paw with his boots in the process.

His "Oh no, no, noooooo!" and the loud cracks of the small bones that compressed and broke under his full weight were drowned out by my loud, piercing yelps.

The yelps brought Gabby and the First Sergeant running. Gabby was the first through the kennel door and when she saw me limping, whimpering, and unable to put any weight on the leg, she went ballistic.

"What the fuck did you just do, Private?" she yelled, brushing him aside to get to me.

"It was an accident!" said Young Billy, almost in tears. "Jesus, I didn't mean to do it!"

"Yeah well, you did!" snarled Gabby, kneeling to inspect the damage and not liking what she found. The paw was hanging at an awkward angle, which is what the First Sergeant saw, as he came through the doorway and found me mewing in Gabby's arms.

"What the hell just happened here?"

"PFC Young just broke Thor's paw…"

"By accident! Swear to God!"

"*Mira!* It looks like you fucked it up good," said Gabby, scolding Young Billy, all the while wincing as she gently went over the injury a second time.

"Oh, you poor baby, poor dog," she said, back to me.

Then to the First Sergeant she added, "Broken carpus for sure. Maybe even the metacarpus. We'll need to get an X-ray and let Doctor Larson know she'll need to look him over. Until then, from what I see, he ain't going anywhere for a while, thanks to this *pendejo.*"

"You sure?"

"Take a look. I'd say it's broken in a few places."

The First Sergeant took a knee and then leaned in for a closer inspection. He saw what the Vet Tech saw and realized that Gabby was right. It wasn't good.

"My, oh my, oh my," he said with a heavy, frustrated sigh and a slow shake of his head, but then, suddenly and uncharacteristically, he did something totally unexpected.

He smiled.

"We'll have to let Headquarters Command know he's injured, Captain Larson, too," he said, trying now to mask the smile and failing.

It took Specialist Gabrielle and me a brief moment to catch on to the reason behind his sudden change in attitude, and when we did, Gabby smiled as well.

"I'd have to say he's no longer of any use to the Army, First Sergeant," she said, nodding. "He's done."

"Why yes, I believe he is."

Because their backs were to him, a very much-distressed Young Billy, who hadn't seen their faces and only had heard their words, started in on a new round of woeful apologies. "Oh God, I'm sorry! I didn't mean to step…"

At that the First Sergeant stood and turned to face the young soldier holding up an open hand that cut off the rest of the excuse.

"No. Of course, you didn't," he said, actually finding the kind Uncle approach the Command Sergeant Major had asked him to try in situations such as this. "In all likelihood, there could have been residual damage we all had missed from his last mission, and maybe it wasn't a good idea of getting him back in service before he was physically ready. Good thing it happened here and not out on patrol. Hooah, PFC Young?"

"Yes, I mean, Hooah, First Sergeant."

"Help Specialist Gabrielle carry your dog into the treatment room."

"Yes, First Sergeant."

"Oh, and your first combat mission is scrubbed, too."

"Scrubbed?"

"Yeah, it's not happening. You and Thor are both out of the

rotation," Hallatt said, surprisingly calm about all that had just happened. "After you help Specialist Gabrielle move Thor I want you to report to the Orderly Room and let Lieutenant Dimmer know your dog is injured."

"Am I in trouble, First Sergeant?"

"Trouble? No. I'll talk to the Lieutenant. By the way, you're going to be the new Detachment Clerk, at least for the time being."

"The clerk?"

"That's affirmative. You'll answer phones, do some typing, and maybe a little driving for him," Hallatt said. "It's only temporary, at least until we get a new dog in for you. Then, of course, you and the new dog will both be put through the required in-country training together, before you can be approved for mission rotation."

"More training?"

"Standard procedure," said Hallatt. " Oh, and PFC Young?"

"Yes, First Sergeant?"

"Let me say this again, you're not in trouble. Accidents happen and that's what this was," said Hallatt. "Right? It's not like you did this on purpose."

"No, First Sergeant. Oh God, no."

"Exactly. And will you tell Lieutenant Dimmer that I'll be along shortly to help him get started on the incident report and the necessary paperwork he'll need for Captain Larson and Headquarters."

"She's...she's going to be mad at me, First Sergeant."

"Naw," Hallatt replied with a shrug. "I'll talk to her as well."

Young Billy nodded, only he wasn't moving just yet. "First Sergeant, I, eh..." said the Army Private staring at the tops of his boots.

"You, eh, what, PFC Young?"

"I..."

"Yes?"

"I can't type."

"You can't type?"

Young Billy shook his head. "No, First Sergeant. I don't really know how to use computers, I mean other to play video games."

"Better and better," replied Hallatt, happy and maybe more than a little relieved that Young's first combat mission was cancelled. The Private wouldn't be getting himself or anyone else injured or killed because he wasn't ready for a field mission, or because the temporary Officer-in-Charge didn't want or know how to look out for the soldiers under his command.

"And better and better for you too, you lovable mangy mutt. You're going home!"

My paw was throbbing and I was still very much in pain, but it was lessened knowing that while all dogs may not go to Heaven, every so often, a very, very lucky one gets to limp into a nice, comfortable home in Virginia.

Shakespeare was right. '*All's well that ends well,*' but it's not bad either when all ends reasonably well, too. Aye, there's a better rub.

ACKNOWLEDGMENTS

This book is a work of fiction, but one that celebrates working K-9 teams for all that they do in difficult situations. To that end I'd like to take the time to acknowledge and applaud the following K-9 professionals I've known or have worked or trained with over the years; men and women that seldom get the applause or attention they so well deserve. Specifically, Jeff Gabel, former Training Operations Supervisor for the Canine Center at Front Royal, VA, Ron Friend, former CBP Senior Instructor/Course Developer, Career K-9 Handlers/Trainers for Silver State K-9, John Kelly and Lauren S. Marakas (formerly with U.S. Customs and the ATFE), former U.S. Air Force Military Working Dog handler and veteran CBP K-9 Officer, Sean Mulligan, former K-9 Officers;Gary Drake, Erik Schmidt, Dennis Brannick, Robin Edmundson, Ken Corpman, and Grant Lightfoot, K-9 Police Officer Kevin Jorgenson, Ron Van Why (former K-9 branch chief for U.S. Customs), former and current U.S. Customs and Border Protection K-9 Officers A.J. Chavez, Tom Leif, and Kris Johnson, former U.S. Army Combat dog handler Ed Beal, Aussie K-9 Handler Mike Murdock, the late K-9 officers; Mike Spencer and Robert Blair,, and finally this; to the wonderful dogs, that I'm certain, the K-9 handlers will tell you, serve faithfully, and always with great love and loyalty.

CPSIA information can be obtained
at www.ICGtesting.com
Printed in the USA
FSHW021950241120
76291FS